"We can get married."

Isabel's jaw dropped as she turned to stare at Dan. "Married? How would it help to marry a total stranger?"

"It would give you a legal name. One that wouldn't jump out at anyone searching a computer bank. Instead of Isabel Delgado, you'd be Bella Gibson. You can apply for credit cards and other forms of identification under that name."

Isabel was silent. "Even if I agreed to this," she said at last, "it's not possible to get married without some proof of identification and citizenship, is it?"

"It's possible," he said calmly, "when my cousin's the county clerk."

She studied him, amazed to be having this conversation and even more astonished that she was actually considering his offer. At that moment another obstacle presented itself.

"This house is so small," she said at last, her cheeks flaming. "And your children are in all the other bedrooms. If we're supposed to be married…"

Dear Reader,

Almost ten years ago, Harlequin approached a number of authors with an exciting new idea. We were given the challenge of helping to create a central Texas town and ranching community, along with a host of exciting, heartwarming characters to populate this setting. The result was the 24-book CRYSTAL CREEK series, which has remained popular with readers since publication of the very first book in 1993.

As an author, I loved everything about writing the CRYSTAL CREEK books. So you can imagine my excitement when the Superromance editors suggested I might want to return to Crystal Creek with a new series of books. I could hardly wait! *In Plain Sight*, the beginning of the new miniseries, will bring back many of your old favorites. Bubba Gibson and Mary are here, still raising their ostriches, along with J. T. McKinney, Manny Hernandez, Howard Blake and Nora Slattery down at the Longhorn. More and more of the familiar townsfolk will pop up in the next two books, along with some newcomers you're going to like, as well.

I loved making this nostalgic return to Crystal Creek. I hope you enjoy it as much as I did.

Warmest regards,

Margot Dalton

Upcoming Crystal Creek titles by Margot Dalton

HARLEQUIN SUPERROMANCE

928—CONSEQUENCES. On sale July 2000
940—THE NEWCOMER. On sale September 2000

IN PLAIN SIGHT
Margot Dalton

HARLEQUIN®

TORONTO • NEW YORK • LONDON
AMSTERDAM • PARIS • SYDNEY • HAMBURG
STOCKHOLM • ATHENS • TOKYO • MILAN • MADRID
PRAGUE • WARSAW • BUDAPEST • AUCKLAND

ISBN 0-373-70914-5

IN PLAIN SIGHT

Copyright © 2000 by Margot Dalton.

This edition published by arrangement with Harlequin Books S.A.

® and TM are trademarks of the publisher. Trademarks indicated with ® are registered in the United States Patent and Trademark Office, the Canadian Trade Marks Office and in other countries.

Visit us at www.eHarlequin.com

Printed in U.S.A.

IN PLAIN SIGHT

CHAPTER ONE

ISABEL DELGADO was a precise, orderly person. She liked things to work the way they were supposed to, and objects to be stored in their proper places. At school she'd sometimes been accused of keeping the contents of her handbag in alphabetical order.

That was an exaggeration, but she did compartmentalize with care.

No messy rummaging for Isabel. She could put her hand instantly on a nail file, a pack of tissues or a library card.

So when it came time to plan her death, she embarked on the project with the same meticulous care.

Everything in her plan had to function smoothly, with no loose ends or messy slipups. Isabel realized all too well that good preparation was her only chance to achieve any possibility of life after death.

For weeks she planned her "fatal accident." She'd driven around the Texas countryside north of San Antonio to scout the best possible locations, imagining the scenario, trying to anticipate anything that could go wrong.

She put an envelope full of cash, the diamonds she'd inherited from her mother and all her stock certificates into a safe-deposit box at a bank in San Antonio. Afterward she wondered how long it would be before she could safely slip back to the city and reclaim this small fortune.

The most time-consuming project of all was obtaining duplicates of her identification papers, getting everything reissued from birth certificate and social-security card to passport, marriage license and divorce papers.

A few weeks earlier when she had everything together, Isabel had driven to Abilene to deposit a bulky envelope containing the documents, along with a generous sum of cash, in a locker at the bus depot.

On the final two days her stomach was knotted with tension, and she was too excited to eat. But though she was almost faint with hunger, Isabel knew that in a few hours—after her ''death'' had been successfully accomplished—she would move onto Abilene, and from there embark on her new life.

The first thing she planned to do was eat an enormous meal, with cheesecake for dessert.

On a warm Friday evening in late September, she was finally ready.

For one last time she stood in the vast foyer of her father's San Antonio mansion, dressed in a running suit of navy blue cotton, with white cross-trainers and a red terry-cloth headband, looking around at the kind of luxury that had been her heritage for all the twenty-seven years of her life.

Isabel Delgado was a true golden girl, and not just because of the enormous wealth and privilege she'd been born into. She was blond and tanned, slim and dainty, with the finely drawn, muscular frame of the dedicated runner. Her tanned skin, her French-braided hair, even the highlights in her hazel eyes were a rich golden-brown.

As a small child she'd been a source of pride to her father, but nowadays Pierce Delgado hardly ever came home, and her old friends were all busy with their growing families. Unless the police came here directly with the news of Isabel's death, it could be a long time before anybody even noticed she was gone. Except for one person...

When Isabel realized how little impact the news of her death would have on almost anybody, she felt chilled and deeply sad.

If her sister, Luciana, had still been around, she'd care about Isabel. But their father's anger and coldness had driven Luce away years ago. By now nobody even knew where she was, though Isabel often thought about her beautiful older sister.

"Well, goodbye, everybody," Isabel said aloud to the silent house, bending to pick up her water bottle and a leather waist pack from the bottom of the stairs. "Hey, it's been great."

She left the house, locking the door carefully behind her, and ran down the walk to her little blue Mercedes convertible, which was sitting at the curb with the top rolled down.

Isabel got in, pushed a cassette into the player and looked back at the stately pile of cut limestone that was her father's house, with its grounds so massive that the equally opulent homes of the neighbors were barely within view.

For the first time she had a stirring of doubt about her plan. But then she remembered the escalating dread of recent weeks, the sheer heart-stopping terror that pervaded most of her existence.

Her life was intolerable, and the fear had to stop. Nobody could live this way.

Isabel squared her shoulders, put the sleek little car into gear and headed down the street.

She drove northwest on the freeway leading out of San Antonio, then took an off-ramp and went up through Fredericksburg, deep into the heart of the Hill Country west of Austin.

Out here, far away from the city and the freeway, the summer evening was beautiful, though it was chilly enough that she was tempted to put the top up.

But that wasn't part of the plan. On the off chance that somebody happened to see her car in the Hill Country and testify about it later, it was important for them to notice that the convertible top had been down as she drove.

So she turned up her jacket collar for warmth, enjoying the way the fading light spilled across the hills, and the mesquite and live oak trees rustled and whispered in the breeze.

Heavy clouds massed behind her to the south, threatening a rainstorm, but by the time that storm arrived, she would be well on her way.

Isabel smiled and tapped her fingers on the steering wheel in time to a country song, looking with pleasure at the countryside rolling by. She'd always loved the Hill Country.

Her mother, Pierce Delgado's second wife, had been friends with the J.T. McKinney family at Crystal Creek, whose successful ranching and more recent wine-growing operation was one of the jewels of

Claro County. Isabel had spent many of her summers there as a child. In fact, the family warmth and hospitality at the Double C ranch had been one of the best things in Isabel's lonely childhood. The McKinneys gave her a view of a life so different from her own, with her absent father, brittle alcoholic mother and a half brother and half sister who were both almost a decade older and busy with adult lives of their own by the time Isabel entered adolescence. The memories brought a hot prickle of tears to her eyes.

But this was no time to give way to emotion. She had to stay cool and alert, or she'd never be able to pull the whole thing off.

North of Fredericksburg she turned off the highway and drove up a side road to park on a rocky outcropping, a lookout point high above the Claro River, known as Rimrock Park.

At this time of year the Claro was a lazy sparkle, reflecting the rich colors of the sunset. It gave no hint of the raging torrent it could become in the spring when it flooded and went thundering through the valley like a freight train, sweeping away everything in its path.

Isabel had selected this particular point because the banks narrowed here; the Claro was certainly deep enough to cover a car and had a current powerful enough to carry a body into the Colorado and on toward Lake Travis.

Also, there was a well-used picnic area below, about a hundred yards upriver on the other side. Even from that distance she could see a couple of families with little kids and pets, their food spread out on tables while a group of men nearby played horse-shoes.

She drove her car forward on the lookout point, as far as she could without slipping over the edge and plunging into the water a hundred feet below. When she turned off the music, a clink of metal on metal from the game of horseshoes drifted up to her, along with the muffled shouts of children and barking of dogs.

The sweet everyday sounds seemed unbearably precious and reminded her painfully of everything she'd lost.

Isabel's jaw set in determination. She drew off the terry-cloth headband and pulled on a navy baseball cap, tugging it low enough over her forehead to obscure most of her face.

Then she took her waist pack and wedged it firmly under the front seat. The leather pouch contained all her ID, including her passport and credit cards.

At first she'd been reluctant to include her passport, because it had been such a hassle to get the new one that now waited for her in that bus-depot locker in Abilene. But Isabel needed to make it look as if she'd been leaving the country and had accidentally driven her car over the cliff while taking one last look at the Claro River.

Probably she'd gone to some unnecessary effort, but the whole scene had to be completely believable.

After all, no one who was faking her own death would choose to sacrifice her social-security card, her passport, driver's license and credit cards.

Time was running out. She had to do it now, while the people were still in the picnic ground and could attest to seeing a small blue car plunge into the river from the opposite cliffs.

Her hands began to tremble with nerves and she clenched them into fists, then checked her jacket pocket one last time to make sure she had her wad of cash and the bus ticket she'd bought in San Antonio. In her shoe, under her heel, she could feel the hard shape of the key to the locker in Abilene.

Finally she got out of the car and stood holding the door open.

One more time Isabel checked to make sure the leather pack was wedged under the front seat. For a moment she considered putting it in the glove compartment for safety, but decided that might look a little too staged.

Nervously she patted her pocket, the one containing her money and her ticket to a new life, then tugged the cap even lower over her eyes.

At last she reached inside to slip the car into neutral, gripped the door frame and began to push it toward the edge of the precipice. As soon as it went over the cliff among the scrub mesquite and cactus, she would set off down the road in the opposite direction from the way she'd come, like a jogger out for a run in the cool of the evening. In the unlikely event that anybody asked, she could say she'd already passed the lookout point and hadn't seen a car there.

Her plan was to jog about four miles—an easy distance for Isabel—to the bus depot in Crystal Creek, which was the nearest small town. There she would use the ticket in her pocket to board a bus, ride up to Abilene, about a hundred miles away, and collect her stash of money and her ID.

She would have to lie low for a while in Abilene, of course, until she knew Eric had finally given up searching for her. Then she could devise some way to get safely out of the country. Maybe she'd try going to Mexico again, or to Canada...

But just as the front wheels of the Mercedes hung in space, ready to plunge over the cliff, one of the back wheels was blocked by a small boulder. Isabel pushed and sweated, trying with all her might to rock the little car free.

Suddenly she heard the sound of an approaching vehicle.

"Oh, hell," she muttered, looking around wildly. "Now what?"

There was nowhere to hide among the scrub mesquite and boulders, and the sound was growing closer. In fact, it sounded like two vehicles, possibly a couple of kids on dirt bikes.

If somebody spotted her up here trying to push the car over the cliff, all her careful plans would be ruined. Worse than ruined, because Eric would know what she'd tried to do, and from now on he'd dog her movements even more relentlessly.

The man was bent on possessing her. If he couldn't, he would surely kill her. And after this, nothing would stop him.

With a despairing sob, Isabel gave one great heave and finally sent the small vehicle over the edge. As it fell she closed her eyes and jumped into the void just behind it.

The next few moments seemed to take hours. She

was conscious of space and weightlessness, of the sun blinding her and of the wind that tugged at her clothes and sang in her ears.

Then she was crashing down through tree branches and rustling leaves, rolling among thickets of brush that scratched her face and hands. At the same time she heard a mighty splash, followed by a chorus of startled cries from across the river.

Isabel lay facedown in the heavy brush, cradling her head in her arms like a woman awaiting a blow. Her chest heaved and her heart raced. She was gasping so hard that she was sure her breathing must be audible all the way across the river.

Gradually she began to realize her body was still in one piece and that, for the moment at least, she was safe. Through the screen of brush she could hear the people across the river, their voices clear and distinct on the evening air.

"It was a car!" somebody shouted. "A little blue car. I saw it just when it hit the water!"

"Was anybody in it?"

"I couldn't tell," the reply came as Isabel strained to hear, trying to calm her noisy breathing.

"Somebody call the fire department! Jimmy, get one of those trucks and drive downriver. See if you can find anybody in the water."

Slowly her panic ebbed. Apparently the people on the opposite bank hadn't noticed her body when she'd jumped off the cliff behind the car. And whoever had been driving up to the summit behind her wouldn't have arrived in time to see her jump.

Isabel sat up and did a cautious assessment of her physical state.

She was covered with dirt, had a lot of scrapes and bruises, and was bleeding freely from a gash on her right arm where the jacket sleeve had been torn to shreds. Her face felt moist, and when she touched her cheek, her fingers came away red with blood.

"Damn," she muttered, her thoughts racing. "Damn!"

It would be impossible to get on the bus in this condition without being noticed. Somehow she had to figure out a way to get herself cleaned up and find a change of clothes.

Maybe when darkness came, she could steal something from a farmer's clothesline. But did anybody even use clotheslines anymore?

Isabel didn't have a clue. She'd never done laundry in her life.

Meanwhile the confusion on the other side of the river seemed to be growing. She heard sirens approaching in the distance, then the frantic barking of a dog.

"Oh, God, I need to get away from here," she said, looking around wildly.

The witnesses clearly weren't sure the car had been occupied when it went into the water. But even if nobody had seen her falling behind it, they would still come over here and search the riverbank in case a driver or passengers had fallen out while the car was in flight and were lying injured in the bushes.

Shivering in the evening chill, Isabel pulled off her jacket, gripped the hem between her teeth and tore a ragged strip from the front to bind her arm, then twisted the length of cloth with a stick until the bleeding stopped.

She wondered if her arm needed stitches and how she was going to get proper medical attention. But when she removed her makeshift tourniquet, the flow of blood was just a trickle, already clotting.

The sky darkened, and Isabel looked up to see clouds massing overhead. Lightning split the air, and a low rumble of thunder came shuddering across the hills. At the same time, raindrops began to land on her face and patter in the bushes nearby.

The rain was a stroke of good luck, Isabel realized. A heavy rainfall would soon wash away any trace of her presence on the riverbank, even if they came and searched with dogs.

But she had to find some shelter. Maybe she could pay somebody to—

With sudden, heart-stopping terror, she paused and looked down at her torn jacket. For the first time she realized that not just the sleeve but most of the jacket's right front, including the pocket, had been completely torn away.

Slowly, numb with dread, Isabel tried to make her sluggish mind work out what had happened.

As she'd pushed the car, her jacket must have caught on it somewhere, maybe the door or the rear bumper. Her pocket had been ripped free, possibly even carried into the water with the car.

And that meant her money and her bus ticket to Abilene were both gone.

She whimpered, then buried her face in her hands and struggled to compose herself.

Panic wasn't going to accomplish anything. She had to think, and there was no time to waste. Emergency vehicles were arriving on the other side of the river, and the shouts and calls of the searchers intensified, though their words were harder to make out now that rain had begun to fall heavily.

She had no time to scour the riverbank for her lost possessions, even if by some miracle they'd fallen clear of the water. It was important to get away from here before people came around to the other side of the river and launched a search in the brush.

Again she tried to think, to assess all the possibilities.

If the bit of torn jacket had gone into the water along with the car, would that alert police investigators to what she'd done?

Not necessarily, she decided.

They weren't going to find a body, of course, so they would be likely to assume part of the jacket had torn free when the body washed out of the car. The bus ticket was printed on such flimsy paper a dousing in the river would turn it to unrecognizable pulp. And a wad of money would carry no significance to anybody. People probably assumed women like Isabel Delgado carried wads of money around with them all the time.

It would be worse, though, if the jacket fragments had fallen free of the car on this side of the river and somebody found that bus ticket. Then someone might work out what she'd been trying to do. But the brush was so thick here at the base of the cliff. And the rain was torrential now—one of those storms that seemed to blow out of nowhere during autumn in the Hill Country.

Though she was starting to feel chilled and sick, Isabel was still grateful for the rain. It fell like a dense silver curtain, soothing her wounds and hiding her from view as she made her way though the brush.

She was almost a hundred yards downriver, away from the shouts and sirens, before the full enormity of her situation hit her.

Without the contents of her jacket pocket, she had no way of surviving. She had no money and no way to get herself—unseen—to Abilene to reclaim her careful stash of identification papers.

When she realized this, she sank to her knees on the carpet of rotting leaves and wrapped her arms around her shivering body.

Her hair was wet and dirty, plastered to her neck and face, and she was gripped by uncontrollable spasms. Moisture dripped from her cheeks, frightening her, but when she touched her face, no trace of blood stained her hands.

High above and upriver she heard calls from the summit where she'd been and the sound of people descending the slope.

Panicking again, she got up and set off once more, crouching low and running along a leafy path in the brush made by deer and rabbits. Rain was still pouring and night had set in with alarming suddenness. She could barely make out the path and stayed on it mostly by instinct. Whenever she blundered into the surrounding thickets, cruel branches and thorns grabbed at her shredded jogging pants and stabbed her legs.

After what seemed like several hours, she slowed her pace. The heavy rain was letting up, and the night was silent except for the rustle of dripping trees and the mournful hooting of an owl somewhere nearby.

The clouds separated and a partial moon drifted out from the lacy screen.

Isabel crawled in among the lower branches of a cedar tree and paused to catch her breath. She was chilled through, badly winded, weak from loss of blood. Her arm had begun to throb painfully. She wondered if the gash could have become infected so soon.

But in spite of the cold and the pain of her injuries, she was most distressed by the fact that she no longer had a plan. Her only thought was to put distance between herself and anybody who might be searching the riverbank. Beyond that, she didn't have the slightest idea what to do, or how to make her way to Abilene so she could use the key that was still safely tucked in her running shoe.

Various possibilities presented themselves, none of them very rational.

She could knock on the door of a farmhouse along the river, tell the owner she'd been in an accident and ask to call her father.

No. Pierce Delgado was in Europe on business.

Maybe she could ask for help from her brother or one of her father's personal staff, but after what she'd seen a few weeks earlier, she didn't really trust any of them. And she didn't want anyone to know Isabel Delago was still alive.

Besides, even making a phone call would mean revealing her identity. Nobody in their right mind would let a stranger into the house to use the phone, even an injured one.

Maybe she could claim amnesia, saying the trauma

of her accident had driven all memory from her mind.

But then they would call the police, and that prospect was so distressing that Isabel, who never cried, began to sob aloud.

Suddenly weary beyond endurance, she stretched out and lay full-length on the soft carpet of leaves. Her head and arm throbbed, and her body ached with fatigue.

I'll just rest for a minute, she thought. *After a little rest I'll feel better, and then I can decide what to do.*

It was her last conscious thought for many hours. Almost at once she fell deeply asleep and didn't wake until the morning sun was high in the sky.

CHAPTER TWO

THE IRRIGATION PUMP had broken down again. Dan Gibson knelt and prodded it carefully with grease-stained fingers, wondering if all it needed was something simple like new washers, or if this was going to be another expensive overhaul. Maybe he'd even have to replace the creaky old piece of machinery.

He couldn't afford a new pump without getting another operating loan. And even Bill Hendricks, the sympathetic bank manager in Crystal Creek, was probably going to tell him that was impossible.

Wearily, Dan sat back on his heels and squinted into the fading sunlight where his children played along the river.

Twelve-year-old Ellie was in the water, wading up to her knees, bent almost double as she searched for arrowheads in the bright shallows.

Chris was four years younger than Ellie, and she wasn't allowed to go into the water unless Dan was with her. She was dragging their red wagon along the river's edge, and she and little Josh were filling it with mounds of colored pebbles they intended to use for some mysterious game of their own.

Josh was only two, chubby and energetic in a blue-denim romper suit. His sisters were in sandals, but Josh wore heavy miniature boots to protect his feet from the rocks along the shore. His golden curls shone in the sunlight, and his voice drifted on the wind, as happy as a little bird's.

Dan grinned briefly and tipped his cap back, watching the children. But his smile faded when he looked around at the hay meadow behind him, then at the stalled irrigation pump.

At least a heavy rainfall the night before had provided some moisture for his rapidly maturing crop. It gave him a little breathing room while he worked on the pump. But if he couldn't harvest this final hay crop and pay back a few loans, his financial prospects for the coming year were going to be damned bleak.

"Ellie," he called, "it's time for the kids to have a bath and go to bed."

The two girls raised a howl of protest, claiming extra privileges because it was Saturday night. Josh chimed in, though Dan suspected his son was objecting more to be companionable than out of any real indignation.

Josh was such an easygoing little boy. He actually loved the routines of bedtime, with his bubble bath and toys and storybooks.

"Okay, fifteen more minutes," Dan said. "But you two have already been up more than an hour past your schoolday bedtime."

A contented silence fell, and he returned his attention to the pump.

Dan was a tall, well-built man in jeans and a plaid work shirt, with a disheveled head of light brown hair that was as unruly as Josh's if it got too long. He had smoky green eyes and a grin that transformed his hard face, though these days it was an increasingly rare occurrence.

As he probed the pump mechanism with a screwdriver blade, something caught his eye and he looked up quickly. A flash of color glimmered in the brush near the water, just downriver from where his children were playing. But whatever was in the thicket vanished as quickly as it had appeared.

He frowned, wondering if one of the McKinney horses had strayed this far from the Double C. If so, he'd have to give J.T. a call.

For a moment he considered going over and checking, then dismissed the thought.

Most likely it was a deer, or a hawk flying low after some scurrying rodent, or even a plastic sack blown along the river in last night's storm, caught and fluttering from a branch.

At least to his immense relief, Dan found the problem with the pump—a ragged washer—and knew the repair was only going to cost a few dollars. He had only to get to the hardware store in Crystal Creek.

Disaster was averted for another day, he thought wryly.

But how many bullets could a man dodge before one of them finally hit him and killed all his dreams?

"Come on, kids," he said, getting to his feet. "Time's up."

There was another brief protest, but this time it was halfhearted. They knew he meant what he said, and it was pointless to argue.

Chris walked at her father's side toward the little farmhouse, holding his hand and pulling the wagon, now heavily loaded. Dan looked down into her earnest, freckled face. "What are you going to do with all the rocks, honey?"

"Josh and I are building a castle," Chris said. "We're starting on it tomorrow. It's going to be awesome, Daddy."

"Awesome," Josh said contentedly, trotting at Dan's other side, clinging to his other hand. "Gonna be awesome."

"You two babies don't have a clue how to build a castle," Ellie said scornfully from behind them. "It'll just be a big mess."

Chris's face turned pink with outrage, and Dan ruffled her hair.

"Maybe I'll have a little time to help with the castle tomorrow, sweetie," he said.

His younger daughter's eyes blazed with happiness. "Really, Daddy?"

"Maybe," he said cautiously.

Chris rounded on her sister in triumph. "Daddy's going to help me and Josh build the castle," she said, "and it'll be the best castle in the whole world. So there, you stupid dummy."

"Stupid dummy yourself," Ellie said, unperturbed. "I wish Gypsy was here," she added. "Does it hurt to get spayed?"

"Gypsy's having a good time at the clinic with all the other dogs," Dan said. "She'll be home tomorrow."

Josh stumbled on a tuft of grass near the house and whimpered, rubbing his eyes with a dirty hand. Dan picked the little boy up and carried him the rest of the way, wondering if he'd be able to keep his

word and find a few minutes the next day to help
Chris with her castle.

He worked from dawn to dark, often eighteen
hours at a stretch. In addition to the hay fields, he
grew grapes for the McKinney winery, kept bees in
rows of wooden hives at the edge of the hay
meadow, a small herd of cattle and some pigs and
goats, anything he could think of to pay the mortgage
and keep his farming operation afloat.

And with three little kids to look after, his life
wasn't easy. In fact, most of the time it was a waking
nightmare.

Still holding Josh, who nestled drowsily against
his father's shoulder with a thumb jammed into his
mouth, Dan followed the two little girls into the
house.

In the kitchen he glanced around and sighed.

The place looked like a tornado had passed
through. No matter how hard he tried, tidiness and
order seemed impossible to attain. Toys and clothes
littered the floor and the sink was stacked with dirty
supper dishes; the girls had fought over whose turn
it was to do them. Through the doorway he could
see into the sparsely furnished living room and knew
how badly it needed dusting.

There were times when Dan longed fiercely for the
simple things, like a clean house and a hot meal on
the table when he came in from work, and some
peace from kids who seem to squabble all the time.

Not that he'd ever want to be parted from his children for long. But sometimes he was just so weary.

He sent Chris into the bathroom to run a tub for
herself and Josh, then began to pick up the things

scattered about the floor. Ellie surprised him by marching over to the sink and filling it with hot water.

Something about her rigid back alerted him. He sat down at the table and watched her thoughtfully.

Ellie's real name was Danielle, which she hated with such passion that nobody ever dared to use it. Of the three children, she was the only one who looked like their mother, and one day she was going to be a real beauty.

She had silky black hair with a touch of curl, clipped short around her face, and big brown eyes that could be lively or sullen depending on her mood. In June, just a month after her twelfth birthday, she'd begun her menstrual periods and been appalled by her body's treachery. It was "gross," she'd said, and burst into tears.

Dan had cuddled her tenderly while she cried. He'd shown her books on female reproduction and explained that what was happening to her was not a tragedy but a wondrous thing.

But her moods were more erratic all the time nowadays, with shifts that left him feeling baffled and hopeless.

He suspected she might be having a tough time getting along with some of the kids at school, though she refused to talk to him about it. When he spoke to her teachers, they said Ellie was bright but very quiet. None of them were aware of any particular problem.

At the moment, however, Dan sensed that his daughter's silence needed to be explored. He sat at the kitchen table, doodling with a blue crayon in one of Chris's coloring books and considering how to go about it.

He could hear muffled shouts and laughter from the direction of the bathroom, and winced at the sound of water splashing onto the worn tiles he'd never had time to replace.

"So," he said casually, "what's up, Ellie?"

She kept her back turned, wiping dishes, rinsing them and stacking them in the plastic rack. "I don't see why we can't have a dishwasher," she muttered. "You should see Aunt Mary's house now, Daddy. She has two dishwashers. Last month Uncle Bubba gave her another one just for pots and pans."

"Good for Mary," he said mildly. "She's worked hard all her life, and her ostriches are making a lot of money for them now. She deserves anything Bubba wants to give her. But we can't afford a dishwasher."

"We can't afford anything," the girl said. "It's so stupid, how poor we are."

Dan restrained himself from making a sharp reply. She was just a child and couldn't be expected to understand his financial situation.

"So what's going on?" he asked again.

"I don't know what you mean," she said, but he could see the way her thin shoulders stiffened.

"You've been real quiet since we came in from outside. Is something bothering you?"

"Of course not." She wiped a plate with unnecessary energy and slammed it into the dish rack. "Except that I have to do stupid Chris's job for her because she's too lazy."

"You might as well tell me, Ellie," Dan said reasonably, "because you know I'm going to find out, anyhow. And I might be upset if something happens to catch me by surprise."

When she turned around, her boyish face wasn't defiant, just troubled.

"Daddy…" She leaned against the counter, one thin brown leg wrapped around the other. Dan could see the bare sole of her foot, dirty and marked with a painful-looking bruise.

"What, sweetheart?" he asked.

"If I found something, would it be mine to keep?"

"I guess it depends on where you found it," he said after a moment's thought.

"I mean, if I found it here on our farm and I knew it didn't belong to you or Chris and Josh."

"So how would it get here?"

She turned away uneasily and looked out the window while Dan watched her with growing interest.

"How about if the wind blew it here?" Ellie said, fixing her dark eyes on him again. "Would it be mine if I found it?"

Dan thought this over, then nodded. "Yes," he said. "If the wind blew something here and you found it, I'd say you were entitled to keep it."

She turned back around, relief shining in her face. She reached into the pocket of her shorts, took a bit of paper out and came over to place it on the table in front of him. Dan stared in astonishment.

It was a wet, crumpled, fifty-dollar bill.

"I found it in the river," she said. "Just floating along in the water."

"No kidding." Dan studied the bill, fascinated, then grinned at his daughter. "Let's get some flashlights and go back out there,'' he said. ''Maybe there's more.''

She laughed, picked up the bill and returned it to her pocket.

''It'll have to go into your bank account,'' Dan told her. ''Unless there's anything you need to buy. Clothes or something for school.''

''I don't want any stupid clothes. Can you put it in the bank for me when you go to town?''

''Sure,'' Dan said. ''And if things get real tough,'' he added, ''I can borrow from you. With fifty dollars in the bank, you'll be the richest person in the family.''

She smiled, then turned away and began drying dishes. An uneasy silence fell.

''So,'' Dan said at last, ''we haven't had a chance to talk much since yesterday, Ellie. What happened with Mrs. Graham?''

Her back stiffened again, and she rubbed a plate without looking at him. ''That woman was such an old cow,'' she muttered. ''And she was mean, Daddy. You should have heard how she yelled at Josh.''

Dan sighed. ''You never give them a chance, honey. Mrs. Graham was the third housekeeper I've hired in the last four months, and she only lasted a few days. That's some kind of record, even for us.''

''We don't need a housekeeper,'' Ellie said. ''Chris and I can do it.''

Dan looked around at the messy kitchen, then back at his daughter. ''She told me you were rude and impossible to manage.''

"She was a jerk!" Ellie said passionately. "I hated her!"

Dan struggled to be patient.

"You hate all of them, sweetheart. But we need some help, and it's not easy to find a housekeeper like Mrs. Graham who's willing to live in Crystal Creek and drive back and forth every day. Most of them want to live in, but we don't have an extra room."

"We don't need her! I hate having strangers in my house, Daddy. Especially jerks like her who don't even know what they're doing."

"She was highly recommended by the last family she worked for," Dan said. "And she was willing to do housework and child care and make a hot meal in the evening. It seemed like a pretty good deal to me."

"But it must have cost a lot." Ellie turned to look at him directly.

"Quite a bit," Dan admitted.

"And you're always talking about how we don't have any money."

"Things are tight, but some expenses are necessary, Ellie. I worry about Chris and Josh. They need more attention than they're getting, and I'm too busy to look after them properly."

"I can look after them," Ellie said stubbornly. "And Chris and I can work harder to keep the house clean. I'm learning to cook supper, too."

"Macaroni and cheese every night isn't exactly a balanced diet, honey."

"Aunt Mary can teach me other stuff. She said I

could come over any time I wanted to learn to cook.''

Dam looked in despair at his daughter. He loved her dearly, but Ellie was the most frustrating, inflexible person he'd ever known.

She's just like you, his wife used to point out. *Everybody in Crystal Creek knows where that stubbornness of hers comes from, Dan Gibson.*

''Do you ever give any thought to what life is like for me, Ellie?'' he said quietly.

''I don't know what you mean.'' She stood on tiptoe to put glasses away in the cupboard.

''Well, you keep telling me how you and Chris can look after things and we don't need a housekeeper. But the two of you are in school all day. That means I have to take Josh with me all the time, no matter what I'm doing. It's not easy to do a full day of farm work with a two-year-old running along behind you. And he still needs a nap in the afternoon, you know.''

She considered this, frowning. ''Aunt Mary would look after him anytime you asked. She loves him.''

''You kids are my responsibility,'' he said. ''Mary and Bubba have been good to us since your mother went away, but I can't ask Mary to be a full-time baby-sitter. She has work of her own to do.''

Ellie put the plastic rack in a lower cabinet and wiped out the chipped sink.

''Well, I still don't see why we need to have some creepy stranger around the house,'' she said. ''And I just hated that Mrs. Graham. She looked in all my dresser drawers.''

"She was housecleaning," Dan said wearily. "God knows, this place could use it."

"Chris and I can clean," Ellie said again. "We can clean as good as she did."

Dan watched his daughter, wondering what made her so prickly and defensive. But he understood her well enough to know he wasn't getting anywhere with the argument.

He'd just have to try again, and see if next time he could manage to hire somebody who wouldn't alienate this difficult child of his.

"I'll go and help Chris put Josh to bed," Ellie told him, sidling from the room.

At least she seemed anxious to appease him.

"Thank you," Dan said, opening up the newspaper. "Call me and I'll come in and read to them when they're in bed."

He barely had time to scan the headlines before Chris trailed into the kitchen wearing what passed for pajamas with both girls—jogging pants and a T-shirt. She carried her old Raggedy Ann doll and was looking for a glass of milk.

Dan gave her the milk and a couple of cookies, then took her down the hall and supervised as she brushed her teeth, ignoring her protests that she'd already brushed them.

He tucked her into the upper bunk, smoothed the blond hair back from her forehead and gave her a kiss while Ellie carried Josh into the room and deposited him in the lower bunk.

The little boy snuggled drowsily into the pillows, his thumb in his mouth again, his teddy bear held close to his face.

The girls had washed and dried his hair, and it smelled pleasantly of strawberry shampoo. Dan bent to kiss his son, then settled on the floor near Josh's bed, reading aloud to the two younger children from an old copy of *Peter Pan*.

Josh didn't understand the story, but he was usually too sleepy at bedtime to care what his father read as long as he was nearby for a while. Chris, however, was passionately caught up in the adventures of Peter and Tinkerbell. Several times recently Dan had caught her trying to fly off the haystack.

Ellie left the crowded little bedroom, heading out to the front porch where she had a private sleeping space on all but the coldest winter nights, when she bunked on the sofa in the living room.

After the younger children were settled, Dan went out through the house and knocked on the door of the little screened veranda.

"Come in," Ellie called.

She was lying in bed, reading a copy of *My Friend Flicka* from the school library.

"I loved that book when I was a kid," Dan told her, pausing near her bed. "There are two more in the series, you know."

"I already got the librarian to reserve them for me. Can I tell you something, Daddy?" She looked up at him gravely.

"Sure. What is it?"

"I'm not sorry Mrs. Graham went away, because she was a real stupid woman, but I'm sorry the place is such a mess all the time. If we don't get another housekeeper, I'll try harder to keep things nice."

"Thank you, Ellie." He kissed her cheek and went

back toward the living room. "Don't leave your light on too long," he said over his shoulder.

"Okay, I won't."

He paused to smile at her. She lay in a warm circle of lamplight while crickets chirped beyond the window and moths fluttered softly against the screens.

"Good night, kiddo."

"Night, Daddy."

Dan wandered back to the kitchen, too tired to think about reading a book himself or even watching television. All he wanted was to have a shower in the damp, cluttered bathroom and fall into bed.

But first he made himself a cup of instant coffee and carried it over to the table to read the rest of the newspaper.

A small article on the second page, accompanied by a photograph, caught his attention.

"Heiress missing after car plunges into the Claro River," the caption read.

Dan scanned the article, realizing the fatal accident must have happened last night, quite close to his farm. A young woman named Isabel Delgado, age twenty-seven, had been in a car and plunged to her death from the rocky promontory overlooking Rimrock Park.

"It is unknown at this time," the article said, "whether Delgado's death was accidental. She is the daughter of well-known Texas industrialist Pierce Delgado, who is on his way home from a business meeting in Belgium. Isabel Delgado was divorced two years ago from Eric Matthias, a police lieutenant in Austin. Matthias told reporters he has not seen his ex-wife for several weeks, but that her behavior has been 'unstable' in recent months.''

The paper went on to report that searchers had scoured the banks of the Claro River, looking for any trace of the woman whose body had not yet been recovered, although the late-model Mercedes had been dragged from the river about twelve hours after its disappearance. A number of the missing woman's personal papers had been recovered from the car, including her passport, but there was no sign of her body.

Of course, that wasn't surprising to Dan. She'd apparently been driving a convertible with the top down, and her body would have been sucked right out into the river.

He'd lived in this county for all of his thirty-five years and was intimately acquainted with the river and its habits. He knew that near Rimrock Park the Claro ran deep, with a powerful undercurrent that had caused many drownings over the years.

He looked at the woman's picture displayed beside the article. She had an unusual face, framed by shoulder-length hair that seemed light, though it was hard to tell from the grainy black-and-white image.

What caught him most were her eyes, looking straight at the camera with a thoughtful, appraising look, and her mouth that lifted on one side in a smile that seemed both quizzical and a bit timid.

It was an interesting face, he thought. She looked like a woman who had some humor and intelligence, and would be fun to talk with.

Then he remembered that Isabel Delgado was dead, and her body would no doubt be washing up in a few days along the banks of the Colorado or the shores of Lake Travis. She would never smile or talk with any man again.

Suddenly feeling unbearably tired, Dan folded the paper to conceal the woman's charming lopsided smile and put it in a wastebasket near the door.

He got up, switched off the kitchen lights and headed for his bedroom.

CHAPTER THREE

ISABEL CROUCHED in the bushes, watching as the lights winked off one by one in the little farmhouse. It had been more than twenty-four hours since she'd plunged over the cliff, and she was in agony.

Her right forearm was definitely infected, swollen and hot, throbbing with pain. The rest of her body was also scratched and bruised. She was filthy, hungry and ravaged with thirst, but afraid to drink the river water.

All day she'd been making her way along the shoreline, struggling through thick brush, hiding fearfully whenever she was in danger of being seen. Now she shivered with cold and felt weak and lightheaded, ready to cry like a child at the thought of spending another night outdoors.

For the past several hours she'd been lying in the brush, watching the farmhouse and the three children who played along the water's edge while a big, rugged-looking man she guessed was their father crouched over some piece of machinery in a field nearby.

The house was isolated, at least a mile from anybody else. Isabel was hoping that like many others in this peaceful, rural area, the farmer didn't lock his doors at night. She had a risky plan.

After the lights were all out and enough time had passed for everybody to be asleep, she intended to sneak into the farmhouse and steal some food, maybe even a change of clothes and some medicine for her arm.

If she found any money lying around, she was going to steal that, as well.

She knew the plan wasn't rational, but she was so hungry and painracked that she couldn't think clearly anymore. In a weird, nightmarish fashion, her mind kept slipping in and out of reality. Occasionally she had images of being at home, lying in the four-poster bed in her spacious living quarters, while sunlight spilled across the hardwood floor and the housekeeper carried in a tray laden with food.

Isabel closed her eyes and pictured the food on the tray.

Golden crisp waffles swimming in maple syrup, little sausages and a cut-glass bowl of fresh fruit, hot sweet coffee with cream...

She moaned and pushed the seductive images aside, trying to concentrate on the house. She could no longer remember if minutes or hours had passed since the last light had been extinguished, but she knew it was late because the night felt so cold. And the moon was high, spilling a cold silver glow over the landscape, turning the slow-moving river to a stream of hammered pewter.

She heard something crash through the undergrowth nearby and looked fearfully over her shoulder. The noise subsided for a moment, then began to recede. Probably a deer or stray cow.

Isabel dropped her chin to her chest, waiting for her heart to stop pounding.

Another dreadful thought struck her.

What if that noise had been made by a dog?

She hadn't seen any dogs outside with the man and the children, but there could still be one nearby. If so, it would surely bark, maybe even attack her when she sneaked toward the house.

The prospect was terrifying, but she was too hungry and sick to care.

Holding her breath, she crept from the brush and crossed the yard toward the darkened house, moving from tree to tree, a ragged shadow slipping through the moonlight.

No dog raised an alarm, and she reached the back door feeling limp with relief.

She eased the screen open and grasped the handle on the inside door. The knob resisted for a moment, then began to turn.

Isabel's heart again pounded in terror. Soundlessly she pushed the door open, stepped into a little back porch and paused for her eyes to adjust to the dimness.

After a while she could make out shapes and spaces, faintly illuminated by moonlight spilling through windows. The room seemed to be cluttered with children's shoes, boots and toys. Rows of jackets hung on pegs. Many of them looked small, and a few were far too large for Isabel.

Still, those big garments would provide some warmth, and she reminded herself to take a few of them as she was leaving.

Through an opening she could see what appeared

to be a good-size kitchen. Rows of cabinets, the dull gleam of appliances, a shadowy outline of table and chairs.

So far, so good. Where there was a kitchen, there had to be food.

Isabel paused in the porch, feeling faint and light-headed again. She grasped the door frame and waited for the dizziness to pass, then shook her head blearily, trying to formulate a plan.

The best thing would be to head straight for the tall bulk of the refrigerator. That was probably a lot less risky than opening cabinets one after another, trying to find food.

By now, her brave plans of searching for money and medicine had completely vanished. She didn't even feel all that hungry anymore, just sick and shaky. It was so terrifying to be in this place, only feet away from other human beings who could wake up at any moment and come after her.

Finally she tiptoed to the rear of the porch and took a big denim shirt from one of the pegs. It was lined with flannel and smelled slightly of engine oil. She longed to put it on her shivering body, but that would have to wait. Carrying the shirt she edged into the kitchen.

When Isabel opened the fridge, she winced at the light that flooded the room. Hastily she spread the shirt on the floor and began to pile food onto it.

Part of a ham, a loaf of bread, three cans of soda, some apples…

At the sight and smell of food, her hunger pangs returned. She had dined in some of the finest restaurants in the world, but she'd never seen a banquet like this. Her mouth watered, and her body trembled with deep spasms. Again she felt dizzy. It was all she could do to concentrate, but she knew it might be a long, long time before another opportunity like this presented itself.

She gobbled a bunch of grapes, blissfully savoring their moist flavor, then tore off some of the ham with her teeth and ate a couple of slices of bread.

At last, trying not to make the slightest noise, she continued to pile food onto her makeshift pack.

DAN HAD ALWAYS BEEN a light sleeper, even more so now that he had the full responsibility of his children. Anything was enough to rouse him, the trace of a cough from Josh, or Chris's soft whimper during one of her nightmares.

Now he awoke and lay staring at the ceiling, wondering what had disturbed him. There was no sound from the small bedroom next door, and Ellie always slept like a log once she switched off her light.

Still, he had a sense of something alien in his house, a sort of menacing whisper drifting on the silent night air.

There!

He heard it again, the soft creak of a floorboard, a distant muffled sound coming from the direction of the kitchen.

Dan slipped out of bed and moved quietly toward the door. When he reached the hallway, he could see the soft glow of light from the open fridge. A quick glance confirmed that Chris and Josh were both sound asleep in their bunks. Through the living-room

window he could see the covers mounded over Ellie's body.

Then another muffled scrap of sound drifted along
the hallway. Dan's skin prickled, and the hair rose
on the nape of his neck. Soundlessly he took a baseball bat that one of the children had left leaning on
the arm of the sofa and crept toward the kitchen door.
Flattening himself against the archway, he peered in.

What he saw made him suck in his breath and grip
the bat tightly in his hands.

A ragged, filthy urchin knelt by the open door of
the fridge, wearing torn dark clothes and a baseball
cap. Moving with clumsy haste, the boy seized food
and piled it onto one of Dan's heavy work shirts,
spread on the floor.

The intruder was so intent on his task that he
seemed unaware of any danger. Dan felt a rising anger at this invasion. He stepped into the kitchen just
as the thief sprang to his feet and stared, wild-eyed
with terror.

Brandishing his bat like a club, Dan gripped the
boy's arm, then looked down in alarm as the kid
seemed to faint in his grasp, crumpling slowly to the
floor.

By the light spilling from the open refrigerator,
Dan realized several things. The slender arm he held
was badly gashed and swollen. The pain he'd in-
flicted when he gripped it had apparently caused the
boy to pass out.

Slowly Dan also realized the thief wasn't a boy at
all, but a young woman in a torn jogging outfit. She
was filthy and covered with caked blood from many
scratches. Her face had a vaguely familiar look,

though her hair was matted and dirty, and her features shadowed under the ball cap.

He knelt beside her, automatically putting the food back in the fridge while he kept watch on her, then tugged off the cap to get a better look. When her eyes fluttered open and she stared up at him, he remembered where he'd seen her.

It was the woman whose picture had been in the newspaper, the heiress from San Antonio whose car had plunged off a cliff and into the Claro River the day before.

She tried to scramble to her feet, but Dan grasped her shoulders. Clearly too weak to fight, she subsided, head drooping, and whimpered in terror.

"I'm sorry," she whispered, sniffling. "I was so hungry, and my arm hurts."

Some of Dan's anger ebbed, but he continued his grasp of her shoulders. "Why didn't you just knock on the door? I would have been glad to help you."

"I can't..." Her head drooped again, and he could see her chin began to tremble.

"What?" he asked.

"I can't let anybody see me." She looked up again with passionate entreaty. "Please don't call the police. Please, I'm begging you, just let me go. I promise I won't bother you again."

"I can't let you go," Dan said. "What will you do? Your clothes are in shreds, you're obviously half-starved and that arm needs some medication right away. Of course I'm going to call the police."

The woman struggled frantically in his grasp. "No!" she cried. "If you do that, he's going to find me!"

"Who's going to find you?"

Her face had drained of color and her lips were blue. She seemed completely irrational. "He'll get to me for sure this time," she said. "Even my father is on his side now. Nobody believes me when I try to tell them what he's like. Please, please, don't let any of them near me. Oh, God, I'm begging you, please..."

Her voice trailed off and she fell heavily against him. Dan held her in his arms, looking down at her with concern.

She was groggy but still conscious, and badly in need of a wash. He put her gently on the floor, then went to the bathroom and began to run water into the tub, adding some of the bubble bath his girls liked to use. As the tub filled, he went back to the kitchen, helped the woman to her feet and supported her down the hallway.

He knew this was probably crazy, bringing a strange woman into the house with his children. Especially one who seemed to be in some kind of danger. But he was moved in spite of himself by her fear, and the fragile look and feel of her body.

In the bathroom he paused awkwardly, looking down at her pale, scratched face.

"Can you manage in here on your own?"

She nodded jerkily and began to fumble with her tattered clothes. After a moment she forced a grimace that he recognized as a smile. "That bath looks like heaven," she whispered. "I don't think I've ever seen anything so beautiful."

"Well, believe me, this place isn't heaven," Dan

said grimly, standing on the tiles and looking at the welter of plastic toys on the tub ledge.

Still, he was moved by her courage, and felt a sudden lump in his throat. "Look, I'll bring a chair and sit in the hall just outside the door," he told her. "Call me if you need anything, okay?"

He left hastily, carried a stool from the living room and set it near the closed door, then listened in silence to the muffled series of small splashes as she lowered her body into the tub.

"Are you all right?" he called in a loud whisper, taking care not to wake the two children who slept just across the hall. "Is the water hot enough?"

"It's lovely," she answered. "Thank you so much. I could stay here forever."

"Stay as long as you like."

After a few more minutes of silence, followed by a lot of hearty, reassuring splashes, he heard the sound of the woman hauling herself from the tub. Suddenly she uttered a soft cry of distress.

Dan hurried into the bathroom to find her leaning against the wall and clutching a towel loosely around her body. She seemed unsteady and very pale, swaying on her feet.

Dan supported her with one arm, grabbed the towel and wrapped it tight again, but not without catching a fleeting glimpse of her nakedness.

Though cut and bruised, her body was lovely, with long slim legs, a slender, tapering waist and high, firm breasts. She had a golden tan except for the skimpy bikini patches across her nipples and around her hips.

Angry at himself for looking, even so briefly, he

turned away and stared grimly at the wall. "Are you all right?" he asked. "Can you manage on your own now?"

"I think so," she said from behind him. "I just felt so...so dizzy for a minute right after I got out of the water."

"I'll find you some clothes," he said.

Dan went into the adjoining room to get one of his shirts and a pair of boxers, then handed them through the partly opened door, setting them on the hamper.

"Thank you," she said from within the room, her voice already sounding a little stronger.

Dan hovered anxiously near the closed door and was relieved when she said, "All right, I'm decent. You can come in now."

The transformation was amazing. Except for the mass of wet hair pulled back from her face, she was exactly like that lovely, thoughtful young woman in the newspaper picture.

"You look a lot better," he said neutrally.

"Almost human?"

"Oh, I wouldn't go that far," he said.

His attempt at humor was rewarded with a weary smile. "Just try spending twenty-four hours starving in the rain and mud," she said with a brief show of spirit. "See how great you look."

He sobered, remembering the seriousness of the situation.

"Okay, let's have a look at that arm, and then you can go to bed."

"You won't tell anybody about me?" she asked. Her eyes were an unusual color, a sort of golden brown, set within heavy dark lashes. For the first time he noticed a faint drift of freckles across the bridge of her nose.

"Will you let me go?" she asked.

Dan hesitated. "We'll talk about it tomorrow," he said.

"Oh, please, you can't tell anybody I was here." Her pupils dilated in terror and her body tensed. "Please, if you—"

"Look, don't start getting all upset again," he said. "I won't tell anybody until we've had a chance to talk. But you'll have to stay in the bedroom and keep quiet," he added, "because I have three little kids living here, and we can't let them catch sight of you if you want to stay secret."

"I'll be really quiet," she promised.

He opened a tube of salve and smeared it over the gash on her arm, then fastened it with a neat row of butterfly bandages and wrapped it in gauze.

"Are you allergic to any antibiotics?" he asked her.

She shook her head.

Dan hesitated, then gave her one of the tablets the doctor in Crystal Creek had prescribed for him recently when he cut his hand on some dirty barbed wire and developed a painful infection. He knew it wasn't smart to use a prescription on another person, but this was an emergency. And, as fearful as she obviously was of being discovered, the woman was hardly going to agree to see a doctor, no matter how he pressured her.

By the time he finished bandaging her arm, she

was drifting off to sleep, her wet head lolling drowsily.

"I need to get you a dryer for that hair," he said.

"Hack it off," she murmured.

"Beg your pardon?"

"I don't want to bother with it. I'm too tired." She looked up at him with bleary appeal. "Couldn't we just get some scissors and cut it all off?"

"But I can't—"

"Please," she said, "it needs to be cut, anyway. God knows, I don't care how it looks. Let's just get rid of it."

With some reluctance Dan got his scissors and razor comb from a drawer and cut her matted, tangled hair, trimming it neatly around her ears the same way he cut Chris's.

He tossed the damp strands in the wastebasket, then toweled her hair so it stood up around her face in damp little spikes.

"It's still wet," he told her. "I'll need to dry it before you go to bed."

She examined herself ruefully in the mirror, touching the little spikes. "At least it won't take long."

She lowered herself gingerly onto the edge of the tub while Dan stood above her to blow-dry her hair. Now that it was short, it looked considerably darker than it had in the newspaper photograph. And the gamine cut was surprisingly attractive with her delicate features.

"You look nice," he said.

She didn't respond, just leaned back with her eyes closed.

"Do you still want something to eat?" he asked.

She shook her head. "Not hungry anymore. Just...so tired."

Dan helped her up and guided her into his bedroom, tucked her into the double bed and pulled the covers over her body. She looked up at him in exhausted silence, her features washed silver by the moonlight.

"Thank you," she murmured. "So wonderful. Thank you."

"Go to sleep," he told her gruffly.

She snuggled down in the covers and he sat on the mattress beside her, trying to think.

There was no other empty bed in the little house. If he slept on the sofa and the kids found him there, they were certainly going to wonder why. Dan had no choice other than to share his bed with her.

He tidied the bathroom and disposed of the drying curls of hair, then returned to his bedroom, closed the door and slid under the covers next to his unexpected guest. Every nerve in his body was conscious of her slender body curled next to him, the clean sent of her hair and the soft sound of her breathing.

Hands behind his head, he stared at the ceiling and wondered what could have happened to make this beautiful woman drive her car over a cliff. Who was after her, and why was she so afraid of the police?

Either the woman was mentally unbalanced or she was involved in something illegal. In either case he'd probably been a fool to bring her into his house. Again he thought of his children sleeping nearby and felt a chill of alarm.

But even though he'd caught the woman raiding his fridge, she hadn't seemed like a crazy person or a criminal. Just a woman in pain, and Dan, who spent his life caring for children and animals, had a hard time not feeling sympathy for anybody who was hurt.

Still, he couldn't take any chances with the safety of his kids. Until he knew what was going on here, he needed to get them away from the house.

Reluctantly, he decided to bundle them all up first thing in the morning and take them over to Mary and Bubba. They could stay a few days, help with the ostriches and have the run of Bubba's sprawling ranch.

Dan's uncle and his wife were always pleading with him to let them help look after the kids, but Dan resisted, stubbornly maintaining that the care of his children was his responsibility.

Now, maybe he'd take them up on their offer. Mary could take the kids to the school bus on Monday morning. By then he should know what was going on with Isabel Delgado, and why she'd turned up in his kitchen trying to steal his food.

Slipping noiselessly from the bed, Dan padded into the kitchen to retrieve the folded newspaper from the wastebasket. He switched on the back-porch light and read the article again, then stared for a long time at the woman's face, her disarmingly lopsided smile and the expensive haircut he'd just demolished.

Finally he went back to his bedroom, carrying the paper, and tucked it away in the top drawer of his dresser. The woman was sleeping peacefully, her face innocent and sweet in the pale moonlight. When Dan settled next to her, she reached out her bandaged arm and touched his shoulder, nestling close to him.

The move was automatic and without seduction.

Dan drew away from her gently, taking care not to hurt her injured arm. She smiled in her sleep, the same, crooked smile the newspaper photograph had caught.

He patted her shoulder, then rolled over and lay alone on his side of the bed, wide awake and troubled, wondering what in hell he was getting himself into.

CHAPTER FOUR

SOMETIMES WHEN ELLIE was deeply asleep, noises that were, in reality, happening around her somehow got into her dreams.

She lay in the darkness, only partially awake, and realized the same thing had just happened. She'd been dreaming about running through a dim cavern, where a bottomless river lapped at her feet and she was in constant danger of falling into the water.

Cody Pollock ran just behind her, his jeering young face exultant with triumph.

"I've got you now!" he shouted, reaching for her, so close that Ellie could see the inflamed pimples on his cheeks. "Now there's just two choices, Gibson. You can come and play nice with me, or you can jump into that river. What's it gonna be?"

In the background of her dream Ellie could hear the voices of other boys and girls who looked on and talked in muffled tones, enjoying her terror.

Frantically she tried to find some way out of the cavern, but she'd reached a blank wall and there was no escape. She saw Cody's horrible face and cruel hands, then the dark, swollen river…

Sweating and whimpering with fear, Ellie awoke fully and lay staring at the window screens.

It was a dream, she told herself, hugging her thin

body. Just a stupid dream. Cody Pollock was nowhere close to her. If he ever came to this farm and tried to hurt her, her father would kill him.

That was when she realized some of the noises from her nightmare were still going on, drifting to her from inside the little house. She could even see a dim light in the hallway, like that partially lit cavern in her dream. And she heard the distant sound of splashing, running water, along with her father's deep voice and an occasional soft reply.

Ellie frowned, wondering what was happening, then relaxed.

Probably Chris had had one of her accidents, and Daddy was cleaning her up. When their mother had first gone away, Chris used to wet the bed all the time, but she was getting a lot better now and it hardly ever happened anymore.

In fact, Ellie thought drowsily, most of the bad stuff started happening two years ago, right after their mother left.

For one thing, Daddy was always upset about how messy the house was. And Chris had been so unhappy she hardly talked to anybody for a while. Only Josh hadn't seemed bothered by their mother's absence.

Of course, the baby had been only six months old when Annie Gibson left her family.

"I stayed long enough to have Josh," Annie once told her eldest daughter, "though God knows I was getting pretty damned anxious to be out of there. But fair's fair, and your daddy was always real good to me. If he wanted that baby so bad, well, I guess I just had to give him the baby once I went and let myself get pregnant. Didn't I, Jelly-Belly?''

Ellie had wanted to ask her mother how she could have gotten pregnant when she didn't love their father anymore, but it was so hard to talk with her about anything serious. Annie's mind was always darting on to something else before you could even start to take in what she'd just told you.

''You should see my new show outfit,'' Annie had told Ellie dreamily, smoothing her daughter's dark curls. ''It's bright red suede, with fringes hanging down to here. It's gorgeous, Ellie. I need to lose a few pounds to fit into it, though.''

''Mama, don't you love us?'' Ellie had asked, trying not to cry. ''How could you leave me and Chris and a sweet little baby like Josh, and go off singing to a bunch of people you don't even know?''

''Why, honey, of course I love you!'' Annie gave one of her rich, booming laughs and gathered Ellie into a fragrant embrace. ''But some women are just naturally cut out to be housewives, and I'm not one of them. I was born to be a star, kiddo.''

And it was true—Annie Gibson was trying very hard to be a star. Her stage name, which she'd invented all on her own, was Justyn Thyme, and she'd already been hired to sing at a couple of big conventions in Nashville, as well as lots of nightclubs. She was earning good money, enough to fly back to Texas and see her children several times a year, and she kept believing her big break was just around the corner.

For Annie's sake, Ellie hoped it was, too.

She'd long since given up hope that her mother

would come back to them if her music career failed. To tell the truth, Ellie wasn't even sure she'd welcome her mother back for more than those brief visits when she swept in carrying presents and took them all out for treats.

Though Annie's company was exciting, after a while Ellie got tired of her mother's constant laughter and chatter and wanted some peace again, the nice feeling of the little farmhouse with just her and Daddy and Chris and Josh, looking after themselves.

Still, it was true bad things had started happening after Annie left them, including Cody Pollock picking on her.

He was a bad boy from Lampasas whose parents weren't able to control him. When Cody was eleven, they sent him down to their cousin, June Pollock, who lived alone in one of the big old houses in Crystal Creek, since her daughter, Carlie, had gone off to Rice University to study marine biology.

June was a strong, quiet woman who'd worked most of her life as a hotel waitress and chambermaid. Everybody in town liked and respected her. No doubt Cody's parents thought she could do something with their son.

And Cody hadn't gotten into much real trouble since coming to Crystal Creek, but nobody knew how mercilessly he tormented Ellie Gibson. The older boy had spotted her almost two years ago when she was just ten years old, and tried to grab her legs when she was on a swing at the park.

Ellie had kicked him, giving him a nosebleed. After that, Cody never left her alone. He took every opportunity he could to trip her or knock her books out of her hands or jab her in the ribs when they passed in the hallways, and usually managed to do so without being seen. In fact, he was always careful not to be seen, especially by June, who had no stomach for bullies. Kinfolk or not, June would have dealt with Cody fast enough if she knew what was happening.

During the rare occasions Ellie ran into him alone, she was terrified. Though she tried not to give any sign of how she felt, it was almost as if Cody could smell her fear, like a dog does, and got some kind of cruel enjoyment out of it.

The situation had grown even worse when Ellie's body began to mature over the past spring and summer. Cody was thirteen by now, with a pimply face and the shadow of a mustache, and his manner toward her had also changed. Now there was real menace about him, a leering expression in his eyes that frightened her more than ever. When Cody got close to her nowadays, he didn't only jab her in the ribs, but also tried to grab her growing breasts, which, to Ellie's dismay, were visible under her loose T-shirts.

Worst of all, he'd gotten his friends involved, a gang of four other rough boys who swaggered across the schoolyard and terrorized everybody with their coarse words and threats of violence.

Ellie was never safe from them. At any moment she could round a corner at school and find Cody and his friends blocking a hallway, keeping her from getting to her next class. Or she would see them in the park, crouching behind bushes to call insults at her, or deliberately jostling up against her on the

street when she walked downtown to Wall's Drugstore.

Ms. Osborne, the middle-school principal, held
regular assemblies where she urged kids to report
bullies if their lives were being made unpleasant.

Unpleasant, Ellie thought bitterly, scowling at the
ceiling. What a stupid word.

Her life was hell, pure and simple. Going to school
every day was like running a gauntlet with no idea
if you'd ever emerge safely.

"Don't be afraid to speak to your parents," Ms.
Osborne told the kids. "Your teachers here at school
and your parents, working together, can keep you
safe from bullies. And those who are threatening you
will be punished."

Ellie rolled over and buried her face in the pillow.

It sounded good, that big promise from the principal, but Ellie didn't believe a word of it. Her homeroom teacher, Mr. Kilmer, was a shy man who was
probably every bit as terrified of Cody Pollock and
his friends as she was.

Ellie's father, of course, wasn't scared of anybody.
But Ellie would die of embarrassment if she told him
the things those boys said to her and what Cody Pollock threatened to do to her.

Besides, what good would it do, anyhow? Her father couldn't kill Cody or make him move away, and
so the bullying would just go on. Probably it would
be even worse because Cody would know she'd told
on him.

But tonight, for the first time, Ellie could see the
possibility of escape.

She thought about the miraculous fifty-dollar bill

she'd found in the river. It was like a present from God, just the same way He'd sent baby Moses floating down the river to lodge in the bulrushes.

And that money was going to give Ellie a whole new life.

She knew fifty dollars wasn't enough for what she wanted to do.

But she had more than sixty dollars already in her bank account, painstakingly saved over the last two years, mostly birthday and Christmas money from Mary and Bubba. And her father had assured her it was her own money, so she could take the whole amount out of the bank anytime she wanted to.

A hundred dollars was just about all she needed. Ellie tensed with excitement when she thought of having so much money.

Her plan was simple. She intended to go into town one day soon, when her father was busy with the haying and couldn't pay much attention to her. Ellie would withdraw the money, buy a bus ticket and go to Nashville to live with her mother.

She knew, of course, that Annie didn't want to be saddled with a twelve-year-old kid when her career was just starting to take off, but she could hardly turn away her own daughter. Besides, Ellie was determined to show how much help she could be. She'd clean Annie's apartment and cook good meals for her when she came home after singing all night, and she'd never, ever be in the way. And soon Annie would be glad her daughter had come to live with her.

Dreamily, Ellie pictured their relationship in Nashville, a whole world away from Cody and his awful friends.

Of course, she didn't want to stay with Annie forever, because she'd get too lonely for Daddy and Chris and Josh. Maybe after a while, when Cody Pollock got tired of waiting for her to show up and found somebody else to bully, she'd be able to come home to the farm.

Meanwhile the fifty-dollar bill lay safely in her dresser drawer, a magical promise of better days ahead.

Within the house, the distant sounds began to fade. She heard her father emptying the bathtub, talking to Chris as he got her ready to go back to bed. Then he came striding through the hallway to fetch something from the kitchen, looking big and hairy in his boxer shorts.

Cautiously Ellie raised herself on one elbow and saw him carrying a folded newspaper back to his room. He must be planning to read in bed.

She settled down under the covers, wondering what Nashville was like, imagining her mother's look of amazement when Ellie turned up on her doorstep. "Hi there," Ellie would say casually. "I was in the neighborhood and thought I'd drop in."

Or she could say, "Howdy, ma'am. I heard you're a big country-music star and I thought maybe you needed a cook and housekeeper."

Annie was going to like that, Ellie thought drowsily. She always loved being called a star.

As she drifted off to sleep, Ellie acknowledged that she wasn't really sure how her mother would receive her. With Annie, you never really knew. It depended on her mood, on whether she was gaining or losing weight and what else was going on in her life at the time.

Still, putting up with her mother's moods was a whole lot better than facing Cody Pollock and his friends every day.

With a final shiver of revulsion, Ellie fell asleep and darkness closed in on the house again.

ISABEL BLINKED in the warm glow of sunlight. She opened her eyes and saw a patchwork quilt over her body, a green wall hung with framed pictures of children, a dusty nightstand and a wicker basket on the floor, piled with laundry.

She had a moment of intense panic, unable to recall where she was or how she'd come to be here.

Breathing deeply, she forced herself to stay calm and concentrate. Like images from some hazy, badly made movie, she saw herself pushing the car over the cliff, then jumping down behind it. She recalled the jarring shock of her landing, the scratches and blood, the hunger and chill and wetness as she fought her way through the brush. And the endless day that followed, when the oppressive heat had emphasized her throbbing pain, hunger and relentless thirst.

And then the sickening terror of creeping into the darkened house and being caught by that hairy giant wielding a club.

Isabel gripped the quilt and looked around wildly. Beyond that encounter, her memories weren't nearly as clear. She'd been taking some food when he sneaked up behind her and grabbed her. After that she could dimly recall being handled and moved, the

sheer bliss of finding herself immersed in warm
sudsy water, and later a man giving her clothes while
she pleaded with him not to tell anyone about her.

Isabel frowned in confusion and lifted her right
arm, examining the neat gauze bandage. The arm was
still swollen, though it didn't feel as tender as it had
the day before.

But had she also asked that hard-faced stranger to
cut her hair?

Surely not. That part must have been a dream, one
of the confused fantasies that kept jostling around in
her mind.

Tentatively, she reached to touch her head and encountered the cropped, silky strands around her ears.
She raised herself on her elbows in sudden alarm. If
that man really had cut her hair, then he must also
have been the one who'd helped to cover her nakedness when she almost fainted right after getting out
of the bathtub. But who was he, and where was this
farmhouse?

She noticed a glass of water and a plastic pill container on the nightstand, sitting on a sheet of paper
with some handwriting on it. Isabel lifted the little
container and saw it held several oblong yellow pills.

"If you've had no adverse reaction," the note
said, "take another antibiotic pill when you wake up.
I'll be back as soon as I can."

The pharmacist's label was from Wall's Drugstore
in Crystal Creek and read "Dan Gibson: Take one
tablet every four hours."

Isabel hesitated, then took one of the pills and
gulped it down with a mouthful of water. She sat
upright on the edge of the bed, feeling dizzy again,

and dropped her head to her knees until the feeling passed.

When her mind cleared she stood up and looked down at what she wore—a man's white shirt and plaid cotton boxer shorts.

In a cheval mirror by the dresser, Isabel caught sight of herself and stared in horror. Her face was scratched and bruised, her eyes darkly shadowed, and the cropped hair stood up every which way. With the baggy clothes and her bandaged arm, she looked like a waif, some kind of pitiful refugee from disaster.

"Well, I guess that's what I am," she said aloud, almost jumping at the sound of her voice in the quiet house.

Moving cautiously, she ventured to the door of the room and peered down the hallway. She could faintly recall the man saying something about having children in the house, and the need for her to stay out of sight in the bedroom.

But nobody appeared to be home at the moment. The place was silent except for birdsong drifting through the open windows, and the distant sound of the river.

Isabel walked slowly into the messy bathroom, recalling her blissful soak in that tub and later the man standing beside her to cut and blow-dry her hair.

She went into the kitchen and found a pot of coffee on a sideboard. The room appeared to have been hastily abandoned, with dishes stacked carelessly on the counter and in the sink. Evidence of children was everywhere. A smeared high chair sat at the table next to a couple of cartoon mugs with lids and straws, and toys littered the floor all the way into the living room and out to the porch.

Isabel poured herself a cup of coffee and added some cream from the fridge, but gave up looking through the disorganized cabinets for sugar. Instead, she toasted two slices of bread and ate them hungrily.

But by the time she'd devoured a banana and most of the remaining grapes, she was starting to feel guilty. Clearly the people who lived in this house didn't have a lot of money, yet she was gobbling all their food and had no way of paying for it.

With sudden alarm she rushed back to the bedroom, moving so quickly that her head began to throb with pain again. On the floor near the window she found her jogging pants and shirt. They'd been washed and dried but were both ragged, stained with blood. Under the clothes were her bra and panties, also clean but tattered, along with the still damp leather cross-trainers.

Isabel's heart sank. She lifted the right shoe and shook it, but she already knew the locker key was no longer there.

"I have the key," a voice said behind her. "I put it away for you."

Braced to flee, she turned to face the man. But this wasn't the hairy, half-naked giant she dimly remembered from the night before. This was a tall, youngish man with light brown hair and green eyes, broadshoulders and a strong, calm face.

"How are you feeling?" he asked.

Isabel stood with the shoe in her hand, at a loss for words.

"Here," he said, opening a wooden box on the dresser. "This is the key I found in your shoe."

He held it out to her. She accepted the key, then merely clutched it in helpless silence.

"How about if I put it back?" he suggested gently. "It'll be right here in this box."

She nodded and gave him the key. His hands were big and square, with callused palms and surprisingly long fingers.

Nice hands, Isabel thought, remembering how they'd trimmed her hair and bandaged her arm with such gentleness.

"Thank you," she whispered. "Thank you so much for helping me."

He was watching her intently. "I didn't have much choice, did I?"

"You could have thrown me out," she said. "Lots of people would have."

"That's not the way we treat folks here in the country." He moved to the door. "Care to join me?" he asked over his shoulder. "I haven't had a chance to eat breakfast yet."

"But aren't your children..." Isabel began nervously.

"I took them over to my uncle's place for a few days. None of them have any idea you're here."

She followed him to the kitchen and sank into a chair at the table while he poured her another cup of coffee. "Cream and sugar?" he asked.

She nodded and he fetched the cream jug from the fridge, then opened a little ceramic canister shaped like a tomato, handing it to her along with a spoon.

"So that's where the sugar is. I didn't think of looking in there," she told him, trying to smile.

He didn't smile back, just popped a couple of slices of bread into the toaster and brought some butter and jam to the table.

"Did you take another pill?" he asked. "Let me see that arm."

She held it up for him to examine.

"The rest of your arm's not as red and swollen today," he said, holding her wrist. "How does it feel under the bandage?"

"It doesn't hurt as much, but it's getting pretty itchy."

"Well, that's supposed to be a sign of healing. I'll change the bandage after we eat, and put some more salve on it."

Isabel watched him, marveling at his calm, capable manner. He acted as if there was nothing unusual about a wild-eyed woman breaking into his house and trying to steal his food, then being dumped in his bathtub, sleeping in his bed...

His bed!

For the first time she remembered him lying beside her in the darkness of the night, holding himself away from her, his body so hard and muscular when she brushed against him that it was almost like sleeping next to a block of wood.

"I'm sorry," she whispered, feeling tears of shame stinging her eyelids. "I've been such a huge bother to you."

His toast popped up. "Want some?" he asked. When she declined, he buttered both slices, then fixed his green eyes on her face. "What are you running away from?"

Isabel stared into the depths of her coffee mug. "I'm afraid to tell you," she said at last. "I don't want anybody to know who I am."

"I already do know. There was a picture and an article about you in the paper last night."

She tensed. "What did it say?"

"It said you were Isabel Delgado, an heiress from San Antonio, and that your car went into the Claro on Friday night, but your body hasn't been recovered yet."

Isabel felt sick with fear. "My picture was there, too?"

"I recognized you right away."

"Oh, no!" She gripped the mug tightly. "I was hoping they wouldn't do that."

"I guess it's pretty big news when a rich girl goes missing. So what are you hiding from, Isabel?"

She glanced nervously around the silent kitchen. "Please don't call me that!"

"There's nobody around," he said. "My nearest neighbor is about a mile downriver."

"Is this farm anywhere close to where the Mc-Kinneys live?"

"That's him. My neighbor, I mean."

Isabel felt a return of that strange, dreamlike confusion and panic. "You mean J.T. McKinney is your neighbor?"

"Why? Do you know him?"

"Oh, God," She dropped her head into her hands. "There's nowhere to hide."

"If it's any comfort," he said after a moment, "I

can tell you that right now you don't look anything like the woman in the picture.''

''I don't?'' She raised her head to look at him.

He grinned, showing even white teeth. ''Haven't you seen yourself in a mirror lately?''

''Yes, but I wasn't sure if…''

''Well, my haircut and all those cuts and bruises have done a real job on you. You look like a totally different person.'' He watched her thoughtfully. ''So what should I call you?''

She pondered. ''Call me Bella,'' she said at last. ''That's what my…my sister used to call me,'' she added wistfully, ''when I was a little girl.''

''Okay, Bella. From now on, that's your name and we'll never use the other one. Okay?''

''Okay,'' she said feeling relieved. ''My name isn't Isabel anymore. It's Bella.''

''Now, Bella, why don't you tell me what you're so afraid of? And then we'll try to figure out what we can do about it.''

CHAPTER FIVE

DAN STUDIED THE WOMAN across the table. Bella Delgado had none of the arrogance he normally associated with heiresses to great wealth. Quite the opposite. She seemed awkward and unsure of herself, and her gratitude was obviously sincere.

For that matter, so was her fear.

"It's my ex-husband," she said at last, looking down at the table. Her eyelashes were dark brown tipped with gold, so long and dense that they cast a shadow on her pale cheeks. "His name is Eric Matthias, and he lives in Austin."

"What about him?" Dan asked when she paused.

"He's been stalking me." She looked up, meeting his eyes directly. "He turns up at a lot of places I go, restaurants and such, even though he works in Austin and I've been living in San Antonio for the past couple of years. At least twice in the last month I've seen him sitting in a car outside on the street, watching my father's house."

"Anything else?"

"He phones me a lot, even after I've changed my unlisted number. No matter where I go, and I mean anywhere in the world, Eric calls me within a day or two just to show how easily he can track me."

Dan watched her thoughtfully. "What do you think he wants?"

"I don't know for sure, but he scares me."

"Did he hurt you when you were married to him?" Dan asked.

"Not physically, though he was emotionally abusive all the time. And he terrified me because he was so intense. Mostly he…" Her voice broke.

"What?"

"Eric was crazy with jealousy. I never gave him the slightest cause, but that made no difference. He'd invent things to be mad about, then sulk about them for weeks. After I finally left and went back home to my father's house, Eric cried and said nobody else would ever have me. I'm sure he means it."

"What makes you so sure?"

Isabel shivered and hugged her arms. "When I told him I was leaving him, Eric…tried to kill my dog."

Dan stared at her.

"Afterward he claimed it was a misunderstanding," she said miserably. "Rufus was a Pekingese, the sweetest little thing. I'd had him ever since I was a girl. He was almost fifteen years old, and stiff with arthritis. I always took such care of him," she said wistfully. "I adored him. Eric was really jealous of Rufus, about all the time I spent with him."

"So what happened?"

"We were arguing, and Eric held Rufus over the edge of balcony, ten floors above the street. He kept threatening to drop him, demanding that I grovel and beg. I leaned way out onto the ledge to get my dog back and almost fell myself. Eric just laughed at me.''

"And your dog?"

"Poor Rufus was never the same. He died a few weeks later."

"Didn't you report that to the police?"

"Eric's a detective lieutenant with the Austin police force," she said wearily. "A fifteen-year veteran and he's very popular with the other cops. At the time he was distraught over our split, and they all felt sorry for him. He claimed I invented the business with Rufus to make him look bad. It was my word against his."

"But you're genuinely frightened of him?"

"I'm terrified." She met Dan's eyes steadily. "I saw his face when he...he was holding that poor little dog out above the traffic. Dan, it was so awful. I still have nightmares about it."

"But why can't your family help you deal with this man?"

"My father assured me he'd hire some extra security to watch the house, though he couldn't do anything about the phone calls. Daddy's always seemed neutral about our split, but a while ago I found out he's really on Eric's side. My father is actually helping my ex-husband to stalk me. It's no wonder," she added bitterly, "that Eric always knows where I am."

"Come on, Bella." Dan felt a rising concern for her emotional balance. "Don't you think that sounds a little paranoid?"

"I saw them," she said passionately. "Last month I dropped in at a pub downtown to meet a friend. It was a day when my father thought I'd gone to Houston for the weekend.''

"What did you see?"

"My father, my older brother and my ex-husband, all sitting together in a booth. They were smoking cigars and laughing," Bella told him. "That was when I knew for certain there was absolutely no hope for me to get away from Eric and have a life of my own unless I could fake my death and make them all believe it.''

"Forgive me if I'm being harsh, but you must realize that sounds a bit melodramatic.''

"I guess it does. But you know what? Life is really like that in rich families," she told him sadly.

"What does money have to do with it?"

"When my mother died, I inherited a whole lot of shares in the family company, plus a monstrous trust fund from my grandfather. My father makes a tidy profit as administrator of the trust, but it's all distributed to charity if I die or become incompetent.''

"So what money is in the safety deposit box?"

"There's money everywhere," she told him simply. "My family's net wealth is close to half a billion dollars, Dan. What's in the box is from my own bank account and some term deposits I cashed.''

"What bearing does that have on your problems with Eric?" Dan asked.

"It's in my father's best interests to keep me safe and happily married. Both my mother and my stepmother were addicts who committed suicide, and my sister left home when she was barely out of college. I guess poor Daddy's afraid all women are going to spin out of control without a strong hand to guide them.''

"And he thinks your ex-husband can provide this strong guiding hand you need?''

"Oh, yes. He always has. Daddy was so thrilled and relieved when Eric and I got married. I could tell he looked on this as a huge problem off his hands. He could go on administering the trust, and Eric would look after me and keep me on the straight and narrow. Now, I believe Daddy's determined to help Eric get me back, and there's nothing I can do about it.''

"What kind of father would want his daughter with a man she was afraid of? A guy who threatened to kill your dog, for God's sake!''

"Daddy's always dismissed that business with Rufus as female hysteria. He likes Eric and thinks I'd be better off living with this nice man who obviously loves me so much. I can't tell him what Eric's really like, because he simply refuses to listen. I'm helpless, Dan. They have all the power.''

"But...'' Dan watched her, eating his toast and wondering how much of this to believe. "With all that money, can't you just leave the country? Why don't you take off and live somewhere you'll be safe?''

"Do you think I haven't tried? I told you, Eric always finds me, whether I go to Switzerland or Japan.''

"How?''

"He uses the resources of the police department, even though it's illegal. And he has private detectives following me, too.''

"The guy can afford that?" Dan asked in surprise. "I didn't think policemen made enough money to hire private detectives."

"I always wondered about that, too. But I don't anymore," Bella said grimly. "When I saw them together last month, I realized my father's probably been giving Eric enough money to keep track of me. After all, he gave us a million dollars when we got married, just as a gift."

Dan mused about a life-style where a million dollars could be offered as a wedding gift. Irrationally, it made him dislike the woman, though he knew that was an unfair reaction.

"If your father was willing to pay that much for your happiness, why wouldn't he be concerned now when you tell him you're afraid of your ex-husband?"

She shrugged. "Daddy wasn't paying for my happiness, just his own peace of mind. It's been months since I've been able to talk to him about anything serious. He's almost always gone, and when he *is* home he avoids me. My father wants me married and out of his hair."

"So what happened with your car Friday night?" Dan asked.

"I pushed it over the cliff."

"You pushed it over?"

"My plan was to make it look like I'd died so Eric would give up and stop looking for me. I got duplicates made of all my pieces of ID and put them away in a bus locker up in Abilene. Then I left everything in the car, all my credit cards, even my passport, so it would look like a real accident."

"You assumed the police would think a woman who was running away was going to need her ID?"

She nodded and took a sip of coffee.

"Did anybody help you plan this?" he asked.

"God, no! I couldn't take the risk of confiding in anybody—too dangerous. I did everything by myself."

"So I assume your father and brother don't know about your plan, either?"

She shook her head. "Of course not. I'm hoping they think I'm dead now, just like everybody else. Not that they're going to care very much," she said without emotion, "except that it'll be messy when my body isn't recovered, because I hold a lot of company stock and they won't be able to transfer ownership for a while. And if I don't resurface in two years, Daddy will lose control of the trust."

"Okay," Dan said after a moment's silence, "so you were intending to push your car over the cliff and into the river. What was the rest of this plan?"

"I was wearing my running clothes, with my hair stuffed under a cap so my face wasn't easy to recognize. I planned to jog down from the lookout point and all the way to the bus depot in Crystal Creek, then get on the bus and go to Abilene. I had the ticket and some money in my coat pocket."

Dan thought suddenly about the fifty-dollar bill Ellie had found floating in the river. Incredible as her story seemed, the woman was apparently telling the truth.

"And the key in your shoe," he said. "That's for the locker up in Abilene?"

She nodded again.

"So what happened?"

"Just when I was pushing the car," she said, "I heard somebody driving up the hill. I couldn't stick around or they'd see me. I had to throw myself over the cliff behind the car."

His eyes widened. "Above Rimrock Park? That's a pretty steep drop."

"The bushes broke my fall, but you know how scratched and bruised I was. And when I got up, the front of my jacket was torn away. I didn't have the money or the bus ticket anymore."

"So your car was already in the water and you were stuck with no ID and no cash?"

"It was terrible. And I had to stay hidden because there were people across the river in the park. That's why I'd picked the spot, you see. There had to be some witnesses, or the whole effort of ditching the car would have been wasted."

Dan watched her, torn by conflicting emotions. Part of him was still turned off by the kind of wealth and privilege she represented, yet at the same time, he couldn't help admiring her grit and ingenuity.

"So what comes next?" he said at last.

"I need to get to Abilene." She looked up at him with timid appeal. "Do you think you could possibly drive me there? With all these bruises and cuts, I'd be so conspicuous if I rode on the bus."

Dan hesitated, wondering how to respond.

"Look, I'll pay you," she said earnestly, misreading his silence. "I have a lot of money stored in that bus locker. Once I get there and have my stuff back, I'd be happy to give you whatever you want. After all, you probably saved my life."

"I'm not looking to be paid for helping you," Dan said coldly.

"Please," she whispered, watching his face. "Don't be angry with me. I'm so sorry for doing this to you. I just need to get to Abilene, and then you'll never see me again."

"All right," he said finally, pushing the chair back and getting to his feet. "Do you feel strong enough to go today?"

"Oh, yes," she said eagerly. "Once I'm there, I'll rent a hotel room and rest for a few days, then decide where to go."

"What if he comes looking for you? Do you think that's possible?"

"I'm never sure what Eric might do," she said. "But if they've searched the riverbanks and haven't found any trace of me and they've recovered my car with all my ID in it, I'm pretty sure he's going to think I really killed myself."

"He told the newspaper reports your behavior had been 'unstable' in recent months."

"Is that really what he said?" She glanced up with a flare of anger. "The rotten bastard."

"He sounds like a real sweetheart, all right," Dan said. "Somebody tells him his ex-wife is dead, and all he can say is that she's been acting unstable lately."

"I hate him," she said with passion.

"Well, maybe you've managed to outwit him this time." Dan hesitated, looking down at her. "I should change that bandage before we leave."

"It's all right," she said. "You've done enough for me. I can see a doctor once I get to Abilene."

"But what are you going to wear? You can hardly turn up in Abilene wearing my old boxer shorts. That's going to make you a little conspicuous, don't you think?"

She glanced down at herself, then up at him. Her brief flash of anger was gone, and she seemed uncertain and frightened again.

"I know what you can do," Dan said after some thought. "My ex-wife sent an outfit to my older daughter last month, and it's a little too big for her. I think it'll probably fit you."

He went to Ellie's room and found the unworn clothes in a bottom drawer, a pair of loose pants and matching top made from pale yellow parachute cotton. When he brought them back into the kitchen, Bella shook both pieces out and looked at them with relief.

"They seem just about right. How old is your daughter?"

"She's only twelve. My ex-wife's got a good heart," Dan said, "but she doesn't pay much attention to things like sizes. I guess she doesn't see the kids often enough to know how big they are."

Her eyes widened in surprise. Dan moved quickly toward the door to forestall any questions.

"Get dressed, Bella," he said. "Use my bedroom. We'll leave as soon as you're ready."

He went out into the front porch to find a pair of Ellie's sandals for his guest to wear, expecting her to take some time. All too well he remembered how long Annie used to spend preparing herself to go out, and his own impatience with his wife's primping.

But Bella Delgado was dressed and back in the

kitchen within five minutes. The only thing she'd done by way of grooming was to brush her short hair.

Even barefoot in the casual yellow suit, without makeup or jewelry and carrying the baseball cap in her hand, she had an air of casual elegance.

"I'm ready," she told him simply.

Dan gave her the sandals. "I just need to check on the dog," he said, "and then we can go."

"You have a dog?"

"Her name's Gypsy. I picked her up this morning from the vet in Crystal Creek."

He picked up the truck keys and led the way outside, locking the door of the house.

Bella followed, hurrying along at his heels while he crossed the yard to the barn where their young Border collie lay drowsing in the sunlight on a bed of old sacking.

"She had surgery yesterday." Dan checked on the water bowl, then pulled a dish of food within easy reach.

Bella knelt by the dog, glancing up with her eyes full of concern. "What's wrong with her?"

"Nothing," Dan said. "She's been spayed."

Bella fondled the dog's silky ears and looked at the shaved portion of Gypsy's abdomen with its neat row of stitches.

"Poor dear," she murmured, scratching behind the dog's ears while Gypsy closed her eyes in bliss and thumped her tail on the sacking. "Poor baby. Does it hurt, sweetie?"

Dan looked down at the woman's eyelashes and the sweet curve of her cheekbone, the silky sheen of her hair. When he remembered his brief glimpse of that naked golden body under the towel, he felt a sudden, alarming wave of lust.

"Yeah, I suppose it hurts," he said with more curtness then he'd intended. "But she's had some medication, and she'll be fine in a few days."

"It's so odd, how a person's point of view can change overnight," Bella said thoughtfully, still stroking the dog.

"What do you mean?"

"When I was hiding out there in the bushes, planning to break into your house, I was so afraid you had a dog. I kept picturing that dog attacking me and how terrified I'd be."

He stood silently by the truck door.

"But now that I've met you and seen your life from the inside out," she said, getting to her feet, "and met your dog, it all looks so different than it did out there in the bush."

"I'll just bet it does." Dan turned away to open the truck door, thinking how messy and impoverished his life must seem to a woman like Bella Delgado. And she hadn't even met his kids. She didn't know the half of it.

"Come on," he said curtly, "let's go. I still have work to get done today."

He could see she was stung by the coldness of his tone. Without another word she hurried around the truck, scrambled into the passenger seat and sat with her hands folded tensely in her lap while Dan drove out of the yard and toward the highway leading to Abilene.

BELLA GAZED OUT the truck window at the rolling hills, brown and sere after the brutal heat of summer, dotted with scrub brush, mesquite and grazing cattle.

She glanced over at the man's hard profile, wondering if he was still angry with her.

"How long have you lived on your farm?" she asked shyly.

"All my life. It was my father's place. My grandfather, Ezra Gibson, owned a lot of land along the river and divided it between his two sons. My uncle still has the property next door."

"And the McKinneys live on the other side of your farm?"

He nodded, keeping his eyes on the road. "Part of J.T.'s property runs down to the river. How do you happen to know them?"

"My mother was good friends with Pauline, J.T.'s first wife. When I was a girl, they used to send me out here for a few weeks in the summer when everybody was too busy to bother with me. I liked to sit all by myself and fish along the riverbank." She smiled, remembering. "I always thought heaven must feel like the Claro River on a summer afternoon."

"How old are you?" He glanced at her, and all at once she was vividly conscious of his square-jawed face, the smoky green of his eyes.

"Twenty-seven."

"Well, I'm about eight years older," he said. "I was probably out moving irrigation pipes around while you were fishing. Maybe I even saw you once or twice, though I don't remember."

"I was just a skinny little kid with braces on my

teeth." Bella looked out the window again. "You can hardly be blamed for not remembering me."

"So where's your mother now?"

"She died about six years ago, drank herself to death. I told you, my father is hard on wives. His first wife committed suicide."

"But you said you had a sister and brother?"

"My father had two children with his first wife. They're ten and fifteen years older than me."

"And neither of them can help you with all these problems?"

"My brother doesn't care if I live or die," Bella said. "As for my sister, she left home almost ten years ago after a fight with my father, and she hasn't been heard from since."

"Nice warm family," he commented.

"Really nice." She looked down at her hands, twisted tightly in her lap. "I'm sure my sister has probably tried to get in touch with me over the years," she said. "At least I hope she has. But my father wouldn't let her talk to me. He's never forgiven Luciana for defying him."

"Pierce Delgado sounds like a pretty controlling kind of guy, all right."

"How about you?" she asked after a brief silence.

"What about me?"

"Do you have brothers or sisters? Are your parents still alive?"

"No, I was an only child. My father died of a heart attack a few years ago, and my mother lives up in Oklahoma City."

"But you said your uncle's ranch is right next door to yours?"

"Yeah, Uncle Bubba and Aunt Mary. They're pretty much the only family I have nearby. They raise ostriches," he added.

"No kidding?" Bella laughed, her spirits lifting for a moment. "I'd love to see the ostriches."

He glanced at her and she turned away, stung again by the cold look on his face.

But the silence was too uneasy, and she was growing increasingly tense as they neared Abilene. She felt compelled to keep their conversation going, even if the man hated talking with her.

"Where does your wife live?" she ventured at last.

"Ex-wife," he said curtly.

"That's what I meant."

"She's in Nashville, trying to become a big country music star."

Bella looked at him in surprise. "But…you have children."

"Yeah, well, that doesn't mean as much to Annie as it does to most women. She's always dreamed of hitting the big time, becoming a star. After she won a local talent contest a few years ago and got the chance to cut a demo, she was wild to get out of Crystal Creek."

Bella thought of all the toys in the cluttered farmhouse, the row of small jackets hanging on pegs. "How old are your children?"

"Ellie's twelve, Christine is eight and Josh is two."

"Only two?" Bella was shocked. "But how could anybody…" She bit her lip nervously.

"Josh was an accident," he said, his gaze not

straying from the highway. "Annie was all set to leave before it happened, and horrified when she found out she was pregnant. Still, she stayed with me an extra year to have the baby and look after him for a few months. Then I gave her a divorce, and she was free to go."

"If you had so little in common, why did you get married in the first place?"

"It was one of those adolescent things. Annie and I went steady all through high school. After we graduated, folks in Crystal Creek started to ask us when we were getting married." He glanced over at Bella. "Around here, a lot of kids drift into marriage that way, long before they've made any important decisions about the future or even figured out who they are."

Questions crowded Bella's mind, but all of them seemed too intrusive.

"So…is her career going well?" she asked at last.

He shrugged. "It's a pretty tough business. She manages to support herself and even sends gifts to the kids sometimes. And she seems a whole lot happier than when we were married."

"Are you sorry she's gone?" Bella ventured, casting another glance at his big lean body and callused hands on the steering wheel. "Do you miss her?"

He appeared to give serious thought to her question. "No, I don't miss Annie. The last few years we didn't have much feeling for each other. We were just hanging on, trying to do the right thing."

"It must be really hard for you, caring for three little ones all by yourself."

"It's hard, all right. And every time I try to hire

a housekeeper, the kids drive her away. Ellie—that's my oldest—she doesn't want anybody else in the house. She's a pretty hard kid to get along with.''

Bella tried to imagine what his life must be like. "So in the daytime," she said, "you have to take the baby with you all the time while the others are in school?''

"He's not a baby," Dan said. "He can walk and talk, and I've even got him mostly potty trained now. But you're right, my life isn't easy.''

Bella thought about the untidy, simple house. "Is farming…profitable?''

"If you work hard enough and can keep the debt load down. I had to take out a big loan to give Annie her share when we got our divorce, because she was entitled to it after ten years of marriage. But it's hard making ends meet.''

Bella nodded, thinking that after she was safely in another country, she would find some way to send Dan Gibson a generous gift of cash. If she sent the money without a return address, he could hardly refuse. And it would be small repayment for the help he'd given her.

The farmer didn't seem disposed to talk any further, so she settled back against the seat and looked at the passing scenery.

CHAPTER SIX

AT THE BUS DEPOT Dan parked and got out, striding around to hold the door for her. Bella tugged the baseball cap low over her eyes, feeling nervous and exposed in the midday sunlight, reluctant to leave the shelter of the truck.

"Come on," he said, holding her arm and walking next to her. "Let's get this over with. Do you have the key?"

She nodded, fingering the hard metal shape in her pocket. "It's right here."

Inside the depot they headed for the row of lockers along a wall in a wide hallway. Benches lined the center of the hall, crowded with people waiting for buses. Children played and shouted in the open space, and a young couple on a bench near the lockers were kissing passionately, oblivious to their surroundings.

"Locker number 1165," Bella told Dan under her breath. "It's right down there near the end."

He nodded and drew her along the hallway, pausing by a scratched brown locker. She fitted the key in the door, opened it and stared in horror.

The locker was empty.

Dan looked down at her with narrowed eyes, his grip tightening on her elbow.

"But I..." Bella stared wildly at the key, then the locker again. "I put everything in here just last week. Two big brown envelopes, fifty thousand dollars in cash, all that ID..."

Dan studied her face for a long moment, then put an arm around her and hustled her toward the door. "Keep your head down," he murmured as they walked. "Try to look casual."

"What's going on?" she asked frantically. "Where could it have gone?"

"Be quiet, Bella," he said in a low tone, gazing straight ahead as they went out through the entrance doors. "Just keep walking calmly toward the truck."

She obeyed, bewildered and terrified. He unlocked the passenger door and bundled her inside.

"Keep your cap on and stay inside," he said. "Don't unlock the doors or get out for any reason. If you see somebody watching the truck or acting suspicious, duck down and keep yourself out of sight."

"But, Dan..." She gripped his arm, feeling the hard muscles under the cotton of his shirt. "Where are you going?"

"To find out where your property is. I'll be right back."

With a final warning look he was gone, striding back across the pavement in the direction of the terminal.

Bella huddled on the passenger seat, wondering if this waking nightmare was ever going to end.

Within a few minutes Dan was back, almost running. He flung himself into the truck, started the engine and backed out of the parking lot, glancing sharply at passing vehicles as he pulled onto the street and drove away.

"Do you think there's anybody following us?" he asked her. "Try to see, but keep your head down."

Bella peeked out the rear window at the quiet Sunday traffic. "I don't think so. One car's in the lane right behind us, but it's... No, it turned the other way. There's nobody."

"I asked at the locker rental desk," he said. "I showed them your key and said the contents of the locker had been removed. They asked where I got the key, and I told them a friend sent it to me in the mail."

"Did they tell you what happened to my things?"

"Apparently the attendant remembered you from last week when you rented the locker. After he saw your picture in the paper on Friday, he called the police. The department in Abilene contacted your father, who sent your ex-husband up from Austin last night to collect the contents of the locker."

Bella's terror was cold and sickening, like a blow to the stomach.

"Eric came up from Austin?" she whispered, staring at him.

"The attendant claimed he was just doing his duty. He thought there might be something important in the locker, maybe a suicide note or a will, so the police should be notified."

"But that means..." Her mind struggled to absorb this new development.

"It means your ex-husband's most likely figured everything out by now. He knows you're probably not dead, after all. He also has your money and all your ID.''

A new thought struck her. "And you think Eric is having the lockers watched," she said. "Don't you, Dan? That's why you wanted to get me away from there in such a hurry."

"As far as I can see it's not a police matter, and I doubt if he'd be able to get a civilian on the job this fast," Dan said. "We didn't see anybody hanging around the parking lot, and nobody followed us or took down our license-plate number, so we should be all right."

"But…" Gradually the true enormity of the situation dawned on her. "This means I'm right back where I was yesterday. I still have no money and no identification."

"You can get more ID," he said. "All you have to do is apply."

"As soon as you apply for anything, your name goes into a computer bank somewhere. And through the police department, Eric has the ability to monitor every government computer in the country."

"Maybe you could apply for some ID under an assumed name," Dan said, frowning at the highway. "It's not illegal to use a different name, as long as there's no intention to defraud."

"But to get any kind of legal document or even apply for a credit card, you have to show some proof of identification," Bella said in despair. "Oh, God, it's all just so hopeless."

In spite of herself, she felt tears gather in her eyes and begin to trickle down her cheeks.

"Eric's won," she said. "He's going to find me for sure. I'm trapped, and there's no way out."

BACK AT THE LITTLE FARMHOUSE by the river, they ate soup and sandwiches in silence. After their meal Bella stayed inside while Dan left to do chores.

"I'll be back in an hour or so," he told her, pausing in the doorway. "Will you be okay?"

"I'll be fine," she said tonelessly. "Take as long as you want."

He lingered as if about to say something else, then left the house and strode across the yard to the barn. She watched out the window as he bent to tend to Gypsy on her pile of sacking. His hands were gentle, and he spent some time talking to the collie before vanishing into the dark recesses of the barn.

Bella made herself a cup of coffee and drank it listlessly, then forced herself to get up and wash the lunch dishes.

The work was a novelty to her, and she was even briefly distracted from her terror by the act of filling the sink with sudsy water, wiping the plates and making them shine.

When that was done, she studied the rest of the messy kitchen, wondering where to begin. Tentatively, she searched out rags and cleaning supplies and found them in an upper cabinet. Before long she was absorbed in her task, removing everything from the countertops, wiping them down, polishing canisters and appliances and setting them back neatly.

She moved on to scrub the big fridge inside and out, enjoying the fresh scent of lemon cleanser, thinking that housework would probably not be such a bad occupation.

Methodically she next tackled the lower cabinets, taking the contents out and spreading them around her on the floor, filling a trash bag with empty cereal boxes and sticky syrup containers. One by one the cabinets emerged, gleaming and tidy, a result that she found immensely gratifying.

Maybe she could get a job somewhere as a domestic. She could live in and work for her board, plus a bit of spending money. Eric would never think to look for her in somebody's kitchen.

But she didn't know how to cook. Besides, even to work as a housemaid you probably needed a social-security number and some kind of ID.

She was unaware how quickly the hours passed until a noise startled her, and she whirled to see Dan standing in the doorway in cap and work boots, watching her in astonishment.

Bella scrambled to her feet amid a collection of utensils from a crumb-filled cutlery drawer.

"I'm sorry," she said, flushing. "I just…had to fill in the time somehow, and I thought—"

"So the Texas princess knows how to do housework," he said with a grin.

"Not really. Actually, I've never done this before." She waved a hand at the tidy countertop, then opened the fridge door shyly to show him the gleaming interior. "I'm just figuring it out as I go along, but it's…kind of fun."

"Cleaning a kitchen is fun?"

"I've never had much chance to do any kind of work with my hands." She turned her attention back to the scattered utensils, putting them into the plastic tray she'd just cleaned. "And I'm enjoying it. You see such great results for your effort, a kind of instant gratification."

He pulled out a chair and sat watching her as she worked. "What did you do to fill your time back in your princess days?"

Bella shrugged. "Driving around in my car, charity work, shopping…"

"That sure sounds like a rich, full life," he said dryly.

She scowled at him. "It's not my fault I was born into such a wealthy family. For most of my life, I'd have given anything to have a normal existence and a job like other people."

"Did you go to college? Do you have any marketable skills?"

"I majored in art history and got terrific grades. I guess I could get a job as a gallery curator or something like that, but those jobs are pretty rare. I wouldn't even know where to start looking."

"I see."

Bella held up an oddly shaped kitchen utensil. "What's this for?"

"It's a potato masher."

"How does it work?"

"You peel the potatoes and cook them until they're soft, then add butter and milk and use that thing to mash them."

She studied the utensil. "I always wanted to learn to cook, but most housekeepers don't want their employer messing around in the kitchen."

"You didn't keep house for yourself even when you were married?"

Bella shook her head. "Another of my father's wedding gifts to Eric and me was a high-rise condo in Austin with a full-time housekeeper."

"You know, if a guy ever tried to give me a wedding gift like that," Dan said quietly, "I'd tell him thanks, but no thanks."

Bella glanced at his hard face. "But you and Eric are completely different men," she said. "He married me for the money and the status, though of course I didn't realize that until it was too late."

"He could have married you for other things," Dan said.

"Like what?"

"Come on, Bella, you're a beautiful woman."

She looked at him in amazement. Until now, the man hadn't given her the slightest indication of being impressed by anything about her. And even now, despite the compliment, he seemed more distant and preoccupied than admiring.

"Look, I've been thinking," he said abruptly, confirming this impression.

"About what?" She put the cleaned cutlery tray in the drawer and switched the heat on under a teakettle. "Would you like a cup of coffee? I think I could use one."

"Thanks," he said absently. "I've been thinking about your dilemma ever since we left Abilene, and I might have a solution. Especially," he added with a humorless smile, "since you've decided you're so fond of housework."

Bella spooned instant coffee into a pair of mugs. ''Great. What's your solution?''

''If you stayed here with me for a while and he was somehow able to find you, is there any chance this guy might come after me?''

She thought it over for a moment, then shook her head. ''I don't think Eric's ever been a danger to anybody except me, and possibly himself. It's some kind of really concentrated obsession, his jealousy over me.''

''Wouldn't he be a threat to me, then, if he thought you were living with me?''

''I doubt it. Eric's too concerned about his career and his reputation to get sucked into that kind of violence. Especially not with you.''

''Why not?''

''Because you're a stronger man than he is,'' Bella said without thinking. ''Instinctively, he'd steer clear of a man like you.''

Dan smiled with such unexpected warmth that Bella felt briefly confused and distracted. She looked down at the scrubbing cloth in her damp hands.

''I mean,'' she said, ''if Eric thought I was with some other man, his reaction would more likely be to punish me, not the man involved.''

He appeared satisfied. ''Okay,'' he said. ''Do you want to hear my plan?''

''At this point, any plan would be welcome. What were you thinking?''

''That we can get married,'' he said.

''Married?'' Her jaw dropped as she turned to stare at him.

''Just as a legal means for you to get some ID

together," he said. "Otherwise it seems to me your situation is completely hopeless."

"But how would it help me to get married to a total stranger?"

"You'd have a legal name then," he said. "One that wouldn't jump out at anybody searching a computer bank. Instead of Isabel Delgado, you'd be Bella Gibson. You could go ahead and apply for credit cards and other things under that name, and gradually start putting an identity back together."

"Dan, that's crazy." She poured boiling water into the mugs, carried them to the table and went to get cream from the fridge. "Totally, completely insane."

"Just hear me out," he said. "You'd be able to stay here in safety for a few months until this guy gives up looking for you. After that you could leave and go your own way, and by then you'd have at least the rudiments of some ID to get you out of the country."

Stay here in safety…

As bizarre as his offer seemed, Bella was suddenly tempted. She heard the distant chuckle of river water against the rocks, trees rustling outside the door and the warble of birds. A dappled ray of sunlight fell across the kitchen floor. From her nest of sacking near the barn, Gypsy barked at some distant cattle.

"Even if I agreed to this," Bella said at last, "how could I legally marry you? It's not possible to get married without some proof of identification and citizenship, is it?"

"It's possible," he said calmly, "when my cousin's the county clerk and she'd do anything for me."

"You have a cousin who works for Crystal Creek County?"

"Mamie Gibson—actually my father's cousin. She's sixty, plump and sweet, never been married herself. But Mamie's a warmhearted romantic who's a real sucker for a love story."

"Some love story," Bella muttered, staring out the window again.

Still, she couldn't stop thinking of that magical word. *Safety.*

And the protection of a brand-new, fully legal identity.

"Is this lady enough of a sucker," she said at last, "that she'd give us a marriage license when the bride has no ID?"

"As long as I swore I'd never tell a soul, I think Mamie could be persuaded. Then once we were legally married, you'd be Bella Gibson, and you could use your marriage certificate to start acquiring some new ID, claiming you'd lost all your valuable papers in a house fire or something."

Bella watched him in sudden suspicion as he gulped his coffee. "It seems you've given this quite a lot of thought."

"What else am I going to do with you, Bella? Take you to the city and dump you out on the street like a stray cat, with no money and no papers? Or drive you to San Antonio to your father's house and let you sit there waiting for him to deliver you back to this jealous maniac?"

"I don't know." She gazed unseeingly at the window where a trumpet vine grew across one corner of the smeared glass. "In fact, I haven't got the slightest idea what you could do with me."

"Well, like you said, I gave this a lot of thought while I was out doing my chores, and this is the only solution I can see."

"What's in it for you?" she said. "You can't be thinking of doing something like this just for my benefit. There has to be some kind of trade-off."

"Of course there is." He watched her steadily over the rim of his coffee mug. "You'd have to agree to give me three months," he said. "Just until Christmas. That's enough time for me to get the haying done and organize my business for next spring, and find a good permanent housekeeper to look after the kids. I really need a little breathing room here."

"Give you three months?" she repeated blankly. "Doing what?"

"Looking after my kids and my house. I can't manage on my own with the busy season coming up, and I've told you how hard it is to keep a housekeeper."

"Three months of housekeeping and baby-sitting isn't nearly enough in exchange for a marriage and a whole identity," she said. "There'd have to be some other way I could repay you."

"Three months of housekeeping and baby-sitting is worth a fortune to me," he said quietly. "In fact, it's beyond measure."

"But I'd also have to give you..." She paused, stunned by the turn their conversation had taken. It was almost as if she'd already decided to accept his offer and they were simply haggling over terms.

"You have no choice, Bella," he told her. "What

else can you do if you're afraid to ask your own family for help?''

"But that's so..." She got up and moved on to the next row of cabinets, taking plates out and setting them on the counter. "It's just not a fair deal. I'd be too much in your debt."

"Okay, then, you can pay me something in addition if that's what it takes to make you agree."

"How much?"

"Tell you what," he said after a moment's thought. "As soon as you find some way to get safely out of the country and have your money transferred, you can pay for our divorce and send me the cash for a new irrigation pump. Then we'll call it a deal."

Bella looked at him over her shoulder, standing on tiptoe to scrub out the empty cabinet. "How much does a new irrigation pump cost?"

"A fortune." He gazed into his coffee mug with a brooding expression.

"How much?" she said again.

"For a good one, I'd say about nine thousand dollars."

"But that's nothing," she said without thinking. "I've paid that much for a dress."

Again his face chilled, and Bella regretted her words.

"You know, this may not be such a ridiculous idea," she said slowly. "You're right. If you really could get a legal marriage license, it would give me a place to hide and a chance to build a new identity. And of course I'd be more than happy to pay for the divorce and buy you a new irrigation pump or anything else you wanted, once I was safely out of the country.''

"Could you stand to spend three months looking after my kids? They're not all that easy to handle, you know.''

"I think I could.'' She was silent a moment, thinking. "But what would you tell them? It's going to look kind of suspicious if I just arrive out of the blue and you marry me. People will gossip, and then it could get back to Eric somehow.''

"How?''

"I don't know. Through the McKinneys, maybe.''

"You'll have to keep yourself well away from anybody who might recognize you. We can tell the local folks you're from Oklahoma City and I met you last year while I was visiting my mother, but we've kept our relationship a secret until now.''

She nodded, amazed to be having this conversation and even more amazed that she was actually considering his offer. But then another huge obstacle presented itself.

"This house is so small,'' she said at last, her cheeks flaming. "And if we're supposed to be married...''

Dan understood immediately, and for the first time looked a little awkward.

"I'll admit there are a few weaknesses to the plan,'' he admitted. "But it's the best thing I can come up with right now. If this guy's as relentless as you say he is, you're not going to be safe anywhere else, and you sure won't be able to get out of the country under your own name.''

"I don't think I...'' She polished a plate over and

over, staring out the window to avoid meeting his eyes.

"It's a double bed, and you don't take up much room," he said, still looking embarrassed. "But if you can't stand the idea, I suppose I could maybe squeeze twin beds in there somehow."

She shook her head. "No, it's not possible. The whole thing's too far-fetched. We'll have to think of something else."

"Okay." He got to his feet and pushed in the chair. "If you come up with a better idea, let me know. But it'll have to be soon, because I need to bring my kids home in a day or two."

She watched him from the kitchen window as he left the house and walked over to his truck with a lithe, easy stride. His shoulders were broad and strong under the denim work shirt, and the sun gleamed on his crisp brown hair.

CHAPTER SEVEN

BY FIVE-THIRTY, Bella had the entire kitchen tidied to her satisfaction, and it seemed like a different room. She stood looking around with pleasure at the spotless cabinets, the tidy counters and gleaming tile floor.

Her hands were raw and chafed from all the scrubbing, and her pretty yellow outfit was soiled and damp, but she felt better than she had for a long time.

At least until she recalled the danger she was in, the general hopelessness of her situation and Dan Gibson's incredible offer.

She put the unhappy thoughts out of her mind and checked the clock, wondering if there was time to start cleaning another room. That big, messy porch would take hours to organize. And the living-room furniture was dusty and smeared with finger marks, the floor littered with toys and discarded clothes. As for the bathroom…

She looked at the clock again and her eyes widened in alarm. He'd probably be coming in soon, looking for his dinner. Farmers liked to eat the evening meal early, didn't they?

Even though she'd refused Dan Gibson's offer, Bella had an irrational desire to show him she could do the job if she chose to. After all, she'd shown him she could clean.

Now she wanted to show him she could cook a meal, as well.

And fortunately, having just reorganized the cabinets, she knew where everything was.

Galvanized with excitement now that she had a plan, Bella took lettuce, tomatoes and cucumbers from the crisper tray and made a salad, which she covered with plastic and put back in the fridge. She'd dress it with the bottled ranch dressing she'd seen there.

After that, her plan became less clear.

A brown paper wrapper in the fridge contained raw steaks, but she had no idea how long to cook them or what kind of pan to use. She'd have to check in one of those dog-eared cookbooks stacked in a drawer.

At least she remembered his description of how to make mashed potatoes. Bella hauled out the sack of potatoes and stared at them uncertainly, wondering how many to peel.

When you ordered steak in a restaurant, you got a single baked potato with it, so presumably one was enough for each person. But what if he was really hungry after hours of outdoor work?

Finally she peeled four good-size potatoes, washed them and cut them in quarters, then set them to boil in a saucepan.

In the freezer compartment of the fridge she found a package of broccoli, but according to the instructions it didn't need as long to cook. She put the package away again, deciding to wait until the mashed potatoes were done before she cooked the broccoli.

Dan came into the porch just after she finished setting the table. She was at the stove poking a fork into the bubbling potatoes, wondering how to tell when they were done.

Dan stood looking around in astonishment at the orderly kitchen. When he saw her probing the cooked potatoes, he gave her the first, genuine smile she'd ever seen from him.

"Well, look at this," he said. "What a nice surprise."

"I have no idea when a potato is cooked enough to mash," Bella told him.

He walked over beside her and took the fork, jabbing it into one of the pieces. She was painfully conscious of his nearness, of his hard-muscled body and the scent of dust and straw and healthy male.

"They need to cook at least another ten minutes," he said, "until they're soft to the fork. Otherwise they'll be lumpy when you mash them."

She nodded, relieved when he turned and started back outside.

"I'll just fire up the barbecue," he told her from the door. "We might as well cook a couple of those steaks and have a real nice dinner, since you've gone to so much trouble."

His praise made her feel unexpectedly happy. She turned away to hide her smile.

Dan started the barbecue, then vanished into the house. She heard the shower running and a male voice raised in song. A few minutes later he reappeared, wearing khaki shorts and a white shirt.

Looking scrubbed and comfortable, he took the raw steaks outside on a big plate along with some barbecue sauce.

Bella remembered to put another saucepan of water to boil for the broccoli, then drained the potatoes, added a dollop of butter and a little milk and mashed them furiously, watching in satisfaction as they swelled into a fluffy mound of white.

Before she was aware of his arrival, Dan stood at her side again with one hand on her shoulder and dipped into the potatoes with a spoon.

"Great," he said, tasting them. "You just need a little more salt, and they'll be perfect. I'll bring the steaks in right away."

Bella added the salt, then turned the potatoes and broccoli out into serving dishes, along with the salad and dressing and a heel of crusty bread from the fridge that she'd warmed in the microwave.

Dan put the plate of barbecued steaks on the table, looking at the food with hungry anticipation.

"This is close to heaven for a workingman," he said. "Looks like we don't have any wine," he added over his shoulder, peering into the fridge. "Is root beer okay with you?"

"Root bear is great."

Bella sat at the table, feeling an inordinate sense of accomplishment when she looked at the food. As they ate, she felt even more gratified when Dan took second helpings of everything.

"But the broccoli's too soft, isn't it?" she said anxiously. "I shouldn't have cooked it so long, even though the instructions on the package said—"

"Here's to you," he interrupted her, raising his

glass of root beer in a salute. "You did a great job, Bella. This is the best meal I've had in weeks."

Afterward they stacked the dishes in the gleaming sink and went outside to his little vine-covered patio to drink their coffee.

Twilight was beginning to set in and mauve smudges lay across the distant hills. Shadows filled the valley, soft and mysterious, and an owl called from a tree by the river.

"It's amazing," Bella said, "how that scene can look so heavenly and tranquil from here and be so scary when you're out there by yourself after dark."

"I can't believe you spent a whole night alone outdoors."

She glanced at his austere profile. "It was a really horrible experience. But, you know, in a way this is even worse."

"This? What do you mean?"

"Because when I was out there, I still had an escape plan. I just needed to get to Abilene somehow, and after that I'd be safe. Now I'm like a lost soul, drifting along with no direction of any kind. You can't imagine how helpless I feel, a woman with no identity and no protection."

"You don't think he'll lose interest after a while and leave you alone?"

Bella drew up her knees and hugged them. "You wouldn't ask if you'd ever seen Eric's face or heard his threats when he gets into a jealous rage. You know, I never thought…" She hesitated.

Dan took a sip of the coffee. "What?" he asked.

"I never thought there was anything about me to

inspire that kind of passion in somebody,'' she said awkwardly. ''It's still hard for me to believe how obsessed and jealous he is, even after all this time.''

''But it may not be you specifically,'' Dan said. ''He'd probably react the same way to any woman who made him feel abandoned and inadequate.''

Bella thought that over. ''You're saying it's something that comes from him, not me?''

Dan nodded. ''You couldn't have done anything to make it turn out differently.''

''God,'' she muttered, resting her chin on her knees. ''If you only knew how long I've wanted to hear somebody say that to me.''

''Was it a rocky marriage right from the start?'' he asked.

''Mostly. We had some good times, but his jealousy was always there just under the surface. It wasn't long before it started to scare me.''

''Scare you in a physical sense?''

''Not at the beginning,'' Bella said, trying to remember. ''It just seemed…excessive, you know?''

She glanced at Dan, who nodded.

''What really scared me was when he started saying I'd never get away from him, and he'd rather see me dead than with another man. Those aren't the kind of threats a woman can safely ignore.''

''They sure aren't.''

''Don't you feel any anger at your ex-wife?'' she asked curiously. ''Would you be jealous at all if she had another man?''

''I hope she does have somebody,'' he said. ''Annie's a real passionate woman, and she'd be too lonely without a man.''

"I can't believe you don't bear any grudges at all. She left you with three kids and all this work, and you don't say a word against her."

"Not much point in being bitter, is there?" Dan leaned back, extending his long legs. His thighs were knotted with hard muscle, his calves thick and dusted with springy golden hair. "Bitterness never accomplishes anything."

"Do the kids miss their mother?" Bella asked. "Is that why they resent the housekeepers so much?"

"It's not all of them who resent the housekeepers," he said. "Just Ellie, the oldest. My two little ones would love to have a woman around the house more. They don't actually miss their mother, but they do miss a woman's touch, I think."

"Not Ellie?"

"I think she misses it, too, but she'd never tell anybody. Ellie's a tough little nut," he said with another of those brief grins. "And I think something's bothering her right now," he added, his smile fading. "Whatever the problem is, it seems to be making her more prickly than ever." He poured more coffee for her from a thermos on one of the side tables, then refilled his own cup.

Bella murmured her thanks. He nodded, then said reflectively, "Tell me. What was your life like when you were small? Did you have lots of friends and go to play at other kids' houses?"

"Not much," Bella said. "My father was always afraid of my being kidnapped. He was over forty when I was born, and really rich by then. So when I played with anybody, the other kids had to come to my house. I wasn't allowed to go out very often."

"What about school?"

"I was taught at home by a tutor until I was nine, then sent to a private boarding school in Massachusetts." Bella shivered, remembering. "I hated that place."

"Why?"

"It was so strict and bare and gray, and far away from Texas. I was homesick all the time for almost ten years."

"But surely you were allowed to come back for the holidays?"

She shook her head, feeling her spirits plummet as she recalled those awful days. "Not all the time. Lots of holidays my parents had something planned for themselves, so they'd arrange with the headmistress to keep me there or send me to some other girl's house."

The shadows deepened so she could hardly see him, only the white blur of his shirt. "I used to beg them to send me here to the Double C ranch, because when I was with the McKinneys, I felt like I'd come home. But my father didn't like to do that too often."

"Why not?"

"I think he didn't want to be overly beholden to J.T. McKinney. Businessmen are like that, you know," she said bitterly. "They want to retain the balance of power in any relationship."

"I had such a great childhood," Dan mused aloud, the fondness of his tone surprising her a little. "Cal McKinney and I played rafts on the river and went fishing, and rode our ponies to town for ice-cream sodas."

"And when you went to bed," Bella asked, "you

had a mother and a father there to read you stories and tuck you in?''

"Yes, I did."

"No wonder you want the same kind of life for your own children," she said quietly.

"I've always had a picture of how I want their lives to be." He stretched and put his hands behind his head. "But I can't give them the kind of childhood I had. Mostly, I just can't seem to find the time."

"You feel that way now because you're worn-out and stressed," Bella told him. "But when they're grown and look back, I bet they'll think it was a wonderful childhood and be grateful to you."

"Thank you," he said with a warm sincerity that touched her. "I don't know if it'll turn out that way, but it's a real nice thing to say."

Bella watched the moon coming up across the river, tangled in the branches of a tree at the corner of the yard.

"Did you ever leave Crystal Creek?" she asked. "Or have you lived here since you were born?"

"I went to college for a couple of years, at Baylor."

"Really? What did you take?"

"Structural engineering." He drained the coffee mug. "I was going to design bridges and skyscrapers."

"Did you like it?" she asked, fascinated.

"I loved it. Never had a grade below a B and couldn't get enough of the classes."

"But you didn't finish your degree?"

He shrugged. "My father had his first heart attack

around that time. I had to come home and run the farm...and let other guys build the bridges."

"You gave up your education and career to run the farm," she said. "And now you're giving up everything to look after your kids."

She was a little disconcerted when he got to his feet abruptly and headed for the door.

"Come on," he said over his shoulder. "Bedtime comes early out here in the country. Let's just change your bandage, and then it's time to hit the sack."

DAN TRIED TO COAX Bella to use the bed again, arguing that it was no problem for him to sleep on the sofa. But she refused, and they finally compromised by having her sleep in Ellie's bed out on the screened veranda.

Long after the lights were out and the house was silent, Dan lay awake, thinking about Bella and wondering what she was going to do about her life.

His hands clenched into fists when he thought about the jealous police officer who was using his position to stalk and terrorize her. For a while Dan even considered driving into Austin and having a confrontation with the man. But in his rational mind, Dan knew that threatening her stalker would only make the situation worse for Bella.

She was really in a trap, especially without money or any kind of identification and no way to trust her wealthy family.

He thought about her shy, lopsided smile, the touching way she'd spent the afternoon cleaning up his kitchen, her glow of pride when he praised the meal she'd made.

And that unsettling moment out on the patio, when she'd commented on his life.

As far as Dan could recall, nobody else had ever mentioned or even noticed all the private dreams he'd given up for his family.

The woman was a bundle of contradictions. At times his heart was touched by her helplessness and fear. Sometimes she seemed womanly and sympathetic, but then in the next breath she'd say something breathtakingly tactless and annoying, such as she'd often spent nine thousand dollars on a new dress.

His face hardened. It was difficult not to resent the ease with which the wealthy spent money without thinking.

He thought about his offer to marry her. He hadn't been acting on impulse, and he still believed a sham marriage might be a reasonable solution to her problem. In addition, their bargain would certainly have offered him the substantial benefits of a temporary housekeeper, plus a new irrigation pump.

Still, the complications would probably have outweighed the advantages. Especially the obvious one that seemed to bother her the most—the fact that they would have to deceive his children by sharing a bed. It was quite obvious Bella couldn't bear that prospect. And it troubled him, as well, but for quite different reasons.

Now that she was recovering from her initial trauma, the woman had become far too attractive. There'd been times during the hours they'd spent together, especially when she smiled at him, that he'd had to fight an overwhelming urge to take her into his arms.

The best course of action, he realized, was to think of some way for her to leave here in safety and be gone from his life.

Maybe if he...

But he fell asleep before he could formulate any kind of plan.

HOURS LATER he awoke to the smell of coffee, and something else he couldn't identify. He dressed hastily and headed to the kitchen, where he found Bella wearing the yellow cotton pants and her own ragged shirt. She was studying a cookbook on the counter and stirring something in a smoky cast-iron frying pan.

"I'm trying to make scrambled eggs," she told him, looking up with a harried expression. "But they don't seem to be—"

"Too much heat." He adjusted the burner. "Scrambled eggs need to be cooked very lightly."

"Oh, hell." She gripped the spatula, staring in dismay at the somewhat scorched yellow mass. "And I put six eggs in there, too."

Dan found himself battling an irrational urge to drop a kiss on the silky nape of her neck. "The eggs will be fine," he said, taking the spatula from her. "Why don't you make some toast, okay?"

She complied without argument, and again he was touched.

While he ate the eggs, which weren't bad in spite of being rather overcooked, she nibbled at some toast and made aimless little circles on the tabletop with her fork.

"Come on, you should eat some of this," Dan said. "I can't handle six eggs all by myself."

She scooped some of the yellow lumps onto her plate, then took a deep breath and looked at him. Her face was pale, her eyes darkly shadowed.

"Dan," she said.

"Yes?"

"I lay awake most of the night wondering what to do, and I can't see any other way out. We have to go along with your plan."

He put down his toast. "You think so?"

She nodded. "I have to make a deal with you about…some kind of temporary marriage," she said, her voice barely more than a whisper. "You're right, I need a legal name. There's no other way I can get ID without Eric finding out where I am."

Dan's heart began to pound. "Okay," he said, "then let's go into Crystal Creek and do it right away, all right? Because I have to bring the kids home tomorrow, and I've already lost a whole lot of work time."

"Look, I'm so sorry about all this. And I'll be as fair as I can," she told him. "I'm going to try really hard to be a good baby-sitter and housekeeper, and as soon as I'm safe and have some money again, I'll be sure to pay you. I promise not to let you regret this."

Dan regretted it already. In fact, he was appalled at what was happening, but how could he say anything when she looked so tense and fragile, and it had been his idea in the first place?

"It's the best way to hide—in plain sight," she said earnestly, as if trying hard to convince herself, as well as him. "I'd be right here on this farm, going about my business like a normal person. I wouldn't be hidden away at all, yet nobody's ever going to think of looking for me here."

"Eat your eggs," he told her. "If you're sure about this, we should get going."

THEY SAT TOGETHER in a quiet office in Crystal Creek's old limestone courthouse. The branches of a live oak rustled against the window, making a soft, drowsy murmur on the glass. Across the desk, a woman looked solemnly into Dan's face while he told the whole story of Isabel Delgado's marriage and the terror of her recent past.

Mamie Gibson, the county clerk, was plump and majestic, with silver hair done in old-fashioned finger waves. She wore a flowered cotton dress, and her face looked soft and matronly. But above the steel-framed reading glasses, her blue eyes were sharp.

Bella listened uncomfortably as Dan recounted the bald facts of her life and identity. By now, she was so accustomed to secrecy and hiding that she felt like some nocturnal animal being dragged out into the light and exposed to terrible danger.

Mamie Gibson gave no indication of emotion as Dan spoke. She merely listened, her eyes resting on Bella's face from time to time with an unfathomable expression.

"So you think the only way out is for her to marry you?" Mamie asked when Dan was finished.

"We can't think of anything else, Mamie," Dan

said. "Can you? Seems to me she's trapped, and she needs a place to hide for a while, plus a bona fide identity she can use to get away and start rebuilding her life."

"And in exchange she'll look after your kids for a few months?"

"That's our deal."

"What will you tell the children and the neighbors?"

"I'm going to tell them Bella's from Oklahoma City, that we met while I was up there visiting Mama, but we didn't want to make a big deal about our relationship until we were sure we wanted to get married."

"Seems like the two of you are about to tell a whole lot of lies," his cousin observed. "And lying always gets folks in trouble, you know."

Bella tensed, casting a glance at the man next to her, but Dan kept his eyes fixed on the imposing Mamie. "This woman's already in a whole lot of trouble. If you can think of a better way to help her, I'd be happy to do it."

After a moment, Mamie nodded and opened a desk drawer. "I'll need some photo identification from both of you," she said, "and verification that your prior marriages are legally ended."

"Come on, Mamie," he said gently. "You've known me all my life. And if Bella had that kind of ID, we wouldn't need to get married, would we?"

While the woman studied him over the rims of her glasses, he took out a newspaper clipping from his shirt pocket and handed it across the desk. Mamie examined the picture in the paper, then Bella's face.

"Who cut your hair?" she asked.

"Dan did," Bella whispered.

Unexpectedly Mamie smiled. But the brief glimmer of warmth vanished as quickly as it had come and turned glacial as she looked at the newspaper clipping.

"I reckon," she said reluctantly, "that we could call this a photo ID. And it mentions your former marriage, too, so that's okay." She placed a form on the desktop, marked with a county seal. "I assume you'll be wanting a confidential license."

"What's that?" Dan asked.

"It's available in most counties in Texas. The license is only valid in the county where it's issued, and only for one month. The details of the marriage are recorded in a private file, but not put into the public record. If asked, the county clerk—me, in this case—will verify that the marriage took place. Otherwise the information remains sealed."

Bella felt a surge of relief. "Oh, but that's perfect!" she said. "Thank you so much, Miss Gibson."

Mamie eyed her thoughtfully, then picked up a rubber stamp and pressed it firmly onto another document. "This will allow you to bypass the three-day waiting period," she told Dan. "I assume you want to get this over with today, so you can bring the kids home?"

"Yes," Dan said, "the sooner the better." He reached for his wallet in the back pocket of his jeans. "What do I owe you, Mamie?"

His cousin waved her hand. "Call it a wedding gift," she said dryly, then glared at him to cut off his protest. "And don't argue with me, boy."

While both Dan and Bella murmured their thanks, Mamie handed over the marriage license, then checked her wristwatch.

"Howard Blake stops by around this time every morning to have coffee with Judge Brower," she said. "If you want to come on upstairs to the judge's chambers with me, Howard can marry you right now. The judge and I will be your witnesses."

The whole thing had a dreamlike quality. Bella walked up the carved oak staircase and stood beside Dan in a book-lined room while an older man with a white mustache heard their vows and pronounced them husband and wife.

Both the minister and the judge kissed Bella on the cheek, while Mamie hugged Dan and whispered something in his ear.

"What did she say to you?" Bella asked as they left the courthouse, heading for Dan's truck.

"Nothing much."

"Come on," Bella urged, opening the passenger door. "What did she say?"

"Okay. She told me you were the prettiest thing she'd ever laid eyes on," he said calmly.

Bella's jaw dropped in astonishment. "She did not. You're making it up."

He gave her a thoughtful glance. "You don't have much confidence, do you?"

She looked down at the ruffled white top and red cotton skirt she wore. Dan had unearthed the clothes from a stack of boxes in a metal shed near the barn and offered them to her a little awkwardly when they were preparing to leave for town.

"The clothes in those boxes belonged to Annie

years ago,'' he'd told her, ''back when she was about thirty pounds lighter. She always hung on to them, swearing she was going to slim down again enough to wear them, but it never happened.''

Bella looked out the window as he drove along the quiet, tree-lined streets of the sleepy little town. ''It's hard to have a whole lot of confidence,'' she said grimly, ''when you've just married a complete stranger, and your wedding dress is a hand-me-down from the groom's ex-wife.''

He chuckled and so did she, which helped defuse the tension they'd both been under all morning.

''Would you like to go out for lunch?'' he asked. ''It'll be our wedding reception. There's a great little restaurant in town called the Longhorn. It hasn't changed at all in the past forty years.''

''I remember the Longhorn.'' She clasped her hands nervously in her lap. ''But I'm afraid of seeing somebody I know, or being recognized.''

''You'll have to face the community sooner or later,'' he said reasonably. ''And you don't look anything like the woman in the newspaper photograph,'' he added with a casual glance at her cropped hair and cheap, ruffled clothes. ''Not a bit.''

''Well, thanks,'' she said dryly as he parked the truck.

But she was terrified all over again when they walked into the restaurant and the first person she saw was J.T. McKinney, sitting with a group of other men at a table near the door.

CHAPTER EIGHT

BELLA HAD TO FIGHT DOWN a shiver of fear when they entered the coffee shop and J.T. McKinney's shrewd eyes rested on her with interest. The rancher was probably over sixty by now, but as lean and handsome as ever, with his weathered face and graying temples under his trademark black Stetson.

"J.T.," Dan said, pausing by the table, "this is Bella. She's from Oklahoma City, and she's come down to stay with me for a while."

His casual announcement was clearly of great interest to the men at the table. Dan went on to introduce the rest of the group, and through a blur of panic, Bella tried to take note of the names.

Manny Hernandez and Tony Rodriguez, the local veterinarians, and the sheriff, Wayne Jackson. Across the table was a rugged, humorous fellow with a Scottish accent. "Douglas Evans," Dan told her. "Local mayor, stockbroker and real-estate agent, and the only guy in town who wears a kilt to parties."

The other rancher apparently was Bubba Gibson, Dan's uncle and neighbor from downriver.

Bubba had been a fixture in Crystal Creek back when she'd spent summers at J.T.'s ranch as a child. But she saw no sign of recognition on either of the older men's faces.

Bella felt herself relax a little, though she was still anxious to get away. She gave Dan a private glance of pleading. But Bubba reached out to grip his nephew's arm, grinning amiably.

"Well, well. No wonder you wanted a little private time without the kids," he said, winking. "It's about time you had some company, son."

Dan smiled. "Are they all doing okay, Bubba?"

"Right as rain. Mary took the girls up to the school bus this morning, and now she and Josh are baking gingerbread cookies."

"Tell Mary how much I appreciate it," Dan told his uncle, resting his hand lightly on Bella's shoulder. "I'll come and pick them up tomorrow after school, all right?"

"Take your time," Bubba said. "Mary's having a lot of fun with them kids."

"I'll get them tomorrow," Dan repeated quietly. "Bella's going to stay at the farm for a while, so she can help me with the baby-sitting."

"Well, that's good to hear," Bubba said, beaming. "That's real good."

Dan took her arm to guide her away from the table, and Bella felt limp with relief. As they walked toward the back of the restaurant, she recovered enough to look around.

"You're right," she murmured. "This place hasn't changed a bit."

The Longhorn coffee shop looked as if it had been lifted out of the fifties and plunked down in a new millennium. The tables were covered in red-and-white checked cloths, with chrome napkin holders and individual jukeboxes. The floor was dark, polished hardwood, worn thin over the years by the scuffing of countless pairs of boots, and the windows were decked in cheery, red-gingham curtains with white ruffles.

They sat down and a thin, sweet-faced woman appeared with a notepad and a couple of menus.

"Hi there, Nora," Dan said cheerfully. "I guess we'll both have some coffee to start and then take a look at the menu."

The woman smiled at Bella and left, tucking her order pad in her apron.

"That's Nora Slattery," Dan said, watching the waitress's slim back. "She's a real nice person."

"Slattery," Bella repeated. "That name sounds really familiar."

"She's married to Ken Slattery. He's been the foreman at the Double C for a lot of years."

"Oh, I remember him now!" Bella craned her neck to look at the waitress behind the long counter. "Ken was always such a nice man, a real old-time cowboy. He taught me how to ride when I was about ten."

"Nora used to be married to Dottie Jones's son. I don't know if you recall Dottie, but she owned the Longhorn back in those days. Gordon Jones was a lot like your ex-husband," Dan said. "He gave Nora an awful life, beat her up all the time. After they were divorced, he kept pestering her, making threats and trouble. Finally got himself accidentally run over by a police car about seven or eight years ago."

"So if Nora and Gordon got divorced, how did she happen to wind up back here at the Longhorn?" Bella asked, fascinated.

"Dottie was always loyal to Nora. She knew what a bad actor Gordon was, even if the man was her own son. Nora stayed on here to help Dottie after the divorce, and when Dottie died a few years back, she left the place to Nora and her grandson."

"So Nora owns this restaurant?" Bella asked. "She's not just a waitress?"

"Nora went back to school after Gordon died and got a college education, became an English teacher. Then a couple of years ago she took over the coffee shop full time. She's a real sharp businesswoman," Dan said. "She's made the place even more popular than it was in Dottie's time."

Bella smiled at the woman when she delivered their coffee.

"Thank you," Bella murmured, watching as Nora went back to the kitchen, awed by the courage of this woman who'd gone through the same kind of nightmare she herself was enduring and had been able not only to survive but to prosper.

"So," Dan said, "I was right, wasn't I? J.T. didn't recognize you at all."

"No, he didn't seem to." Bella shuddered as she poured cream into her coffee. "But it was scary having him look at me up close like that."

"Do you know any of the other McKinneys well enough to be worried they might recognize you?"

She shook her head. "If J.T. didn't, I doubt anybody else will. Tyler and Cal were already grown men when I spent those summers at the ranch, and they never paid much attention to a skinny little kid hanging around underfoot."

"How about Lynn?"

"She was away at college by then, and off with her friends most of the time. I think Pauline would have known me," Bella added, thinking about J.T. McKinney's first wife. "But she's been dead…how long?"

"More than ten years now. Have you met J.T.'s second wife?"

"Her name is Cynthia, isn't it?"

He nodded, sipping his coffee.

"I saw her and J.T. together at a charity function in Austin a couple of years ago, but we were never actually introduced." Bella looked down at herself ruefully. "Anyway, I doubt Cynthia would recognize me in these clothes."

"You're not all that impressed with Annie's taste, are you?" he asked with a teasing grin.

Bella flushed. "Look, I don't want to seem ungrateful. Considering the state I was in when I arrived at your house, I'm lucky to have clothes to wear at all. And there are a lot of jeans and shirts in those boxes, things I'll get good use out of. I just…" She moved awkwardly under his keen gaze. "I guess I'd choose…different styles for dressing up."

He smiled again but refrained from comment, examining his menu, instead. "The Longhorn burger's real good. They make it with lean Texas beef and the best home fries you ever tasted."

"Is that what you're having?"

"I think so. And afterward maybe we'll have room for rhubarb pie. It's a little slice of heaven, Nora's rhubarb pie with ice cream."

"Okay," she said. "I'll have the same thing."

Bella watched the laughing group of men at the

table near the door. They all seemed so happy, teasing one another and the waitress. The sight brought back memories of those sun-drenched summers of her childhood and how she'd always loved the atmosphere of this little ranching community.

"You know, I remember your uncle Bubba visiting the Double C," she said aloud. "He was always so full of fun."

"He used to be, but he's weathered some hard times since the days you were here."

"What kind of hard times?"

"Bubba went through sort of a bad midlife crisis. Had an affair with a young woman, spent too much money and almost lost his ranch. Eventually he was in so deep that he even got involved in insurance fraud and spent some time in jail."

Bella stared at Dan, then looked cautiously at the laughing, gruff-voiced rancher. "Really? I never would have imagined anything like that could happen to Bubba."

"It was a real tough time for Bubba and Mary. She was the one who had the idea to start raising ostriches, and it saved the ranch."

"But...wasn't she upset about his affair?" Bella asked.

"I reckon she was, but in the end she forgave him and took him back. And Bubba's never forgotten how lucky he was."

Their conversation was interrupted for a moment as Nora came back to take their orders.

"Dan," Bella said after the woman left, "I've been wondering how this is going to work." She avoided his eyes, concentrating on her own blurred reflection in the chrome of the napkin holder. "Getting myself new ID in my…my married name. How will we go about it?"

"The best thing," he said, "would be to start with a driver's license, since that's what they usually ask for, isn't it?"

"I guess I'll have to take a driver's test."

"Sure, but that's no problem, right? You can use my truck."

"But the only official ID I have right now is our marriage certificate, and it also shows my maiden name. So if I have to present that certificate to get a driver's license, I'll be putting myself in the same danger as before, won't I?"

"You won't be presenting the marriage certificate to anybody," he said calmly. "You'll just tell Stella Metz, who does the test and issues the driver's license, that your name is Bella Gibson, you're married to me and you live at my farm, so that's your legal address."

"But will she actually issue a driver's license without seeing any ID?"

"She will after she calls Mamie," he said with a brief grin. "Because Mamie's going to tell her to go ahead and give you the license, since she was a witness at our wedding and she can testify that Bella Gibson is your legal name."

Bella's worries began to ease slightly. "I see what you mean. And then I can present the driver's license, in the name of Bella Gibson, to get a credit card or open a checking account."

"It's a pretty good start. I think you'll probably need to use your maiden name for a passport or to get copies of your birth certificate and social-security card, but those are things you can look after a few months from now, once you're safely out of state somewhere and ready to move on.''

For the first time in months, Bella felt herself breathing a little easier, actually contemplating some kind of future.

''Thank you so much, Dan,'' she said gratefully. ''Really, I can't tell you how wonderful it is to feel safe again and have a name I can use without looking over my shoulder all the time to see if somebody's following me.''

''You should be all right,'' he said, ''as long as you don't attract any attention to yourself.''

Bella glanced at the group of men by the door, who were now getting up to leave. Bubba Gibson waved at his nephew, then tipped his hat in Bella's direction with awkward gallantry before he went outside, his boots clumping on the scuffed hardwood floor.

''What's your uncle going to say when he finds out we're actually a married couple and I'm not just a friend who's come down from Oklahoma for a little visit?''

''If I know Bubba,'' Dan said dryly, ''he's going to tell everybody what a lucky son of a gun I am.''

When she realized what he meant, her cheeks warmed.

''I would have told him we were married just now,'' Dan said, ''but I want the kids to hear it from me first. I'm afraid,'' he added, frowning, ''that Ellie's going to be pretty upset about it.''

Bella looked at him in alarm and was grateful for

the diversion when Nora arrived with heaping plat-ters of burgers and delectable-looking home fries smothered in rich gravy. She picked up her fork and dug in, surprised to realize how hungry she was.

"How does your arm feel today?" Dan asked, gesturing with his burger at the neat bandage he'd applied the night before.

"It hardly throbs at all anymore," she said, chew-ing blissfully. "Oh, you're right, these home fries are wonderful!"

He smiled and picked up the ketchup. "For a rich girl, you have pretty simple tastes in food. And a good thing, too," he said ruefully, "since meals at my house aren't fancy."

"I really mean it, Dan." She looked at him across the table. "It's a wonderful, generous thing you've done for me, and I want you to know I'm very, very grateful for everything."

"Don't be too hasty. You might not be all that grateful once you meet my kids and see what you've gotten yourself into. Could be you'll decide I'm the one who made the best deal."

She watched him for a moment, but he kept his eyes fixed on his plate, eating steadily. Bella fol-lowed suit, losing herself in the delicious meal and wondering if she would ever learn to cook anything nearly as good.

ERIC MATTHIAS sat in his office in Austin, looking at the contents of the bulging envelopes spread out on his desk. His eyes burned with angry tears when he picked up his ex-wife's passport and examined the photograph.

"Damn you," he whispered, staring at her shy, crooked grin and her gentle eyes. "Pretending to be so innocent, and all the time you were planning a trick like this."

Actually, knowing Isabel, he was a little surprised at the complexity of her escape plan.

Dumping the Mercedes into the river to fake her death, getting duplicates made of all her ID, depositing enough money in that bus locker to take her a long way from Texas—it was a pretty smart move and must have required a lot of organization and thought.

If an alert locker attendant at the Abilene bus depot hadn't spotted her picture in the paper and notified the police, Isabel might even have gotten away with this.

Eric frowned, still holding the passport. He was a handsome man in his late thirties, with dark hair graying at the temples and a smooth tanned face, but his looks were somewhat marred by eyes of such a pale gray that they seemed almost without color.

He glanced at the busy squad room beyond his office window, then looked down again at the pile of documents on his desk.

No need to get upset, he reminded himself, because she hadn't managed to get away with her little plan and was now in a worse fix than ever. Eric had her ID, her escape money, her whole life right here in his hands. She couldn't go anywhere.

So where *was* she?

At first he'd had a terrible fear she might have gone into the river, after all, and died before he could find and confront her. Eric couldn't even fathom a world without Isabel. She was the sole reason for his existence.

But then they'd called Eric from Abilene on Sunday morning to report a young man asking about the contents of the locker, claiming he'd been sent a key in the mail.

As bad luck would have it, the guy had arrived at the depot just a few hours before Eric was able to get a private investigator into position to watch the lockers, which meant another golden opportunity had slipped through his fingers. None of the idiots at the bus depot had even thought to check what the man was driving.

But whoever he was, the man must have Isabel stashed away somewhere, and by now they both knew her secret little plan had been blown sky-high.

So what would they do?

Eric tried to put himself in Isabel's head and think what her next move might be. He knew she didn't trust her father or brother. He also knew she had lots of her own money, but she'd be aware that he was monitoring her banks and credit-card statements, watching for any sign that she was trying to get duplicate ID issued anywhere in Texas.

Maybe she was smarter than he thought and this whole thing was really elaborate. What if she and her boyfriend had a third set of ID made and were planning even now to flee the country?

Eric tensed in fear, then relaxed, leaned back in his swivel chair and stared at the wall.

If they'd had another set of ID, the guy wouldn't have taken the risk of turning up in Abilene at the bus depot, knowing he, Eric, would probably have had it staked out.

His brain hurt from the effort of trying to anticipate her next move. And no matter how hard he concentrated, he kept seeing the unknown man the locker attendant had described as a ''big, good-looking guy, kind of a farmer type.''

He imagined the unknown man holding Isabel, kissing her and stroking her slim, naked body while the two of them laughed together at how they'd managed to outwit Eric Matthias.

Pain rose in him…and a hot, choking storm of jealousy. He took his handgun from the holster under his arm and fondled it absently, comforted by the polished smoothness, the cold, deadly weight. Then, frightened by his own emotions, he put the gun away again.

That wasn't the way to go and he knew it, though he was increasingly troubled by dark fantasies of cruelty and revenge.

Most of all, he simply wanted to get Isabel's attention, have her thoughts focused on him while he explained everything to her.

He wanted her to know he hadn't really meant to hurt the stupid dog; he'd just been overcome by emotion in the middle of their fight. Also, he wanted to make her understand how important she was to him, how he felt sometimes that he'd die if he couldn't have her, or if some other man possessed her. Eric still believed that if he could just somehow force her to listen, Isabel would realize how much he loved her and come back to him.

All his assets, all his energy outside of work and,

if truth were told, even a good deal of his time on the job had become directed toward this single purpose.

Pierce Delgado was on Eric's side and his association with Isabel's family had given him enough money over the years that he wouldn't need to work anymore if he chose. But his career had always satisfied Eric's craving for power and given him an identity.

And in recent years, it had also provided him with the means to track and monitor Isabel's behavior. He couldn't bear to give that up, at least not until he had her back and his life was in order again.

"I'm going to find you." He touched her smiling image on the passport, stroked the curve of her lips with a trembling finger. "I'm going to make you understand how I feel, no matter what it takes. And your new boyfriend, whoever he is, that bastard's going to be sorry he ever even *met* my wife."

A timid knock sounded at the door. "Lieutenant Matthias?" a secretary called. "Are you in there?"

Hastily he put the papers away in the file and leaned back. "Yeah, I'm here. Come in."

The young woman popped her head inside the door and smiled at her handsome boss. "Almost time for the department briefing."

"You're a slave driver, Ashley," he told her with a charming smile, then got up and strode past her into the squad room, while she stood watching his tall, erect figure with frank admiration.

CHAPTER NINE

LATE TUESDAY AFTERNOON, Dan drove to Bubba's place to pick up the kids. He kissed his aunt, who stood in the doorway wearing an apron patterned with cartoon ostriches.

"Thanks a lot for doing this, Mary," he told her, watching the kids pile into the truck. "It was real nice of you."

"I hear you have a...a friend visiting you." Her cheeks turned faintly pink. "Allan says she's real pretty."

Mary Gibson was the only person in the community who insisted on calling her husband by his given name. She never referred to him as Bubba.

Dan smiled at her gentle face, then glanced over his shoulder toward the noisy crew by the truck.

"Do you want to know a big secret?" he asked, leaning close to his aunt.

"Well, of course. I love secrets," she replied solemnly.

"Like I said, this is a big one." Dan hesitated, looking down at her. "I'm married to that 'friend,' Mary. We're husband and wife."

Her mouth fell open and she stared at him in astonishment. "Dan Gibson, go on! You're joking with me, surely."

"Believe me, it's no joke. But I didn't want to tell anybody else until I had a chance to tell the kids about it."

"So nobody knows you're married? Not a soul in Crystal Creek?"

"Except for Howard who married us, and Mamie and Judge Brower, who were our witnesses. But I guess folks need to get the news eventually," Dan said with a faint grin, "so you might as well tell Bubba when he comes in for supper."

Mary chuckled. "Telling Allan is like putting it in the *Claro County Courier*. You know what a gossip the man is."

"I know, but like I said, the neighbors have got to find out sooner or later."

"Dan, sweetie, what's going on?" Mary reached out to hold his arm gently. "Are you happy? Is everything all right?"

Dan found himself reluctant to meet her shrewd gaze. "Sure, I'm fine. Everything's just great, Aunt Mary."

"Well," she said a little dubiously, "you bring this girl over to meet me, you hear?"

"Bella's going to be happy to meet you," Dan said. "She doesn't know a whole lot about cooking and housekeeping, so she'll probably want some advice from time to time."

"You know I'll be tickled to help out any way I can," Mary said with automatic courtesy, but her gaze was increasingly puzzled.

Dan smiled and hugged her, dropping a grateful kiss on her cheek. "Thanks again for watching the kids,'' he said, then turned and strode to his truck before she could say anything more.

Ellie and Chris had strapped Josh into his car seat in the rear compartment and were settled in the front. Dan reached over to check the fasteners, stroked the little boy's round face and halo of curls, then smiled at his daughters.

"Do up your seat belts, girls,'' he said. "Both of you.''

He ignored the usual chorus of argument, sitting placidly with his left arm on the window ledge. "I'm not starting this truck,'' he told them, "until both of you have your seat belts fastened.''

Grudgingly they obeyed, then turned to wave at Mary who still watched them from the kitchen door with a quizzical expression.

"I need to tell you kids something,'' Dan said as their truck topped a rise above Bubba's Flying Horse ranch and started to bump across the back country toward his own farm.

On the passenger side, Ellie stared out the window while Chris looked up at him, her freckled face serious. "What is it, Daddy?''

Dan hesitated. Now that the time had arrived, he didn't know how to start.

"While you were over at Mary's,'' he said at last, "I did something that's…going to be a big surprise for everybody.''

Chris's face blazed with happiness. "You built the castle for us!''

"No, sweetheart,'' he said gently. "I'm sorry, I didn't have time to work on it. This news has nothing to do with your castle.''

Apparently Ellie was struck by something in his tone, because she turned away from her examination of the passing countryside and leaned forward to stare at her father.

"Okay," she said tensely, "so what's the big surprise?"

"I got married yesterday," Dan told them. It sounded harsh and abrupt even to his own ears, but he couldn't think of a more tactful way to tell them.

Both girls stared at him, speechless. In the back seat, Josh was singing garbled lyrics to "Itsy Bitsy Spider" and doing the hand motions for his own entertainment. His voice was the only sound in the silent cab.

"You got married?" Ellie said at last.

Dan nodded. "To a nice lady named Bella," he said. "I met her in Oklahoma City when I was up there last year visiting Nana."

Ellie kept watching him, her eyes hard and suspicious. "We were with you when you went to visit Nana. You never talked about meeting a lady."

Dan hated the necessity of lying to his kids. It was something he almost never did, because it made him so uncomfortable.

"Well, maybe I don't always tell you everything," he said, trying to smile. "Just take my word for it, okay? Her name's Bella and she's my wife, and she's going to be living in our house from now on and helping to look after you."

Chris spoke for the first time, her face taut with anxiety. "Do we...do we have to call her Mama?" she whispered.

Dan's heart ached for this gentle middle child of

his. "No, honey," he said huskily, putting an arm around her. "You can call her Bella. She's very nice," he added, trying to sound hearty and casual. "I think you're really going to like her."

He stole a glance at Ellie who gripped the hand-hold on the door. Her face was pale, and he tensed when he saw the ominous stiffness of her body.

"Ellie, look," he said. "Don't be upset. At least give Bella a chance, okay?"

But Ellie didn't reply, and soon afterward they pulled into their farmyard. The girls got out, looking dazed, and headed reluctantly for the back door while Dan unstrapped Josh from his car seat.

When he walked into the kitchen, Chris and Ellie were still in the doorway to the porch, staring at Bella who stood nervously by the kitchen sink, giving the girls a bright, forced smile.

She looked so awkward that Dan's heart ached for her. God, he thought wearily, what a mess I've made for everybody.

Bella wore a pair of Annie's old khaki shorts and a green plaid shirt. Dan vaguely remembered the clothes, but they looked very different on Bella. Something indefinable about her graceful bearing gave flair and style even to this kind of casual garb, and set her apart from any woman he'd ever known.

Again he felt that familiar mixture of admiration and resentment that colored so much of his association with her.

"Bella," he said, drawing the two girls forward, "here's Chris, and this is Ellie. And this little fellow—" he lifted the wide-eyed toddler into his arms "—is Josh."

"Hello, everyone." Bella waved a hand toward the table and gave the three silent children another anxious, timid smile that made him ache for her all over again. "I made some…I made mashed potatoes for supper. I sure hope you like them."

SOME HOURS LATER, Bella lay rigidly beside Dan in the cool darkness, staring at the ceiling and feeling desolate.

What made things even worse was that she had to share his bedroom now that the children were home. Otherwise she could have closed the door, buried her face in a pillow and given way to the tears she could feel threatening. Maybe after a good cry she'd feel a little better.

But the man was right next to her, wearing his boxer shorts and a clean white undershirt, close enough to touch though both of them kept scrupulously to their own sides of the bed.

"Your children hate me," she murmured, her voice trembling. "All of them."

"Of course they don't hate you," he said patiently, then switched on his reading lamp and opened a book as if to dismiss further conversation. "This has been a bit of a shock to them, but they'll all warm up soon enough."

"What makes you think so?"

"Well, Josh and Chris were already willing to let you see their castle."

Bella thought about the pile of rocks by the back door. "They're hoping I can help them make it into a real castle. But I don't know how. There's nothing

I know how to do," she added with sudden passion. "Nothing that's worth anything."

He grinned. "You can make pretty good mashed potatoes."

His teasing smile faded when she glared at him in the dim circle of lamplight. "Stop making fun of me!" she whispered furiously, but her voice caught, ending with a sob.

Dan sighed and lay the book on his chest. "Look," he said reasonably, "this is going to be tough on everybody for a while. It's a big change for the kids—they'll have to get used to you. And you're right, there's a lot you need to learn, even to get along here for just a few months. But I'm willing to teach you, and so is my aunt Mary, and after a while it's all going to be easy for you."

"One of the first things I need to do is learn to cook something besides mashed potatoes." She frowned at the ceiling. "I spent the afternoon looking at recipes, and I think tomorrow I'm going to try spaghetti. It looks pretty straightforward."

"There you go," Dan said with obvious relief. "The kids love spaghetti."

He picked his book up again, then glanced sidelong at Bella who had taken a cookbook from her nightstand to read and was twirling a strand of hair around her finger in thoughtful silence.

She felt his eyes on her, and looked over at his book. "What are you reading?"

"A novel by James Michener," he said. "It's really interesting."

Her eyes widened in surprise, and she could see the way his jaw tightened.

"What's the matter?" he asked abruptly. "Did you think a dumb guy like me would never read anything but the *Farmer's Almanac?*"

Bella met his gaze calmly. "Actually, I've never given your reading tastes much thought at all," she said, with a coolness she didn't entirely feel. "But since I knew you took structural engineering at college, I would assume you were at least semiliterate."

She pretended to immerse herself in the cookbook again, conscious of his eyes resting on her with puzzled speculation.

The bed was beginning to feel smaller all the time, even when she kept herself plastered right over by the nightstand. There was always a danger she might brush him with her toe when she stretched, or roll into his hard-muscled body when she turned over.

Briefly she considered suggesting some kind of barrier down the middle of the bed, a pile of cushions or a rolled blanket, but the idea seemed childish. Also, she didn't like the implication that unless they were restrained somehow, they wouldn't be able to keep themselves apart.

Because she could certainly keep herself apart from this big, arrogant farmer who found it entertaining to tease her all the time and who made it clear just how much he disapproved of her background and her wealthy life-style.

"Hmm?" she said, realizing he'd just asked her something.

"I asked, why did you marry this guy in the first place?"

"You mean Eric?"

"Unless you've had other husbands you didn't tell

me about.'' He smiled, his teeth flashing white against his tanned face.

A lock of thick, sandy hair had fallen over his forehead, and Bella was distressed by a sudden, wholly irrational urge to reach up and brush it back.

She gripped the cookbook tensely and thought about his question.

''My family has a beach house on Lake Travis,'' she said at last. ''I went there alone a few years ago and found it had been broken into. I called the police, and Eric was the detective who came to investigate.''

''And the handsome cop swept you right off your feet?''

''Not really.'' She frowned, remembering. ''I was scared and upset.'' She turned her head to look at the man beside her. ''It's a really terrible feeling, you know, having your house broken into. You feel so vulnerable and violated.''

Again he grinned at her, his eyes dancing.

''What?'' she asked, puzzled, then remembered the dark night when she'd slipped into his house and begun emptying the fridge. ''That's not the same thing!'' she said indignantly. ''Not at all.''

''Well, I felt pretty damned violated at first. But—'' his smile broadened ''—I have to admit, not all that vulnerable.''

Bella glared and swatted his arm with the cookbook, making him wince, then returned to her story. ''Eric was very kind and understanding, and explained everything the police were doing. For weeks afterward he kept dropping by to see if I was all right.''

"You didn't think that was a little odd for a busy detective?" Dan asked.

"No, I just figured Austin had a really wonderful police force."

"But it turns out the officer had his eye on the heiress?"

Bella stared at the ceiling, thinking about his question.

"You know," she said at last, "I don't think the money was his primary interest, at least back in those days. Eric was really, really attracted to me. I mean, he was head over heels." She gave Dan an awkward smile. "As difficult as that may be for you to believe."

"I don't find that difficult to believe at all," he said quietly, with a look in his eyes that made her turn away quickly.

They lay together in silence for a while as Bella leafed through the pages of the cookbook, pretending to search for a recipe.

"So were you attracted, too?" he said after a while. "Was this a mutual passion?"

"Not really. Eric's a nice-looking man, but kind of...serious. And he's almost ten years older than me, you know. Though after a while, that started to seem appealing." She paused. "I mean, the man had all that power and authority, and he seemed so confident..."

"And you've spent your whole life looking to find some confidence, haven't you?"

She glared at him. "So you're a psychoanalyst, too, among all your other talents?"

"But am I right?"

"I guess you probably are," she said reluctantly. "At any rate, I started to accept when he asked me out, and I'd let him look after me. It felt good to have a powerful man care about me so much. And he never gave the slightest indication of what he was really like. All that obsessive jealousy and insecurity—I never saw a trace of it when we were dating."

"You know, that's a little hard to believe," Dan said mildly.

"I suppose it is. Maybe I was just seeing what I wanted to see," Bella replied frankly. "And Eric was being extra careful in those days, of course. I guess with more experience I might have noticed a few warning signals. But when you're in your early twenties and not all that confident, and this big man adores you so much he never wants anyone else looking at you, it can be really flattering."

"Not so flattering when the jealousy starts getting out of hand, though."

"It was awful," Bella said with a shudder. "After we were married, he called home every hour to see what I was doing. He came by the house on routine sweeps to make sure nobody was parked outside. He even fired the pool-maintenance guy when he thought the poor kid was looking at me in my bathing suit."

"No kidding?"

Bella shook her head. "Eric threatened and terrified the kid, and he was on duty at the time. I'm sure the police department probably had to hush it up and make some kind of arrangement with the family to keep from being sued."

There was a long, tense silence.

"What about you?" Dan said at last. "Did he ever threaten you?"

"Sometimes. I started getting really scared of him," Bella frowned. "He was just so…intense. At first I could joke him out of it, or we'd…have sex, and that would make everything okay for a while. After a time, though, nothing could get him to settle down for long. And if I didn't seem to be paying attention to something he was telling me, or if he thought I was too interested in some good-looking man on television…"

"But he wouldn't hit you, would he?"

"No. I think in an odd way that would have been less scary. If he'd ever hit me, I could have packed up and left him. But he'd just get broody and sullen and pick a fight, and then make these veiled threats that really terrified me. Afterward he always seemed so needy and miserable that I felt guilty. I guess I kept believing it was my fault, because I couldn't ever seem to do enough to make him happy."

"No doubt he wanted you to feel that way," Dan said. "But that's what a good relationship is about. Nobody is responsible for providing happiness for another person. We're supposed to do that for ourselves."

"I know that now," she said. "I guess I finally realized it when he…when he tried to hurt Rufus. The very next day I left him and went back to my father's house."

"So what did he do then?"

"He came to the house and cried and pleaded for hours," she said tonelessly. "He told my father it was an accident, that we'd been fighting and he was so upset he might have lifted Rufus up without realizing it, but he never intended to hurt him.''

''And your father believed this?''

''He wanted to believe. Daddy didn't want me hanging around the house again, maybe starting to drink like my mother. He wanted my marriage to be a success, so he convinced himself Eric was telling the truth.''

''And what was it like after you went back?''

''From then on it was a nightmare, with fights all the time except for a few peaceful interludes when he'd be sorry and beg for my forgiveness. I didn't stay very long, and when I absolutely couldn't stand it anymore, my father finally had to let me come home and file for divorce.''

''But Daddy still believes the problem was all your fault?''

''I think he'll always believe that. My father has an infinite capacity to believe what suits him. And Eric can be very charming, you know. I'm sure Daddy thinks I'm lucky to have a man who loves me so much.''

''Obsession isn't love, Bella.''

''I understand that clearly now. Believe me, it was a brutal lesson to learn.'' She was trembling, reliving the horror of her past months and years.

''You're really terrified of this guy, aren't you?'' Dan watched her thoughtfully.

''It's horrible to be the object of somebody's concentrated attention, especially when you know he's unbalanced. And especially when nobody believes you. I think Eric spends almost all his time thinking about me and searching for me. And I don't know—'' she faltered briefly ''—I honestly don't know what's ever going to make him stop doing it.''

Dan put a hand on her arm. She felt the warmth and hardness of his palm, saw the muscles of his forearm. His touch was very comforting. Her breathing slowed and her heart stopped racing.

''But in spite of everything, I feel safe here,'' she said in a low voice. ''For some reason I have the impression he won't be able to find me.''

''Let's hope he can't,'' Dan said, releasing her arm and picking his book up again. ''And in a couple of months you'll be able to leave and get on with your life again.''

''Do you really think so?''

''Of course I do.'' He smiled at her, his eyes crinkling warmly. ''That's why we're doing this, isn't it?''

Bella returned the smile a little uncertainly, then tried to concentrate on her cookbook. But the print blurred in front of her eyes as she thought about the days and weeks ahead, the three children and the daunting task of learning to care for them, to cook and clean house and fulfill her part in this bizarre pact she'd made with their father.

CHAPTER TEN

BELLA AWOKE IN THE HALF LIGHT of dawn and looked drowsily at the bedside clock. It was just past six o'clock, but Dan's side of the bed was already empty, and his neat pile of work clothes gone from the top of the hamper.

Grateful for the moment of solitude, Bella lay there wondering how all this had happened to her. It was hard to believe she'd actually spent the night in bed with a virtual stranger, a man who hadn't been tempted to touch her.

All Dan Gibson wanted, pure and simple, was a housekeeper and baby-sitter.

And the grimmest irony of all, she thought miserably, was that he couldn't have found a less-qualified woman for the job if he'd gone out and searched for a year. She had no idea how she was going to cope in the days and weeks ahead.

But huddling behind the closed door of this bedroom wasn't going to accomplish anything. Reluctantly she slipped out of bed and tiptoed down the silent hallway to the bathroom, which looked considerably better after she'd spent more than an hour scrubbing and tidying it the day before, along with the rest of the house.

By now Bella had a couple of inexpensive cosmetic bags containing such personal necessities as a toothbrush and dental floss, a comb and a tube of lipstick.

As she washed and dressed, she thought about her bathroom back in her father's house, with its expanse of marble, brass and gleaming mirrors, the colorful array of bottles containing all kinds of lotions and ointments and perfumes, the adjoining dressing room that was probably bigger than Dan Gibson's whole house.

She dabbed on a bit of cheap lipstick, frowning at her image in the dresser mirror. It was amazing how little a person actually needed. All those mountains of clothes and possessions were really unnecessary. Most of the time they just weighed you down. Though she wouldn't mind a small jar of really good face cream, and something for these reddened hands.

Sternly, Bella put all thoughts of luxury out of her mind, made the bed and went down the hall to the kitchen, past the room where the two smaller children slept.

Dan had made a pot of coffee, and its welcome aroma filled the little house. Bella helped herself to a cup and stood in the back doorway, hugging herself against the chill of early morning.

Silence lay across the hills, except for scraps of birdsong and the ever-present murmur of the river. A mist rose from the valley floor, swirling up to shroud the trees and the humped shapes of sleeping cattle. Above the layers of mist a rising sun warmed the rounded hilltops that rolled off as far as the eye could see, turning them from brown to ever-lightening shades of mauve in the distance.

Dan was working down near the barn, loading wooden beehives onto the back of his truck with the help of a small hand-operated crane. Bella watched his shoulders strain under the flannel shirt, and the lithe movement of his body when he bent to lift the heavy crates.

Gypsy seemed a little more chipper this morning. The Border collie walked stiffly at Dan's side as he moved back and forth from the barn to the truck. Her tail wagged with happiness whenever he stopped to rest a hand on her satiny head.

That man's my husband, Bella told herself with a cold shock of surprise. *Legally, for a little while at least, he's actually my husband.*

For the hundredth time, she wondered what Dan Gibson really thought about their arrangement. Could anybody be that desperate for a baby-sitter and cook?

Her thoughts were interrupted by a sound from the kitchen. She went inside to find Josh standing in the middle of the floor, trailing his teddy bear by one leg. The little boy wore a blue terry-cloth sleeper. His curly hair was tousled, his eyes still a bit drowsy.

"Well, good morning." Bella smiled at him. "Ready for breakfast?"

"All wet," he said, frowning and tugging at the bottom part of his sleeper.

"Oh, dear." Bella looked down at him uncertainly, trying to remember what Dan had told her about this the night before.

Josh wore a diaper to bed at night. But he was in something called "training pants" for daytime, and his clothes were piled on the arm of the sofa so he could be dressed without bothering either of his sisters, who slept later than he did.

Bella took the child's hand and led him into the living room, gratified by the way he trotted obediently at her side.

She took off the sleeper, enchanted by his sturdy little body, and frowned as she figured out how to unfasten the sticky tapes on the diaper. Awkwardly she wiped his damp bottom with one of the moistened tissues from a flat plastic case beside his clothes, then pulled on the heavy padded underpants, the little denim trousers and clean shirt that Dan had laid out the night before.

Finally she put the boy on her lap, nuzzling his curls while she pulled on his socks and tied his diminutive sneakers. He rested against her, solid and warm in her arms, giggling when she finished by kissing his cheek.

"Now Josh is all dressed," she said, bundling up the sodden diaper with a huge feeling of accomplishment. "Let's just throw this old thing away and wash our face and hands. Then we'll be all ready for breakfast."

"Brekbuss," he repeated with pleasure, trotting at her side into the bathroom and holding up his face to be washed, though he grimaced and struggled when she applied the cloth with too much energy.

Bella cleaned his hands and her own, then took him into the kitchen. "What do you want for breakfast?" she asked. "I think your daddy told me you like to eat toast."

"Toast and nana," he announced, scrambling onto

his high chair and watching with interest as she fastened the tray in place.

"What's nana?" she asked.

"Nana." He frowned and hammered his pink fists on the tray.

Bella glanced around the kitchen and caught sight of a bunch of bananas on the counter. "Okay, little guy," she said, "I see what you mean." She hurried to put some bread in the toaster for him, then filled and capped his milk cup and peeled a banana, setting it on his tray.

"Now," she said, "I have to make these school lunches. I wish you could help me, Josh. I don't have a clue how to make a lunch."

There was sudden clatter in the hallway. Ellie passed the kitchen door on her way to the bathroom.

"Ellie!" Bella called hopefully. "I'm so glad you're up. Could you just tell me what..."

The girl paused and glanced into the kitchen, scowling, then turned without a word and vanished again.

Bella sighed and took a loaf of bread from the fridge, along with cheese, peanut butter and jam. She made two sandwiches for each little girl, wrapped them carefully in waxed paper and put them into paper sacks, adding a couple of cookies, an apple and a juice box for each one, then looked at them dubiously.

"I guess that's all right," she said to the boy in the high chair, whose face by now was smeared with toast crumbs and bits of banana.

Too late she realized that Josh should have worn his bib. Now she would have to change his shirt before the day had even begun. And that meant more laundry, another daunting task she would soon have to deal with.

Josh's little golden eyebrows drew together over suddenly stormy blue eyes. "I want lunts," he said, banging a spoon on his tray.

Bella looked at him uncertainly. "Darling, I don't know what—"

"Lunts!" he shouted. "Want lunts!"

"Lunch," Bella said with relief. "You want a lunch, too, dear?"

"Lunts," he agreed. His face cleared and a dimple showed in one cheek.

"Tell you what," Bella said. "I'll make a lunch for both of us, since we're spending the day together. Lunch for Josh and lunch for Bella." She dampened a cloth and wiped his face, then tried ineffectually to clean some of the butter and banana smears from his shirt.

He took his milk glass in both hands and drank thirstily, watching in satisfaction while she made two more sets of sandwiches.

"See?" she told him, holding up the smaller sack. "This is Josh's lunch, and this is Bella's. I'm putting our lunches away in the fridge now," she added, matching actions to words, "and they'll be all ready for later. Josh and Bella will go outside and have a picnic."

"Pitnit," he repeated, looking blissful. "Josh and Bella have a pitnit."

"Who's having a picnic?" Chris asked, appearing in the doorway. She was barefoot, wearing the ragged T-shirt and plaid jogging pants she used as pajamas.

"Pitnit!" Josh yelled at his sister, banging his spoon on his tray. "Josh and Bella!"

Chris edged across the room to stand by the little boy's high chair, looking at Bella with round, frightened eyes.

Bella smiled at her, touched by her timidity, wondering how it would feel for an eight-year-old to wake up one morning in this house and find a complete stranger in the kitchen.

"I made a lunch for you, honey," Bella said timidly, "but I don't know if you're going to like the sandwiches."

"What are they?" Chris asked.

"One is cheese and dill pickle, and one's peanut butter and strawberry jam."

"Yum," Chris said, her face brightening. "I love cheese and dill pickle."

"You know what I used to love? Cheddar cheese and strawberry jam," Bella said, setting plates on the table. "When I was little, I always used to hang around in the kitchen and ask the cook if she'd—"

She fell abruptly silent, but Chris seemed not to have noticed. The little girl was leaning against the table, looking around, her freckled face earnest.

"I really like this," Chris said shyly.

"What do you like, dear?" Bella paused, her hands full of cutlery.

"I like how the house is all clean and nice. It feels good."

Bella stared at the child, astonished and pleased. "Well, I'm glad to hear that," she said, stroking

Chris's short blond hair. "I worked really hard yesterday to get it all cleaned up. And I'm not very good at housecleaning," she confessed. "I'm sort of learning as I go along."

"I'm not good at it, either." Chris watched gravely as Bella set the table. "Ellie says I'm a big dummy and can't do anything."

"But that's not true!"

As if summoned by the mention of her name, Ellie appeared in the doorway and stalked through the kitchen to the porch, ignoring the group at the table. Bella watched the older girl with a sinking heart, intimidated by Ellie's pale, angry face and the rigid set of her back.

"Ellie," she said cautiously when the girl reappeared, carrying a pair of running shoes, "I packed a lunch for you, but I don't know if you'll like—"

Ellie cut short her timid words by yanking open the fridge door and taking out one of the lunches. She opened it without a word, removed the wrapped sandwiches and shoved them back into the fridge, then carried the sack of fruit and cookies from the room with her.

Bella watched in silence, then exchanged a glance with Chris.

"Ellie's real mad," Chris whispered.

"Why?"

"Because Daddy married you and didn't tell us. She says it was an awful thing to do."

Chris edged closer and stood on tiptoe. Bella leaned down so the little girl could whisper in her ear.

"Ellie cried at night in her bed. I heard her."

Bella's heart twisted with painful sympathy. "Oh, I'm so sorry," she murmured, drawing away to look down at her informant. "What can I do?"

Chris shrugged and went to get a box of cereal from the cupboard. "You can't do anything," she said. "When Ellie gets mad, nothing makes her happy again for a long time."

Helplessly, Bella gripped the knives and spoons in her hand, turning as Dan came into the kitchen and crossed the room to wash his hands at the sink.

"Pitnit!" Josh shouted at his father, bouncing in the chair. "Josh and Bella!"

Dan turned and looked at her with raised eyebrows. She flushed a little under his direct, inquiring gaze.

"Josh was having his breakfast when I made school lunches for the girls," she said. "He wanted one, too, so I made lunches for both of us and told him we'd go for a picnic later."

"A picnic," Dan said, pausing to hug Chris and give her a noisy kiss on the cheek while she giggled and clung to him. "Now, that sounds like fun."

"You can go on the picnic, too, Daddy," Chris told him, "because Ellie didn't want her sandwiches. She took them out and put them back in the fridge."

Dan's smile faded at this news. He exchanged a quick glance with Bella, then strode through the house in search of his older daughter while Chris scampered off to the vacant bathroom.

ELLIE SAT ON THE SCHOOL BUS next to her little sister, staring out the window at the passing countryside, where horses and cattle grazed placidly behind vine-covered fences.

"I like Bella," Chris said with a cautious sidelong glance at Ellie. "I think she's pretty. And she's nice to Josh, too."

"Shut up," Ellie said rudely. "You're so dumb you make me sick."

"But she's really nice." Chris's freckled face took on a look of uncharacteristic stubbornness. "This morning Bella told me she was—"

"Shut up," Ellie whispered fiercely. "People are going to hear you."

Chris subsided, and Ellie returned to her gloomy contemplation of the fields beyond the bus windows, thinking about this dreadful new calamity that had come out of nowhere to ruin her life.

Married, she thought. How could they possibly be married?

Ellie hadn't expected anything like this to happen, not in a million years. Her father never went anyplace where he could meet ladies. The idea of being forced to deal with a new woman living in their house forever—not one of the housekeepers who could be easily driven away—had simply never occurred to her.

She pictured Bella's slim body, her dark-blond hair that was cut as short as Chris's but still looked great. And she was pretty, too, with those big golden-brown eyes and a shy smile that tipped up on one side. No wonder their daddy was...

Ellie couldn't bear to think of it.

When the bus stopped, she got up and marched down the aisle, her chin high. She headed across the schoolyard and into the building, ignoring a group of friends who called for her to join them in an elaborate skipping game.

Normally Ellie loved skipping; she was one of the best in the school. She could do double Dutch with her feet flashing so quickly they were almost invisible when she jumped in time to the rhymes the girls chanted.

But today she couldn't bear to look at anybody or hear what they were going to say. Daddy said Uncle Bubba already knew about her father's new wife, so that meant that everybody else in Crystal Creek would know by now, too.

Gloomily she trudged down the hall to the library, where she found Ms. Osborne working all alone at a table near the front desk. The school principal was copying something out of a reference book.

Ellie hesitated in the doorway, her courage almost failing her.

Ms. Osborne was one of the most beautiful, terrifying people in the world. Ellie worshiped the woman, but seldom exchanged a word with her from one school year to the next. The principal was slim and tall, with blond hair that she wore in a short, sophisticated style. One of Ellie's daily routines was to check out the clothes Ms. Osborne was wearing. There were so many of them, and they were all wonderful. Smart black suits, trim, pleated pants and dainty blouses, a gray dress that looked as soft as a shadow on her willowy body. And she had a beautiful, simple piece of jewelry for each outfit. Ellie knew every accessory by heart.

The principal looked up, caught sight of the girl by the door and took off her reading glasses.

"Good morning, Ellie," she said. "Come in. I'm just doing a bit of research."

Ellie hesitated a moment longer, then edged shyly into the library, feeling awkward in her faded jeans and runners. She put down the copy of *My Friend Flicka,* which she'd just finished, and checked the reserve book pile to see if *Thunderhead* had arrived yet.

"So how are you today?" Ms. Osborne asked to Ellie's surprise and dismay.

The beautiful principal was usually cool and distant, and didn't tend to talk much with individual students. Ellie approved of this, because she didn't think the principal should be everybody's friend. It was actually best if the kids were a little scared of her. That way, whenever anybody got called to the office, they knew they were in big trouble.

"I'm fine," she muttered, starting toward the reference books at the rear of the library.

Ellie had never been called to the office for anything, not once since she'd come to this school, and she would die if such a thing ever happened to her.

"You must be very happy today," Ms. Osborne said, leaning back in her chair and rubbing her temples with long, graceful fingers. "I hear your father has remarried."

Ellie was so startled that she paused by the table, wondering what to say.

"It will be really nice to have somebody looking after the house and your little brother and sister again, won't it?"

Ellie nodded without speaking and ducked behind a stack of books, her heart thudding. She watched through some gaps in the shelves as Ms. Osborne gathered her books and shoulder bag and left the library, her tall body gliding into the hallway.

When the principal was gone, Ellie pulled out a big atlas, opened it to the index and flipped through it to the map that showed Nashville, Tennessee. She sank into a chair and sat for a long time, studying the colored map.

Nashville looked so far away from Texas, all those miles of highway and mountains and prairie. It was a long, long way for a kid to travel alone, she thought fearfully.

But she had no choice now. She had to go, because she—

He loomed up in front of her before she was even aware he'd come into the library. For such a big, tall boy, Cody Pollock was able to move with unnerving quietness. Now he pressed close to her chair as he stared down at her with the leering grin she dreaded more than anything.

"Well, well," he sneered. "It's little Ellie Gibson. How are you, pig?"

"Shut up," Ellie said, trying not to show how scared she was. "You're the pig, Cody Pollock."

"Oink oink," he chanted witlessly, following her as she shoved the atlas back on the shelf with trembling hands. "I'm a pig. Oink oink."

"You're a stupid pig," she muttered, moving toward the door.

But Cody blocked her path, dancing along in front of her. He bobbed annoyingly in whichever direction she turned as she tried to get past him, and reached out to poke at her shoulders and arms with his fists.

"Come on, Cody, get out of my way." Ellie held her chin high though her heart was pounding with terror.

"'Get out of my way,'" he mimicked. "Real bossy little thing, aren't you, Ellie Gibson?"

"Leave me alone." She peered past him with rising desperation, wishing frantically that somebody would come into the empty library.

Usually she was careful not to get caught alone with him like this. But today she'd been so upset by that woman in their house, she hadn't been thinking straight.

"I'll never leave you alone," he said with a coarse laugh. "You know why?"

"No, and I don't care." She tried to push past him, but Cody gripped her shoulders so hard she winced. He leaned toward her, almost touching her with his pimply face.

"Because I like bugging you," he said. "It's fun."

"Small things amuse small minds," Ellie said with an attempt at dignity. "Get your hands off me, you gross pig."

"You're a real big talker, Ellie Gibson." Cody's face darkened. "But one of these days you won't talk so big. You know why?"

Ellie didn't respond, just stared at the door, straining in his grasp. Why didn't the librarian come? It was almost time for school. Somebody should be here by now.

"Because," he whispered, looming above her, still

gripping her shoulders, "one of these days I'm gonna get you all alone, and you know what I'm gonna do?"

She struggled and kicked at his legs, keeping her head lowered.

"I'm gonna do the same thing your daddy's doing to his pretty new wife," the boy said, his eyes glittering.

"Shut up!" Ellie exploded.

"At night when they're in bed," he went on, moistening his lips as he stared down at her, "you know what your daddy does to her, Ellie? He rips all her clothes off, and when she's naked, he takes his big ol'—"

Ellie was too outraged to be afraid. She pulled back her arm and punched Cody's grinning face as hard as she could. Blood spurted instantly from his nose and he yelled in surprise and pain, reeling and clutching at his face.

Before he could grab her again, she ducked out of the library and fled down the hall toward the girls' washroom. Her heart thundered and tears flowed down her cheeks while Cody stood in the doorway and swore at her, hissing threats that echoed dangerously in the morning calm of the still-empty school.

CHAPTER ELEVEN

DAN WAS HUNKERED DOWN in his alfalfa field, the midday sun warm on his shoulders as he tinkered with the intricate knotting mechanism on an old hay baler.

As he worked he kept an eye on Bella and Josh. He'd joined them under the tree for lunch, to Josh's delight, and had been surprised at how pleasant it felt in the middle of a busy workday to lie back in the shade while the leaves of a spreading oak tree rustled overhead and his little boy clambered all over him, shouting with laughter.

Now he was back at work, and Josh and Bella were involved in some kind of game that involved pulling petals from the wild daisies growing at the base of the tree. Together they chanted lines from a nursery rhyme she'd been teaching the child, and occasionally Dan heard a peal of laughter.

While he watched, Josh stood up and ran away from her, looking over his shoulder. As she was clearly expected to, Bella got up and gave chase, at last sweeping up the giggling little boy into her arms. She carried him back to the shade of the tree and eventually he settled drowsily in her lap, his thumb jammed in his mouth, curly head resting against her shoulder.

Dan forced his attention back to the hay baler, frowning. He'd been a real fool to get himself so deeply involved in this painful, confusing mess. But what choice did he have? The woman had been terrified and completely helpless.

If only he'd just given her shelter, let her stay at the house in safety and do some work to earn her keep. He should never have taken the drastic step of actually marrying her.

Dan shook his head wearily and tugged the cap lower over his eyes.

Because they were married, it was necessary for them to share a bed. Otherwise the kids were bound to say something to Bubba about the odd situation at home. Word would start to travel around the community that there was something funny about Dan Gibson's marriage.

And living this close to Austin and her ex-husband, Bella couldn't afford to become conspicuous in any way, or she would be in danger again.

But the truth was, this simple act of sharing a bed with her was turning out to be the hardest thing he'd ever done. Dan had actually thought their sleeping arrangements would be no problem for the brief time she would be in his house. For one thing, he was always so tired at night that he slept like a dead man. And when Bella had first arrived, she'd been such a wretched little thing, pitiful as a wet kitten. He hadn't given enough consideration to the possibility of his being physically tempted by her.

But today, after spending the whole night lying at the woman's side, pretty much all Dan could think of was having wild, passionate sex with her.

The darkness of their bedroom, her slim curved body so close to his under the covers, her soft even breathing in the stillness of the Texas night...

He groaned and continued working on the baler. Then he saw Bella stand up, holding Josh in her arms, bending to pick up the picnic basket and blanket. "I think it's nap time," she called to Dan.

"I'll come into the house with you and help get him settled." He got to his feet and brushed dust from his jeans, then crossed the field and took the picnic things from her.

She smiled at him, making his heart pound wildly. Then she turned away, obviously unaware of the effect she had on him, and began to walk across the field toward the farmhouse.

Dan followed, watching the way her hips moved enticingly under those faded khaki shorts, the gentleness of her manner as she held the little boy in her arms.

God help me, he thought in despair. *Please help me not to feel this way. This isn't her world and it never will be. She'll be gone in two or three months. All she wants is to get away...*

In the house she washed Josh's face and hands, then carried him into the bedroom and tucked him in the lower bunk, bending to brush the curls back from his forehead and kiss his cheek.

"How long will he sleep?" she whispered to Dan, who looked on from the doorway.

"It depends," he said. "Two or three hours."

"Well, that's wonderful." Bella straightened. "It'll give me time to tidy the porch and get ready to cook dinner, too."

She paused in the doorway and smiled at the sleeping child with such a look of tenderness that Dan's head started reeling again.

"What a darling he is," she murmured. "You know, I've never had much to do with little kids."

"You seem pretty good at it," Dan said neutrally, following her into the kitchen.

"It's so much fun. I guess in some ways I never really grew up myself." She knelt to get the scrubbing pail from a lower cabinet.

"Or maybe you never had much of a childhood," he suggested, standing by the table and watching her, enjoying the glow of her bare tanned arms. "So now it's all new to you."

She glanced up at him, clearly startled, and her face softened.

"You may be right," she said, carrying the pail to the sink and turning on the hot-water tap, adding some pine-scented cleanser as if she'd been doing housework for years.

Dan left the kitchen. He hesitated in the back porch, wishing he could stay in the house all afternoon and talk with her about everyday things. Finally, he took his cap from a hook by the door and headed outside.

When he was halfway across the yard with Gypsy at his heels, he heard the phone ring twice, then stop. After a moment she appeared in the doorway, shading her eyes against the afternoon sun.

"Dan!" she called. "Can you come back and answer the phone?"

He returned to the house, pausing for a moment in the porch to look at her in surprise. She was so pale that her normally faint freckles almost stood out in relief and the hands gripping the scrubbing cloth trembled a little.

"What is it?" Dan asked, his shoulders tensing. "Has something happened? Did he find out you're here?"

"No, no, nothing like that." She turned away, her voice muffled. "It's the principal of Ellie's school. She wants to talk to you."

Dan's fear shifted abruptly to concern for his children. "Why? Is something the matter with Ellie?"

"I don't know. She just said she needed to talk to you."

Dan strode through the kitchen and grabbed the telephone receiver while Bella stood by the table, watching.

"Mr. Gibson?" the principal's cool voice said at the other end of the line.

"Yes. What's the matter? Is Ellie okay?"

"No major problem," she said. "We've just had a little disturbance at the school this morning. I thought I should probably mention it to you."

"What kind of disturbance?" he asked, still conscious of Bella's wide hazel eyes on him. God, she looked pale. Apparently just answering a ringing telephone frightened her.

"It appears Ellie was involved in some kind of scuffle with an eighth-grade student—a boy" the principal said. "I can't seem to get a straight story from either of them, but he's accusing her of attacking him without provocation. He's suffered a rather serious nosebleed."

"Who's the boy?" Dan asked.

"Cody Pollock."

Dan pictured the loutish teenage nephew of June Pollock, who was now living with her in Crystal Creek.

"You know, it's a little hard for me to imagine Ellie attacking a big kid like that," he said.

"Cody claims he was doing homework in the library when Ellie sneaked up from behind and hit him with a book. When turned around, he says, she punched him in the nose. He's going to have quite a black eye, I'm afraid."

"And what does Ellie say?"

"That's why I'm calling you, Mr. Gibson. Ellie refuses to say anything at all. After I heard Cody's story, I called Ellie down to my office, but she sat the whole time staring at her shoes and wouldn't answer my questions."

"So what do you think?" Dan asked. "Did she really attack this kid for no reason?"

"Well, it doesn't seem to me like the sort of thing Ellie would do. We've never had any discipline problems with her. But Cody Pollock is adamant that she attacked him viciously for no reason at all."

"Is she going to be punished?" Dan asked.

"I think she's probably suffered enough just from being called to my office," the principal said. "It was obvious the whole thing made her terribly uncomfortable. But I thought you should know just the same. Perhaps you can talk to her at home tonight and get her to tell you what happened."

"I'll do my best," Dan said. "Thanks for calling, Ms. Osborne."

He hung up and stood with his hand on the receiver, thinking about Ellie's stubborn face and rapidly maturing body, her occasional passionate outbursts of temper.

And her deep upset over the sudden arrival of a stranger in their household.

"What is it?" Bella said behind him.

"The principal says Ellie attacked a boy at school. She hit him with a book and then punched him. Gave him a black eye and nosebleed."

"What's the boy like?"

"He's a big, tough kid, a real troublemaker. Cody Pollock had to be sent down here from Lampasas to live with his aunt because they couldn't handle him at home."

"And what was this boy doing to provoke Ellie?" Bella asked.

"Apparently nothing. He claims he was just sitting at a table in the library and she came up and hit him for no reason."

"Oh, sure, that's a likely story," Bella scoffed, turning away with her scrubbing pail. "As if Ellie's going to pick a fight with a boy like that for no reason."

Dan watched her thoughtfully. "You don't believe Cody?"

"Not a word of it." She glanced up at him with a grim smile. "You see, I know a bit about bullies. They're usually pretty good liars, too."

"Well, I'll talk to her about it tonight and see if I can find out what's going on."

Again he headed for the door. Bella was already on the porch where she stood on tiptoe to scrub the top of the window. Dan looked at the gracefulness of her body and uplifted arms, the clean, pure line of her cheekbone against the smeared glass.

"Bella," he said abruptly.

"Hmm?" she said.

"When you came out to tell me about the phone call, you looked really upset. I wondered why."

She shook her head without looking at him. "It was the principal's voice," she said, bending to soak the scrub rag in the pail. "It kind of startled me, that's all."

"Why?"

"That principal—what's her name?"

"I don't know what her first name is. The kids always call her Ms. Osborne."

"Her voice seemed familiar somehow, but I can't think who it reminded me of."

"Somebody you know?" Dan paused with his hand on the doorknob.

"No, more like... Anyway, it doesn't matter. Really, it was just silly of me. My nerves are overwrought, I guess." She smiled at him over her shoulder, making his heart begin to pound again.

He needed to get a grip on himself, or something disastrous was going to happen. The last thing this poor woman needed was another man to betray her trust.

"Dan," she asked with a frown, clearly unaware of his discomfort, "how do I keep the windows from looking all smeared after I wash them?"

He gestured at a cabinet on the opposite wall. "There's some glass cleaner there in a plastic bottle. You spray it on and then wipe the glass with paper towels or crumpled newspaper to make it shine."

"Okay, that sounds easy enough." She gave him another of those charming, crooked smiles that took his breath away. "I might just do the rest of them this afternoon, too. Wouldn't it be nice to have every window in the house clean and sparkling?"

"Sure, Bella," he muttered, his throat dry and tight with sexual hunger. "That would be real nice."

He left the house and strode across the farmyard, hurrying to get away from her before he was overwhelmed by the urge to sweep her into his arms and carry her up to the bedroom.

AT DINNER THAT NIGHT, the whole family sat around the table waiting expectantly. Bella was at the sink, straining a big pot of cooked spaghetti through a metal colander.

She felt tense. This was the first meal she'd planned and cooked entirely on her own. Along with a salad, she'd prepared tomato sauce, mostly from a jar but with mushrooms and Italian seasoning added, and green beans and garlic bread.

After Josh had woken from his nap, they'd finished washing the windows together, with the little boy scrubbing solemnly away at the lower panes. Then Bella had taken him out to pick the bouquet of wildflowers that now sat in a vase on the center of the table.

"Bella, do you need any help?" Dan asked.

He'd come in early from the hay field, showered and changed into shorts and a clean shirt. Bella liked the way he looked after a shower, with his hair still damp and shining.

She dragged her mind back to the task at hand.

She turned the spaghetti out into a serving bowl, sprinkled it with grated Parmesan and carried it to the table, then brought the tomato sauce.

"Yummy!" Chris cried. "Spaghetti. I want lots and lots."

"Pagetti," Josh echoed, waving his fork. "Want lots."

Ellie said nothing, just sat behind the centerpiece of flowers, looking sullen.

"This looks great," Dan said warmly, reaching for the salad. "Doesn't it, kids?"

Bella served spaghetti onto the plates of the two smaller children, returning Chris's shy smile and touching the little girl's cap of golden hair.

"After we eat and tidy the kitchen," she said, "maybe we'll have time to start on that castle. Josh and I found some really neat rocks today, didn't we, dear?"

Chris beamed up at her, and Bella's heart melted.

"Wassed windows," Josh told his sisters importantly, waving his fork again. "All the windows."

"Is the spaghetti all right?" Bella asked anxiously, watching as Dan cut Josh's pasta into bite-size lengths and tied the little boy's bib in place.

"It's too soft," Ellie said, the first words she'd spoken since arriving at the table.

"It is not," Chris said indignantly, speaking with her mouth full. "It's just perfect, Bella. I love it."

Dan looked at his older daughter. "The school principal called today," he said casually. "Something about a fight with Cody Pollock?"

Ellie's face turned crimson. She got up, preparing to bolt from the table, but Dan reached out and grasped her arm. The girl sank into her chair again and brushed awkwardly at her hair with a trembling hand.

"What happened, Ellie?" Dan asked.

"Nothing," Ellie muttered.

"Cody told the principal he was sitting at a table in the library and you came up for no reason and hit him. Is that true?"

The girl's flush deepened. "If he says it's true, I guess it must be," she muttered.

"Then I'll have to punish you," Dan said. "If you're starting fights at school, you can't ride your pony for a month or go over to Mary and Bubba's on the weekend when the other kids go."

Ellie opened her mouth to protest, then clamped her lips together. The flush of color had faded and her face was pale. Though Bella was intimidated by this sullen, angry child, she still couldn't bear to witness the girl's pain.

"Ellie, when I was about your age, there was a big boy at my school," she said. "He didn't like me and he was always picking on me, trying to make me mad. He told lies all the time." Bella turned her gaze to Dan, who was watching her in startled silence. "I don't think Ellie should be punished so harshly until we know what happened."

Ellie's dark eyes flickered in surprise.

"Sometimes," Chris volunteered, "when Cody sees Ellie on the playground, he says—"

"Shut up!" Ellie said furiously.

Chris subsided, looking frightened.

"Cody Pollock's just a stupid jerk," Ellie told her

father. "That whole thing in the library was...like an accident, sort of," she concluded lamely.

Bella watched the girl, but Ellie avoided her eyes, looking down at the plate of spaghetti and sauce.

"If that's true, why didn't you tell Ms. Osborne?" Dan asked.

"I just wanted to get out of her office, not sit there talking about...about Cody Pollock." Ellie took a hasty swallow of milk.

For a brief moment Ellie met Bella's eyes, and Bella was shocked by the pain and fear she saw in the child's face. Instinctively, Bella recognized the same kind of helpless terror she was dealing with in her own life. The impression was so strong that her heart ached. For the first time in their uneasy relationship, she longed to take Ellie into her arms and hold her until the girl confided the truth about what was happening between her and Cody Pollock.

But the moment passed as quickly as it had come. Ellie stared at her plate again, her thin shoulders stiff with tension.

Bella glanced at Dan to see if he was angry at her for interfering in a disciplinary matter with one of his children.

But he didn't seem upset, merely puzzled.

"Well, okay," he said at last. "I guess we'll let Bella have the call on this one. No punishment for Ellie right now, but if I hear about any more problems with Cody Pollock, I'll want to know the truth about what's going on."

Again Bella caught a glance from Ellie. Was that gratitude she saw in the child's eyes?

But at that moment Josh dropped a heaping forkful of spaghetti on the freshly scrubbed floor tiles. By the time the mess had been dealt with and order restored, Ellie's face was as cold and shuttered as ever.

CHAPTER TWELVE

LATER THAT NIGHT, Dan switched off his reading light and they lay side by side in the bed, carefully distant from each other. Moonlight drifted through the window and across the quilt like a ghostly coverlet.

The curtains lifted and stirred softy in the evening breeze, accompanied by a rich chorus of nighttime sounds. Down near the stock pond, bullfrogs croaked and crickets chirped. The hoot of the owl that had once terrified Bella now seemed like an old friend.

She stretched out wearily, enjoying the drowsy sense of peace as she thought about the day. "Was the spaghetti really all right?" she asked, turning her head to look at his silvered profile. "You know, that was the first entire meal I've ever made on my own."

"It was fine," he said.

Disappointed, she turned away to gaze out the window again.

It was probably unreasonable to expect praise from the man when she was no more than a refugee and housekeeper, and he was doing her such a huge favor already. Still, the curtness of his manner often hurt her.

Especially, Bella was unsettled by the occasional times when they'd be having a pleasant conversation, laughing and enjoying themselves, and all of a sudden he'd get that cold, withdrawn look and abruptly walk away from her, as if recalling more important things he wanted to do.

Their whole situation was undeniably artificial and embarrassing. Still, it wouldn't last forever, and at least, she and Dan could try to be civil to each other for the time she was staying here, couldn't they?

She wasn't ready to sleep and would really have liked to spend a few minutes talking about the children, especially Ellie. But as if reading her thoughts, he rolled away from her pulling the covers up around his body in a dismissive manner.

Bella glanced cautiously at the breadth of his shoulders, the silvered crispness of his hair against the pillow, and had to fight a sudden distressing urge to reach out and touch him. She wondered how it would feel to cuddle up behind him and nestle her body close to his warm back.

Badly unsettled, she tried to analyze her wayward emotions. It was just such a long time since she'd been close to a man. She had enjoyed sex a great deal during the early years of her marriage. Eric had been skilled and experienced in bed, and their lovemaking had usually been the only means for them to achieve any kind of real closeness.

But her attraction to Dan, though frankly sexual, also had a good deal more depth and complexity. She liked the way he thought, and was impressed by the quiet, methodical way he approached problems. She liked his gentleness and strength, and the unexpected wit he concealed under a laconic demeanor.

If you could ever get really close to a man like this, he'd be a delightful lover…

Bella knew this was a crazy, dangerous thought. But part of her was already wistfully constructing a fantasy where she stayed safely at the little farmhouse by the river, looking after the children, cooking and cleaning. And she'd spend her nights with Dan Gibson, in his bed and in his arms.

She shivered and hugged herself in the chilly moonlight. Of course it was impossible, all of it. He wanted no part of her beyond their bargain—his manner made that clear enough. He thought she was rich, frivolous and useless.

Besides, even if by some miracle Dan should begin to care for her, she could never stay here, anyway. Not when her very presence put the whole family in danger. She'd told Dan that Eric would never hurt the children, but there was always the possibility he might be upset enough to hurt Bella in their presence. Even if he didn't, his anger would frighten them.

She pictured Eric finding her in this cozy hideaway, as he surely would if she didn't leave soon. She imagined him creeping along the river with his out-of-control jealousy, to the same place where Josh slept with his teddy bear and Chris built castles out of rocks.

Involuntarily she whimpered aloud, then covered her mouth with her hand when she realized Dan had heard and rolled over to look at her.

"What's the matter?" he asked.

"I'm sorry," Bella whispered. "I didn't mean to wake you."

"I wasn't sleeping yet," he said curtly. "What's wrong?"

"It's just…my arm hurts a little," she told him, improvising hastily.

He switched the lamp on and leaned up on one elbow to look at her bandage.

"Does it throb?" he asked, holding her arm gently. "Is it feeling hot?"

No, she thought wildly, *my arm's not the part of me that feels hot…*

The mere touch of his hand had the most electrifying effect. Trickles and rustles of sexual desire swept all through her body, building like a forest fire, threatening to carry her away in a mighty roar of heat and flame.

"Bella?" he asked, frowning at her. The errant lock of hair flopped onto his forehead.

"I guess," she said, "I must have just rolled over on it for a second. It's fine now."

"Good. Go to sleep, then, and we'll change your bandage and put some more salve on it in the morning."

"Thanks," she murmured. "Good night, Dan."

"Good night."

But he didn't release her arm. Instead, he kept staring at her with an odd, troubling intensity.

"Dan…" She gazed back at him, mesmerized, holding her breath.

He groaned and drew her into his arms, strained against her and kissed her mouth with a passion that took her breath away.

Bella was conscious of wildly scattered impressions, a blur of sensation. His lips, cool and surprisingly soft against her own, his big, hard body, the exciting breadth and solidity of him, the strong leg he flung over her own, the clean scent of his skin...

His tongue thrust between her lips, exploring her mouth. She pressed closer to him, moving her hands over his shoulders, chest and neck, stroking his hair.

She'd never felt so totally surrounded and enclosed by a man. His arms were a place of warm safety, but also of passion and pure delight. She writhed against him, shameless in her need, and gasped when his hands began to explore her body, then slipped under her nightshirt to caress her bare skin.

She could feel his arousal, the thrusting strength of him. More than anything, she wanted to feel him all around her, inside her—

But then, as suddenly as the embrace had begun, it was over.

He pulled away, shoving Bella almost roughly to the far edge of the bed, and rolled over to lie on his side.

Stunned and trembling with sexual desire, Bella looked cautiously at his rigid back. Her body felt like a moist bruised flower, open and yielding, fully exposed. She yearned to be back in his arms, lost again in that rich tide of passion.

"Dan," she whispered, touching his shoulder. "What's wrong?"

"I'm sorry," he muttered without looking at her. "Go to sleep."

"But I just—"

"Don't talk about it anymore," he said. "I was wrong to do that, and I'm sorry. It wasn't supposed

to happen. But I'm a human being and it's not easy
to share a bed with a woman every night and not
touch her. We'll have to think of some other arrangement.''

She longed to ask him why it would be so wrong
just to give in to their feelings. What harm could it
do, when she wanted him so much and they both
knew it was only temporary?

"You don't have to apologize," she said timidly.
"It was as much my fault as yours."

"Look, I don't want to talk about this now,
Bella." His voice sounded harsh and strained, and
she could see the knotted tension in his big shoulders.
"Let's just go to sleep, all right?"

"But we need to talk about it," she protested.
"How can we ever get through the day tomorrow if
we don't talk about this?"

"Okay," he said wearily. "Then we'll talk about
it tomorrow. Now go to sleep."

Still troubled and breathless, her heart racing, she
curled up on her side of the bed and closed her eyes.
But it was some time before she slept.

DAN WAS UP AND GONE before daylight. He took a
lunch down to the field with him, leaving Bella to
give the girls their breakfast and send them off on
the school bus.

After the bus lumbered off, she and Josh spent the
morning doing laundry, a task she found absorbing
in spite of the tumult of her emotions.

Before leaving for school, Chris had shown her
how to sort the clothes into the washer and how
much detergent to use. During the lesson Ellie had

sat on an upturned laundry basket and watched impassively, saying nothing.

"Most everything goes in the dryer afterward, like the jeans and stuff," Chris had told her. "But usually we hang the sheets and towels out on the clothesline. They smell nicer when they dry outside."

Bella took an armful of sheets off the clothesline and carried them into the house. In the warm autumn breeze, the cotton took less than an hour to dry. And it did, indeed, smell wonderful, like armfuls of freshly mown grass and sunshine.

She folded sheets while Josh squatted at her feet and worked on a pile of his own small T-shirts, trying hard to tuck in the sleeves and fold them as she'd shown him.

"We're quite a pair, aren't we?" Bella told the little boy ruefully. "Both of us are struggling to learn things everybody else in the world already knows how to do. But you've got an excuse, darling." She picked him up and hugged him. "You're only two years old."

He nestled against her and put his arms around her neck, resting his head against her cheek. Bella sat down on the couch, still holding him, overwhelmed by a sudden flood of love.

Her emotions seemed so dangerously close to the surface these days, as if she'd lost her protective covering and was fully exposed to the world. Whenever she thought of Dan and remembered their fiery kiss and his humiliating rejection, it was all she could do not to roll herself up in a little ball of pain—or grab a change of clothes and run away from the farmhouse by the river.

But where would she go?

Until she could build her new identity and get some of her money from San Antonio, she remained utterly, completely trapped.

She made lunch for herself and Josh, tucked him into his bunk and sang to him until he fell asleep, his thumb in his mouth. After he was settled, Bella removed the thumb gently, kissed his cheek and pulled the blanket up around his shoulders. Then she went out and took the last load of clothes from the dryer.

She had the ironing board set up in the living room as Chris had shown her and was figuring out which heat setting would be required to iron blue jeans when she heard the back door open and close, followed by footsteps in the porch.

With a wildly pounding heart, Bella switched the iron off and went into the kitchen. Dan looked tired and strained as he sprawled in a chair and put his cap on the table. Avoiding his eyes, she crossed the room to the coffeepot and took down a couple of mugs.

"Hi!" she said with forced brightness. "How's the haying?"

"It's okay. Any problem getting the kids off to school?"

"None at all." She poured him a mug of coffee, added sugar and cream and brought it to him, then prepared one for herself and sat down at the table. "Chris showed me how to do laundry. I finished the last load just after lunch. Now I'm trying my hand at ironing."

"Yes, I saw the sheets hanging on the line earlier. Is Josh asleep?"

This was ridiculous, Bella thought. They sounded like a couple of strangers having a conversation on a park bench.

"He's been such a good boy all morning. He was helping me fold laundry," she said, "but then he was tuckered out."

"So tell me, Bella, are you any good at ironing?"

She heard a trace of teasing in his voice and glanced at him quickly. He looked incredibly handsome in his dusty work clothes. It was all she could do to keep from flinging herself into his arms.

"It's really kind of interesting," she said pleasantly. "Chris told me to spray the jeans first, then iron. Works like magic. And it smells so nice," she added, smiling over her coffee mug. "I love that warm, clean smell."

"Oh, Bella," he said softly.

But when she looked up, his face was impassive, almost cold.

"You look tired," she ventured.

"I'm afraid the baler's about to break down again. That'll be more repairs I can't afford," he said, extending his booted feet wearily. "First the irrigation pump and now this."

"How much would it cost to replace both of them?" Bella asked.

"A hell of a lot more than I can lay my hands on right now."

"How much?" she persisted.

"I haven't even added it up. I guess about sixty thousand dollars."

"Dan," she said after a brief silence, "has running this farm always been such a financial struggle?"

"No, the place was profitable when my parents were running it. They had a comfortable life here for a lot of years. And it's going to be that way again," he said, "if I can just keep my head above water for a few more years. But I'll tell you, it's not easy."

"What's happened recently to make it so difficult?" Bella asked, troubled by his plight.

"Well, after Dad died I had to mortgage some of the land to give my mother a good chunk of cash. She worked hard all those years, and she was entitled to retire without any worries. Then when Annie left, I had to take a second mortgage to give her money, too. All that debt's left me in a pretty big hole."

"How much would it take for you to be out of the hole?"

He laughed without humor. "I'd need to win a lottery. Right now I owe almost three hundred thousand dollars. Just paying the interest on those two mortgages eats up a lot of my profit, no matter how hard I work."

"But the land itself must be—"

"Hell," he said, "the land's worth a fortune. If I ever wanted to sell, I could pay off my mortgages and be one of the rich people, like you. But then what would I do with my life?"

His words stung. *I'd be one of the rich people, like you.*

She looked down at her hands, clasped tensely in her lap.

"Look, about last night..." he began, setting down his cup.

She got hastily to her feet and went to get the jar of cookies from the counter.

"Dan, I think you're right," she said with her back still to him. "We should just forget about it. Let's call it a moment of temporary insanity, okay? That's what it was, nothing more."

"I can't forget about it," he said quietly. "I'm really sorry, Bella. We had a deal, and I violated it. Now I think we need to set up some ground rules."

"Ground rules?" She carried the cookie jar to the table and set it in front of him, then sank into her chair again and sipped nervously at her coffee.

He examined the cookies, frowning, then took one.

"You know, I'm going to learn how to bake those oatmeal ones," she said, chattering in her nervousness. "I found a recipe in one of the cookbooks, and it seems pretty straightforward. In fact, I told Josh if there's time when he wakes up, maybe we'll even bake some before dinner."

"Bella," he said, "how long are you planning to stay here?"

She looked up at him, surprised by the question. "Just until I can get a driver's license and some credit cards in my new name, and figure out how to get hold of the money I left in San Antonio."

"And then you're leaving the country?" He watched her steadily.

"I have to," she said, tracing the flower pattern in one of the place mats. "If I don't, he's going to find me, Dan."

"What if I went to talk to this guy?" His face

hardened, and his green eyes were suddenly cold. "I'd like to go to his office and tell him to leave you alone, or I'll break his neck."

Bella forgot her nervousness and stared at him. "Oh, you can't do that!" she said. "Please, please, don't even think about it."

"Why should this bully be allowed to get away with terrorizing a woman?"

"Dan, this isn't two kids fighting in the schoolyard like Ellie and Cody Pollock," Bella told him. "Eric is obsessed, and his job gives him an awful lot of power. If you confront him, he's going to find out who you are and where you live, and then..." She couldn't go on.

His hands tensed on the coffee mug. "You honestly think this guy would be a threat to me?"

"Oh, God." Bella fought a rising tide of helpless misery. "I should never have stayed here," she whispered. "I'm so afraid of what I've brought into your life. I don't want to wait two or three months, Dan. I need to leave here as soon as I can."

He was silent a moment, staring at the ruffled curtains above the sink. Finally he selected another cookie and met her eyes. "You've mentioned this money in San Antonio," he said. "How much is there?"

"It's hard to say. The value fluctuates of course, because only about three hundred thousand is in cash. The rest is diamonds and stock certificates."

"Make an estimate," he said.

Bella shrugged. "I really don't know. Maybe two or three million."

"So," he said, his face expressionless, "I assume

that would be enough to keep you in comfort for the rest of your life? Or would you need a whole lot more?''

"I guess it's enough. I don't have much idea what things cost,'' she told him honestly. "When you're…when you have a lot of money, you don't tend to deal in cash at all.''

"You just put things on your credit card and your accountant sees that they're paid,'' he said with that same remote look.

"Yes,'' Bella agreed, puzzled and a little hurt by his manner.

The conversation seemed to have moved well away from that searing midnight kiss. All he wanted to talk about was money.

"So these valuables of yours—where exactly are they kept?''

"Everything's in a safe-deposit box in a bank in San Antonio.''

"I've never had much need for a safe-deposit box,'' Dan said dryly. "How do you access something when it's stored like that?''

"It's very secure,'' she said. "In fact, the precautions seem almost ridiculous. First you have to sign in, using your name plus a code number, and then your fingerprint is scanned for identification to make sure nobody else can access your box.''

"Where in the bank are these boxes?''

"They're kept in a locked room at the rear of the bank. The whole room is lined with metal deposit boxes, all different sizes. There's a table, two chairs and a surveillance camera.''

"Two chairs?''

"When you've been signed into the room, a bank employee accompanies you, takes out your box and sits in the other chair to watch while you go through it. Then he replaces it and locks the room when you leave."

Dan frowned. "So are you required to give some kind of personal identification—I mean, a driver's license or passport—when you first ask to get into your box?"

Bella shook her head. "Just my name, code number and finger."

"Would people recognize you there now?"

"Oh, I don't think so." She touched her hair and tried to smile at him. "With my new hairstyle and wardrobe, I think I'd be pretty safe. Still, I've been reluctant to go to the bank until I have some kind of clear escape route planned."

"So your plan…?"

"I want to get enough ID to travel safely. And then, last thing before I leave Texas, I'm going to stop by the bank, collect my money and buy a one-way ticket out of the country."

"Good." He got to his feet and reached for his cap. "So let's get busy on that. We'll go in tomorrow for your driver's test, and as soon as you have the license, we'll use it to get a credit card or two, a library card, any kind of ID we can think of to establish Bella Gibson as a real, legal person. Then we'll start planning where you can go and how to get there. You should be able to leave here as soon as you want."

Bella realized they were, indeed, still talking about that midnight kiss. Dan Gibson was upset by her presence in his house, and he wanted her gone as soon as possible. It was as simple as that.

"I thought," she told him, looking down at the table, "part of our deal was that in exchange for marriage and a legal name, I'd give you a few months of housekeeping and child care."

"I'm prepared to waive that deal. I think it's best and safest for you to get on with your life, not hang around here."

"You're right." She got up and began to wipe the counter. "That sounds like a good plan. I'll start thinking about where I want to go."

He nodded and left the house. She watched him stride across the yard toward the hay meadow. Then she tidied the kitchen and went to check on Josh.

The little boy still slept peacefully, holding his teddy bear. He lay on his back, one plump arm up-flung next to his face, flushed cheeks surrounded by curls. He murmured something in his sleep, then fell silent again.

Bella bent to kiss him, softly so she wouldn't wake him, and felt tears gather in her eyes. She'd only been here a short time, but she loved the place and its occupants already.

Isabel Delgado, who had visited some of the love-liest homes and most luxurious resorts in the world, had fallen in love with this shabby little farmhouse on the banks of the Claro River, occupied by three children and a man who didn't want her around.

She went back out to the living room and resumed ironing, while she thought about Dan's suggestions for her immediate future. They all made sense, and she intended to follow through.

With the exception of one thing.

She wasn't going to wait until she was leaving Texas before she visited that safe-deposit box with its rich contents. As soon as she had her driver's license, maybe even in the next couple of days, she planned to borrow Dan's truck and drive to San Antonio.

When she was there, she would slip into the bank unrecognized, take out enough of her stock certificates to pay off Dan's mortgages and bring them back here to Crystal Creek. She frowned, spraying more water onto a pair of Ellie's stiff new jeans.

How could she convert those stocks to ready cash without endangering herself?

She thought of Douglas Evans, the handsome young Scotsman who served as mayor, real-estate agent and stockbroker for the citizens of Crystal Creek. When Dan had introduced him to her that day at the Longhorn, she'd been impressed by Evans. And Doug Evans, according to Dan, was a man who could be trusted. If she gave him those company stock certificates and swore him to secrecy, Evans could probably arrange the transaction for her.

Then on the day she was planning to leave, she would hand the money to Dan in a big envelope and express her gratitude for what he'd done.

And by the way, Dan, she'd say as she walked out the door, *I know it's too late for this and you probably don't care, anyway, but I think I've fallen in love with you and your family.*

A couple of tears trembled on her eyelashes and

slipped down her cheeks. They dropped onto Josh's faded denim overalls forming patches of darker blue.

Beyond the window, birds twittered drowsily in the noonday heat, while Bella ironed piles of little jeans and spun her sad, lonely fantasies.

CHAPTER THIRTEEN

ERIC MATTHIAS leaned back in his padded swivel chair and frowned at the ceiling. His desktop was bare, with just a few files resting neatly in a wire box, unlike the clutter that overflowed all available surfaces on the desks of most detectives.

Eric was compulsively tidy and a tireless worker. He didn't believe in letting his personal life interfere with the job. Especially not now, when it could bring unwelcome notice from higher up. Eric wanted no scrutiny of his current activities.

He worked late into the night to keep abreast of his caseload, took on extra assignments without complaint and kept himself in a strong position with his superior officers. *A model policeman,* the department was always saying. *We could use a lot more detectives like Eric Matthias.*

So at the moment Eric was not pleased by the man sitting across the desk from him. His visitor was overweight and sloppy, wearing creased khakis and a plaid sport shirt, the buttons straining across his belly. Even in the air-conditioned coolness of this police-department building, the man was sweating unpleasantly. Wide circles of moisture had formed at his underarms, and his brow glistened with beads of perspiration.

Eric steepled his fingers over his chest and leaned back. "What did I tell you about coming here last time we talked, Manny?" he asked.

The fat man shifted in his chair. "You told me not to come to your office. You said if I had any news for you, I should call you at home."

"And yet here you are," Eric murmured, fixing the man with a level gaze. "Now why is that? You didn't hear me, or what?"

"Don't be mad at me, Eric," the other said uneasily. "It's not easy, what you hired me to do. Takes a lot of time."

"I know it does. I'm paying you for your time," Eric said. "So why are you here?"

"I've been trying to call you for three nights," Manny said. "You're never home. I always get the service or the machine or the police dispatcher or some other damn thing, but never you."

"We've had four homicides in three days." Eric sighed wearily. "Must be the full moon or something. You should just keep trying, Manny. You shouldn't be driving all the way down from San Antonio to bother me at my place of work."

The private investigator scrubbed an arm across his damp face. "But I've got something really important this time," he said. "I knew you'd want to hear about it."

Eric sighed and got up to lock the door, then sat behind his desk again. "Okay, Manny. Tell me what you have."

"I made friends with a girl in the bank where the Delgado family keeps most of their money."

"A girl?" Eric raised an eyebrow.

"More like a woman," Manny amended. "She's in her forties, never been married, lives with her mother. A lonely person."

"And you mean you've been getting close to this woman?"

Manny grinned. "It ain't hard. A couple of dates, a box of candy. Once I sent her flowers at work, and she just about wet her pants."

"So you're having a nice social relationship," Eric said impatiently. "What exactly does that do for me, Manny?"

"This woman says Isabel has a safe-deposit box at the bank, and she's used it recently."

"What?" Eric stood up, leaned forward and grasped the man's damp shoulder.

Manny beamed, obviously gratified by this response. "Yeah, Isabel visited this box just a couple of days before she sent her Mercedes for that little swim in the Claro River."

Eric settled back, tapping a pen thoughtfully against his palm. "Well, well," he murmured. "I'll be damned."

"Angie—that's my new friend—works in a cubicle just outside the safe-deposit room. She sees everybody who gets escorted in there."

"And if your friend sees Isabel, she's going to call you right away?"

"Yeah, that's right." Manny beamed with self-satisfaction.

"So what reason did you give Angie for your interest?"

"I told her Isabel's sick and ran off without her

medication. The family's desperate to find her before she hurts herself.''

Eric felt a stab of annoyance at this clumsiness. "That's not too subtle, Manny. How many people are your girlfriend going to tell that story to?"

"None," Manny said. "You don't understand, Eric. This woman, she's in love with me. I told her I'm working for the family and I'd lose my job if any of this got around. I know I can trust her."

Eric smiled with reluctant admiration and took a checkbook from a desk drawer. "Well, you'll need to hire some help and rent a surveillance room close to the bank," he said as he wrote. "Send me the bills at home for any expenses you incur if this isn't enough. We need at least two men on the job, because you could be in the men's room or out for pizza and miss the call."

"So if Isabel goes to the bank again and I get the word from Angie, you want me to head right over there and grab her?"

"No, I don't want you to do that!" Eric nearly shouted.

Manny quailed back in the chair.

"What I want," Eric said in a calmer tone, trying to get a grip on his emotions, "is to have her followed. I want to know exactly where Isabel goes when she leaves that bank."

"But we could lose her that way. Wouldn't it be safer if—"

"At the bus depot in Abilene," Eric interrupted, "some man went to the attendant and asked about Isabel's locker. It was a young, good-looking man. I want…"

Again the familiar jealousy began to churn, almost choking him.

"I want to know who that guy is, Manny," Eric said. "I want to know where he lives and if she's there with him. I need to know what I'm dealing with before I talk to Isabel."

Manny's plump face began to sweat again.

"Look, Eric, I don't want no part in anything…you know."

"Of course you don't," Eric said. A painful lump formed in his throat when he thought about Isabel's pretty face and curvy body, the sparkle of laughter in her eyes. "You just have to find her, Manny, and tell me where she goes. The rest is up to me."

"I just gotta follow Isabel," the man repeated doggedly.

"You follow her and tell me where she goes." Eric forced himself to drop a hand on the man's shoulder again, though his fastidious nature recoiled in distaste from the damp feel of it. "You've done real well, Manny. I'm grateful to you."

The last thing he saw was Manny's pitiful look of appreciation and the straining rear seam of his khakis as he left the office.

Eric settled back in his chair again, frowning as he turned the pen in his hands. This safe-deposit box of Isabel's was big news. Maybe it was even the breakthrough he'd been waiting for. He should be celebrating. So why did he feel miserable and scared?

They'd already cleared out her little stash in Abilene, and she couldn't get far without cash. Sooner or later, Isabel Delgado would have to go in person to that bank in San Antonio to take some valuables from her safe-deposit box.

And when she did, Eric's men would be waiting to tail her and let him know where she went.

"I've got you, sweetheart," he whispered, grasping his pen. "I can hardly *wait* to see you again."

He was alarmed when the pen broke in his hands, spitting ink. Eric grabbed a couple of tissues and wiped the polished wooden surface of his desk, then tossed the whole mess into a wastebasket and sat looking down at it.

Not for the first time, he was a little frightened by the intensity of his emotions and uncertain whether he could handle them on his own.

When he finally saw Isabel again, especially if she was with another man, how would he react?

The damned private investigator was right—this kind of situation could escalate into something dangerous. Eric had seen it often enough in his career. Domestic problems were the ones that tended to become violent, destroying lives and careers.

Maybe he should go down right now and talk to one of the department counselors, try to get some help.

But a counselor would probably demand that he leave Isabel alone, and Eric couldn't bear to give up now. He needed to see her just one more time and do whatever it took to convince her that she should come back to him.

Hell, even her father and brother believed she'd be better off with him!

He couldn't let this opportunity go by. If he did, Isabel would be gone and he'd never find her.

Eric buried his face briefly in his hands, then he sat up, squared his shoulders and reached for another file.

LATE FRIDAY AFTERNOON, Dan and Bella left Crystal Creek in the truck and headed for home, with Josh in his car seat behind them. Bella was driving, and Dan found it odd to be sitting in the passenger seat.

He glanced over the top of the seat at his son, who clutched his teddy bear and gazed happily at a bulging white paper sack on the floor near him. "Hamburgers in there," the little boy said pointing.

Dan reached behind to ruffle Josh's golden curls. "Bella gets a holiday tonight," he told Josh. "No dinner to cook. We're having a party for her."

"Party tonight," Josh repeated, extending a chubby bare leg to examine his sandal contentedly. "Party for Bella."

"Yeah, right," she scoffed from behind the wheel. "Some party."

Dan glanced over at her. It was the first time she'd spoken since they'd left town. She looked unhappy, her gamine haircut standing up in unruly spikes that melted his heart.

"What's the matter?" he asked, leaning back in the seat again. "You should be happy. You just passed your driver's test on the very first try."

"What's that woman's name?"

"What woman?" he asked.

"The lady with the big hair who gives the driving exam."

"Stella Metz," Dan said, wondering what this was all about.

"Well, Stella more or less told me I didn't pass at all, but she was just giving me the license as a favor to your cousin Mamie. She also complained that I needed to provide some valid ID, and it took me about fifteen minutes to talk her into proceeding with the paperwork, even after she called Mamie, who confirmed that I was really Bella Gibson."

"She's a bureaucrat," Dan said mildly. "They're all the same. You got the license in the end, so what's the problem?"

"She claimed I didn't do a proper over-the-shoulder check before I changed lanes. But I always do a proper check," Bella said passionately. "I'm a good driver, Dan, not an idiot."

Dan watched her profile as she drove, increasingly curious.

"You know what I think?" Bella went on. "I think she was jealous. She kept asking about you and how we met and how long we'd known each other, stuff like that. And I could tell it was just killing her. I think that woman's nuts about you."

"Stella Metz?" he asked in genuine astonishment. "Nuts about me?"

"How long have you known her?" Bella glanced at him with those beautiful golden eyes.

Dan shrugged. "All my life. I went to school with Stella Metz. But I don't think she—"

"The woman's nuts about you," Bella repeated flatly. "Men are so dense about things like that. Boy, did she ever want to fail me on that driver's test."

He studied her thoughtfully.

"I felt like telling her not to worry, this marriage doesn't mean a thing," Bella said. "'Stella honey, it's not going to last, so you don't have to worry. We might be married, but we can hardly stand each other.'''

"What's the matter?" he asked again.

"Nothing," she said curtly, turning onto the highway leading out of town. "I got my driver's license. Let's have a party."

"Bella…"

She swung her gaze to him briefly, her face taut with emotion. "You look so tired, Dan," she said. "And it makes me feel really guilty."

"Why?" he asked.

She glanced in the rearview mirror at Josh, who was bending forward in the car seat to play with a strap on one of his sandals.

"Because," she said in a low, furious tone, "you're working like a dog all day, then last night you sat up half the night waiting for me to fall asleep before you came to bed. You must be exhausted."

"It's not that bad," he said, faintly embarrassed. "I fell asleep in my chair watching television, then woke up and went to bed. So I got two sleeps, instead of one."

"What's your problem?" She squinted at a farm truck loaded with pigs, looked back over her shoulder and pulled out expertly to pass the squealing vehicle, then settled back into her driving lane. "You think you can't trust me? If we share a bed while I'm awake, you're going to be attacked or something?"

"You weren't the one who—"

She slapped her palm on the wheel, muttering something under her breath.

"Look, I don't know why you're so upset about this," he said at last. "I'm just trying to protect you. We both know it's not a good idea to—"

"Sure," she interrupted wearily. "We both know that. Let's not talk about it anymore, okay?"

"Fine with me," he said. "So what should we talk about?"

"When can I use the truck to make a quick trip down to San Antonio?"

Her words chilled him. "You want to do that soon?" he asked.

"As you keep pointing out, there's no reason to wait." Again she glanced at Josh in the rearview mirror. He was now singing to himself. "If you're really prepared to release me from our business deal, then I may as well get this thing moving. I have a driver's license now, and credit cards will be easy enough to get. I'm on my way."

"I'll need the truck to haul hay bales for the next few days," he said. "But early next week, you can head down to San Antonio."

"Will you be able to take care of Josh for the day while I'm gone?"

Dan gave her a level, measuring look, his heart aching. "I took care of Josh for a whole lot of days before you came along, Bella."

She flushed, and her face lost some of its coldness. "Yes," she said quietly. "I guess you did."

She was silent a moment as they skimmed along the road beneath the arching trees. A couple of Mary's ostriches looked up from the field.

"Does Annie ever call the kids?" Bella asked

abruptly. "In all the time I've been here, there's been no word from her at all. How can she stand it?"

"Annie's busy with her own life," Dan said. "Often a whole month or more goes by before the kids hear from her. They're used to it."

Bella shook her head in disbelief. "What about when she visits? Doesn't it drive them crazy when she leaves again?"

"Not really. Josh doesn't know her at all, and Chris barely remembers her. My aunt Mary's been more of a mother to those kids than Annie ever was."

"What about Ellie?"

"It's harder on Ellie," Dan admitted. "She still remembers when Annie was home, not spending her nights running around singing at every bar in the county, then sleeping all day. She misses her mother more than the other kids do, but..."

"What?" Bella asked when he paused.

Dan shifted awkwardly in the seat and gazed out the window at his own small herd of Hereford cattle, glossy with their autumn fat.

"Annie's a warmhearted person," he said, "more like a little girl herself than a grown woman. She has fun with the kids when she visits, but I think they find it tiring to be with her a lot, even Ellie. They seem almost relieved when she says goodbye and heads back to Nashville."

Bella glanced down at her faded jeans and white cotton shirt. "There are times I think she must be a complete monster, neglecting her kids the way she does. And then I start to feel guilty because here I am, wearing the woman's clothes."

"Annie's not a monster," Dan said quietly. "She's just not a mother."

The school bus pulled off the highway ahead of them, and Bella stopped behind it. Ellie and Chris got out and climbed into the box of the pickup truck.

Bella smiled back at the girls through the window, then drove carefully into the farmyard and parked by the barn. Gypsy got to her feet, her tail rotating furiously.

Chris jumped down from the back and ran to the driver's-side window, her freckled face pale with excitement. "Did you pass?" she asked. "Did you?"

Solemnly, Bella held up the new driver's license in its plastic case.

"I knew it!" Chris shouted, dancing from one foot to the other. "I knew you'd get it! Hey, Ellie, look at this—Bella passed her driver's test."

"Big deal," Ellie muttered over her shoulder, trudging toward the house. "Dad, where's my red backpack, the one I used last year when we had the school field trip to Austin?"

"I think it's in the attic," Dan said. "What do you need it for?"

Ellie disappeared inside the house without answering, while Chris hurried around the truck to release Josh from his car seat.

"Hey, look!" Chris shouted, discovering the white sack. "We got McDonald's for supper!"

"It was your daddy's idea," Bella told her. "He thought we should have a party to celebrate my new driver's license."

Chris ran over to hug her father. "I love you, Daddy! And I love Bella, too," she added shyly, looking up while Dan caressed her hair. "I love both of you."

"Love both of you," Josh echoed happily, hugging Dan's legs. "Daddy and Bella."

Dan looked at Bella, who stood nearby, holding the truck keys and watching the two children. She seemed almost on the verge of tears.

For a moment their eyes met and he felt a searing jolt of desire, a physical urge so powerful it was all he could do not to ease the kids aside, cross the farmyard in two strides and take her in his arms. She was so adorable with her crooked smile, tanned face and lovely body, and that cute haircut…

It was the armchair for him again tonight, Dan told himself grimly. Unless he could somehow get these lustful thoughts under control, he wasn't going anywhere near that woman while she was in bed and still awake.

"Come on, kids," he said aloud. "Let's go set the table for Bella, okay? And then after supper, I want all of you to come outside and help me load hay bales onto the truck."

"Even Bella?" Chris asked, trotting along between them, holding the sack of hamburgers and fries. "Is she helping, too?"

"Of course she is," Dan said with a casual grin that hid the turmoil in his mind. "Bella's going to drive the truck while we load the bales. Might as well get some use out of that shiny new driver's license, right?"

They trooped into the house and began to set the kitchen table. Ellie climbed down the folding steps from the attic, holding a big red nylon backpack.

Dan glanced over at his daughter. "What's that for, honey?" he asked.

"We have to take a knapsack to school on Monday," she said without looking at him. "Mr. Kilmer's taking us on a nature walk next week down in Rimrock Park, and we're going to collect specimens of fossils and rocks."

"It's not like you to get ready so far in advance." Dan leaned in the kitchen doorway, watching thoughtfully as she headed for her room.

"I got lots to do," Ellie told him with an evasive shrug. "If we're hauling bales all weekend, I don't want to be looking for this at the last minute."

She closed the door to the front porch with firm deliberation.

Feeling vaguely uneasy, Dan moved away and returned to the laughing group in the kitchen, who were now making a big salad to go with their burgers and fries, and earnestly discussing the possibility of creating milk shakes in the blender.

CHAPTER FOURTEEN

LATE THAT SAME EVENING, after her sister and brother were in bed and the house was quiet, Ellie put her book aside, slipped out of bed and crept to the screened window to peek out.

The yard was bathed in moonlight. It tipped every leaf with silver and cast scary pools of shadow. When she pressed her cheek against the screen and peered to the side, she could see her father sitting on the patio, almost hidden behind the creeper vine on its wooden trellis. Ellie had heard him mixing a drink for himself in the kitchen, something he hardly ever did, and the soft click of the door when he went outside.

Now he sprawled in a big cedar chair, his head resting wearily against the back, the glass sitting half-empty on a table beside him.

What was he doing out there? Ellie wondered. Bella had finished her bath and gone to bed in their room, so why wasn't he with her?

For the thousandth time she heard Cody talking about all the gross things her father did to Bella in the darkness of their bed, and threatening to do the same things to Ellie. Whimpering with fear, Ellie turned and hauled her backpack onto the bed. She began to rummage feverishly through her dresser, deciding which clothes to pack. The problem was, she needed to take practically everything she owned, because she wasn't just going on a little trip.

When Ellie left home and got on that bus, she would be gone forever.

Her plan was to leave on Monday morning. She'd go to homeroom period so she wouldn't be recorded absent, then slip out while the other kids were walking down the hall to math class. The bus station was only a few blocks from the school, so within minutes Ellie could be on the nine-thirty bus, headed out of town.

She usually kept to herself during the schoolday, hiding out in the bathroom or doing special projects in the library to avoid Cody Pollock, so there was a good chance nobody would miss her until the end of the day—when she didn't get on the bus with Chris.

By then she would be far away, probably not even in Texas anymore.

Ellie stopped packing, suddenly struck by the reality of what she was doing. It was terrifying.

Worst of all was the fact that she didn't really want to leave, not now. In spite of herself, she had to admit that life was more pleasant at home since Bella had come along.

Her father's astonishing marriage had happened just a few days ago, but somehow since Bella's arrival, everything had miraculously become clean and shiny. There were real dinners on the table. Josh was happy all the time, and when she and Chris came home from school, the place felt cozy and welcoming.

Not that Ellie would ever admit any of this to a

living soul. She was still mad at her father for going off and marrying somebody without telling them.

But in the privacy of her own heart, she had to admit she could understand why he liked this new wife of his. There was just something so nice about Bella. She wasn't a phony like lots of other grown-ups who pretended to be kind to you but really didn't care a bit about what was going on in your life.

Bella was so good to Josh and Chris. She couldn't keep herself from hugging and kissing them any time they were around.

And when Daddy praised a meal she'd cooked or said how nice the house looked, her face shone. Bella's smile was so pretty, in fact, you hoped people would say things to make her happy, just so you could see her face light up.

Ellie scowled and began to jam things into the pack again.

It was crazy to be thinking that way. She had to remember how mad she was at her father, and how he'd dragged this woman into their life with no warning to anybody. Most of all, she had to remember Cody Pollock. Ellie stuffed a couple of T-shirts into the pack. Cody was getting worse every day. Something about her father's sudden marriage had caused this, it seemed. Nowadays he taunted Ellie without mercy, whispered to her in the hallways and followed her around on the playground, talking about her daddy's pretty new wife and the things that went on in their bed.

His threats were getting crazier all the time, even more scary because Ellie didn't understand half of what he said. She just knew he was dangerous, and that if she didn't get herself far, far away from him, he was going to hurt her.

A timid knock sounded on the inside porch door, interrupting her thoughts. Ellie froze, staring wildly around her makeshift bedroom. Before she could get the pack off her bed and out of sight, the door opened and Bella's cropped head appeared.

"Ellie," she said, "I'm sorry to bother you, but I saw your light was still on and I wondered if you—"

She stopped short, looking from the pack on the bed to Ellie's face. Hesitantly she took a few steps into the veranda and closed the door behind her.

She wore Dan's boxer shorts and one of his cotton shirts, hanging halfway down her slim brown legs.

"Go away!" Ellie whispered, her heart thudding as she tried to block Bella's view of the backpack. "Get out of here!"

Again Bella looked hesitantly from the bed to the T-shirts Ellie was holding. "What are you doing, honey?" she asked in that same gentle voice.

"None of your business," Ellie said, then realized Bella would tell her father about this if she got suspicious. "I'm just trying on a few of my clothes," she said sullenly. "I want to know what still fits and what I can give to Chris. She's growing so fast she needs some new things."

Bella continued to watch her gravely. The woman's eyes were calm and full of concern, and Ellie had the uncomfortable feeling they were looking right through her.

"Is anything the matter?" Bella asked. "Something I could help with?"

All at once Ellie longed to tell somebody the

whole story, all about Cody and the awful things he kept saying, and how scared she was and that she had to run away to Nashville to get away from him, even though she was terrified at the thought of getting on a bus all alone. And also worried that her mother wouldn't be all that pleased to have her turn up on her doorstep.

"If there's a problem," Bella said in her soft, coaxing voice, "I'd be happy to talk about it with you, Ellie."

Sure you would, Ellie thought bitterly, getting herself under control again. But then after their little talk, Bella would go right outside and tell her father the whole story.

The thought of him hearing about the things Cody was saying made Ellie's head whirl with shame. She simply couldn't bear it.

"Nothing's the matter," she said. "And if there was, why would I talk to you about it? You'd just tell my dad."

"I won't tell your dad anything you don't want me to Ellie," Bella said quietly. "I promise."

Again Ellie wavered. But when she thought about Cody's obscene whispers, his pimply face and big hulking body, fear overcame her urge to confide, and all she could think of was escape. She turned away deliberately, put the shirts back in the dresser drawer and shoved the pack under her bed.

"Well, I guess there's only a few things to give away," she muttered, climbing back into bed and picking up her book. "Most of this stuff still fits me."

She peeped over at Bella who hadn't moved an

inch and seemed on the verge of saying something more.

"Good night," Ellie said, forcing her voice to sound casual. "I'm glad you got your driver's license."

Bella gave her one of those sweet, lopsided smiles. "Why, thank you, Ellie," she said. "That's very nice of you."

Ellie stared at her book, wishing the woman would just go away.

"The reason I bothered you," Bella said awkwardly, "is that I was wondering if you know where your father is."

Ellie glanced up in surprise. "He's out on the patio."

"What's he doing?"

"Just sitting there," Ellie said. "He's got a drink and I think he's half-asleep."

Bella's face looked sad again, her eyes big and dark. "Okay," she said. "Thank you, Ellie. See you in the morning."

"Sure," Ellie said, reaching over to switch off her light and end the conversation.

BELLA OPENED the kitchen door and padded out onto the patio in her bare feet. Despite the chilly night air, the flagstones were still warm with the day's heat.

"Dan?" she whispered.

He looked up, his face shadowed and hard to read. "Is something the matter?" he asked. "Are the kids okay?"

"Josh and Chris are both sound asleep. Ellie was

still reading a minute ago, but she's just switched her light off.''

Bella hesitated, thinking about that pack on the bed, the shirts in Ellie's hands and her strangely furtive manner.

She'd promised not to talk to Dan about it, and she wouldn't for now. But she fully intended to draw Ellie into conversation tomorrow and coax the girl into telling her what was wrong.

"I think Ellie might be softening a bit," Dan said, extending his long legs. "She doesn't seem quite as prickly anymore, does she?"

Bella sank into the chair beside him, battling the familiar urge to reach out and touch his arm, stroke his shoulder and snuggle close to him.

"Just now, she told me she was glad I got my driver's license."

"No kidding." In the dimness she could sense his smile. "Well, that's some progress, isn't it?"

Bella stared through the trees at the slow-moving river, her throat tight with emotion. "Why are you sitting out here?" she asked at last.

"I'm just having a glass of rye. It's a nice evening to sit and think."

Again she had to fight the urge to reach out and touch him. "I want you to come to bed," she said abruptly. "This is ridiculous."

"Bella," he said quietly, "don't do this to me. Leave it alone and go to bed."

"I want you to come with me," she said again. "Right now."

She was conscious of the way he shifted in his

chair and the glimmer of moonlight in his eyes as he studied her face. "What are you saying, Bella?"

"You know what I'm saying." She looked down at her hands, clenched tightly in her lap.

"For God's sake," he whispered in a low, passionate voice. "How much do you think a man can bear?"

Bella summoned all her courage. "I don't see why you have to make such a big deal out of this." She kept her gaze on the river. "You're a man. I'm a woman. We're sharing a bed, and we want each other. Why does it have to be so complicated?"

"Because you're leaving next week."

"Yes, I am," she said. "But I'm here now."

He sipped his drink in silence.

Deliberately, Bella brought her hand to his shoulder, let it trail over the hard muscle and down his chest, toward the waistband of his jeans.

"Bella," he whispered, "stop it." But he made no move to prevent her actions, and she heard his sharp intake of breath.

Her heart pounded wildly. Almost dizzy with her boldness, Bella let her hand drift lower, exploring the bulge at his crotch, stroking and caressing while he groaned softly, keeping his face turned away from her.

"You want this as much as I do," she whispered. "I know you do. Come to bed, Dan."

He drained the glass, got up abruptly and took her arm, pulling her to her feet. With a hunger that thrilled her, he began to kiss her mouth, his lips moving and seeking. Bella smelled the clean, masculine scent of him, tasted the whiskey on his breath, felt the firmness of his mouth and the faint bristle of whiskers against her cheek.

She melted into him, on fire with passion, muttering incoherently as his hands slipped under her shirt and stroked her body.

Breathing hard, pausing frequently to kiss and caress each other, they stumbled into the house and down the hall to their bedroom, where he pulled her inside and closed the door, then lifted her and carried her to the bed.

Bella could never remember being so utterly lost in passion, even during the early years with Eric when they'd been crazy about each other physically.

Tonight she was behaving like a complete wanton, practically hauling the man off to bed. She couldn't keep her hands off him, couldn't fight the urge to press her body against his, murmuring and whimpering with need, tugging blindly to remove her own clothes, as well as his.

When they were both naked under the cool sheets, Bella had a brief sense of peacefulness. It was so good to feel the warmth of his skin, the strength of the arms enfolding her.

Though completely new to her, his body had a sweet familiarity. She realized it was because of all the times she'd imagined this moment during the nights she'd lain next to him in the darkness, struggling to keep from touching him.

She sighed in bliss, nuzzling the warm hollow of his throat. "You feel so good," she whispered. "I knew you'd be like this."

"Oh, Bella." He stroked her tousled hair, kissing

her eyelids and mouth and neck. "You're going to kill me, girl. No man could stand this."

"Yeah, right," she teased, reaching down brazenly to cup and fondle him. "It sure feels like you're suffering, all right."

He shuddered at her touch and held her closer. "Oh, Lord. If you only knew."

"Don't think so much, Dan." She shifted so she could gaze earnestly into his eyes. "Can't you forget about what's going to happen next week and just make love to me tonight? Nobody's made love to me for such a long time," she whispered, her voice breaking. "You can't imagine how lonely I've been."

He gathered her into his arms and held her tenderly, running a gentle finger over her nose and across her lower lip. "You're a woman who should never be lonely, Bella," he told her huskily. "You were born to be held and loved by a man."

"Really?" she asked shamelessly, hungry for more. "Do you like holding me, Dan?"

"I like everything about you." He cupped her breasts, then dipped his hand into the hollow of her waist. "I like this…and this…"

She laughed, pushing the hair back from his forehead and smiling into his eyes. "Go on," she prompted. "What else do you like?"

His hand strayed lower, his fingers gentle and seeking. "Well, I'm really fond of this…"

"Are you, Dan? I like this, too, you know." She held him again, fondling and stroking, then slipped lower in the bed to caress him with her mouth.

After a moment he groaned and drew her gently

back up into his arms. "If you keep doing that," he whispered hoarsely, "this whole thing's going to over in about twenty seconds. It's been an awfully long time for me, too, Bella."

"Oh, no," she said, smiling. "Well, we don't want our fun to be over that quickly. Although," she added, "we do have all night, you know."

"Yes, I guess we do."

"So, Dan, tell me what else you like about me."

He cupped her buttocks, pulling her close to him. "I surely do like this," he told her. "This cute little bottom of yours. You don't know how many times I've wanted to touch it in the past few days."

"Yours isn't bad, either," she said solemnly, stroking him there. "And I must confess, a few times I've also had to battle the urge to touch."

"You're so incredibly warm and beautiful," he told her, still caressing her body with long, slow strokes. "Just delicious. You're a woman who was created for lovemaking, Bella."

Her smile faded, and she buried her face in the hair on his chest. "Toward the end, Eric used to complain I was frigid. He got very upset with me."

"The man's a jerk and an idiot," Dan muttered darkly, stroking her hair again. "If you'd let me, I'd go and smash his face in."

"Sorry, I shouldn't have mentioned him. I don't want to think about Eric." She began to kiss Dan across his chest and onto his shoulders. "I want to think about you. I've wanted this so much, you simply can't imagine."

Dimly, through a rising mist of passion, Bella was

amazed by how comfortable and familiar it all seemed.

Dan Gibson was a man who, until now, she'd never held in a sexual embrace, and there had only been a few in her life before him. But this man seemed to be her natural lover and playmate. There was no strangeness between them, just a sense of rightness and belonging, a rich feeling of homecoming.

"We fit together so well." She climbed on top of him and lay full-length on his body, kissing his mouth while she ran her toes up and down his bare legs.

"How do you know how well we fit?" he teased. "That specific alignment still needs to be measured."

"So speaks the mechanical engineer," she whispered, smiling down at him.

But his words and what they suggested struck a chord in Bella, moved her passion to a new plane. Suddenly she was so desperate for him she could wait no longer. Wordlessly, she lifted her hips and settled down onto him, gasping as he filled her.

Dan's eyes closed and his face against the pillow took on a hard, concentrated expression as he held her hips and moved her on top of him, manipulating her body effortlessly. Bella's passion escalated with every thrust, and she felt a blaze of heat that rose from her core and hammered in her ears.

When she reached orgasm, she arched her back and sat erect on top of him, stifling her moans of pleasure while he held her breasts and caressed the nipples gently. At last she collapsed into his arms, shuddering and cuddling against him.

Dan kissed her tenderly. With that same careful, easy strength, he rolled her over in the bed, then entered her again, his big body moving above her. Incredulous, Bella felt herself moving toward orgasm a second time, something that had never happened to her before. She had only a moment to marvel at this before she was lost in that shimmering haze again, hot waves of sensation ebbing from her body.

He lay spent in her arms, gasping, his face buried against her shoulder while she stroked his hair. "I certainly hope you're finished," she said primly. "Because a girl can only stand so much of that kind of thing."

He kissed her shoulder and her neck, laughing softly. "Yeah?" he said, his voice husky. "Well, a guy can stand a whole lot more of it than I've been getting lately, let me tell you."

"Really? How much more?" she asked, smiling into the darkness.

"About a hundred years more." He drew away and gazed down at her, his face taut with emotion. "Don't leave me, Bella. Whatever this problem is, let's work it out together."

Her heart contracted with fear as she watched his profile against the silvery paleness of the curtains. "Dan, I don't want to talk about that," she whispered. "Please, just hold me."

He took her in his arms again. Bella buried her face against his shoulder, cuddling into him warmly, but she could feel the tension in his body.

"So this is just sex?" he asked against her hair.

"Just a night of sweet release for both of us and next week you'll disappear from my life?"

She lay still in his arms, thinking about his question. How easy it would be to give in, to yield to her own longings and stay with him.

Bella indulged in another of the wistful fantasies that filled most of her waking hours nowadays. She saw herself learning to be a really good homemaker and farm wife, getting skilled and competent at cooking and all the other duties that were part of caring for a home and family.

She saw the children growing up in warmth and happiness, and Dan looking less harried and overworked because her money would make his life so much easier. Maybe he'd even decide to go back to college and finish his engineering degree.

And every night they would share this bed, hold each other and talk and laugh together, and merge their bodies with a passion that was indescribably wonderful…

But on top of those wistful visions, Bella also saw the cold reality.

She knew Eric would find her sooner or later, because he always did. But this time, if she'd been weak enough to give in to her longings, she wouldn't be the only one to suffer.

Bella realized her own life didn't really matter that much anymore. After she left Dan and the children, the future would have little meaning. All her hopes were going to die the moment she walked away from them, and nothing Eric might do to her afterward would ever hurt as much.

With this newfound courage, Bella knew she

would calmly face her stalker when she had to, somewhere far away from Texas. But she could never expose any of the people in this house to that kind of danger.

Still, she was afraid that if Dan coaxed her, if he looked into her eyes and told her he loved her, begged her not to leave, she wouldn't be able to resist him.

Don't say it, she thought, lying rigid in his arms. *Please don't ever tell me you love me...*

The silence between them lengthened while gentle nighttime sounds drifted through the open window. She heard the soft raggedness of his breathing close to her ear.

"Sure, Bella," he said at last, "you're right. This is just great sex, that's all. Next week you'll be gone. I won't try to hold on to you."

Relief swept over her, coupled with a deep, aching disappointment she was afraid to analyze.

"But I'm here now," she said, hugging him fiercely. "And the night is young."

His face softened in the moonlight. "What a woman. How will I ever keep up with you?" he said, echoing the lightness of her tone.

"Maybe I'll have to get up and feed you some oysters," she whispered. "Even a dummy like me can serve oysters, because you eat them raw."

"Believe me, I don't need oysters to get me going, Bella." He bent to kiss her breasts. "I just need you."

He drew her into his arms again, and for a long time there was no more serious conversation, just muffled laughter and broken whispers of passion.

CHAPTER FIFTEEN

HOURS LATER in the stillness of early morning, Dan held Bella while she slept, his heart aching with tenderness. He gazed down at her beautiful face on the pillow, so gentle in sleep. The softness of her mouth and the fan of eyelashes shadowing her cheek made her look so innocent. Yet last night she'd been passionate and womanly in her lovemaking.

His heart began to pound with renewed lust when he thought about her whispers and teasing in the darkness, her frank sexuality and the openness of her responses to him. God, what a woman.

Dan felt himself growing hard. He wanted to wake her up and make love to her all over again.

But, he thought, there are limits to a man's selfishness, even his. Instead, he drew her close and rested his face against her hair, kissing her gently, brooding over the things she'd said to him.

Can't you forget about what's going to happen next week and just make love to me tonight? Nobody's made love to me for such a long time....

"Oh, Bella," he whispered, his arms tightening around her. "You sweet darling."

Dan had never before encountered a dilemma like this. He believed in taking action and not being intimidated. In the face of threats, he protected his own. All his instincts told him to go to Austin and look up this cowardly stalker, have it out with the man and force him to leave Bella alone.

When he thought about her fear and desperation, his hands hardened into fists. How satisfying it would be to pummel the man into submission, let him know how it felt to be terrorized by someone who was physically stronger and utterly relentless.

Dan had few doubts about his ability to overpower Eric Matthias. But he was also painfully sensitive to Bella's fear.

Still, it was galling to give in and let himself be pushed around. Under different circumstances, Dan knew he would probably take action regardless of any warnings. But where Bella was concerned, he hesitated, simply because he wasn't sure of her.

It could well be that he'd go to Austin all on his own, confront this cop and have it out with him, and by so doing complicate Bella's life unnecessarily when she really wanted to leave Texas anyway. After all, she was adamant about going away. She said it was to protect Dan and the kids from her stalker. But what if that was just a convenient excuse?

It was reasonable to suppose that Bella would be deeply reluctant to get involved with a single father who lived in a shabby farmhouse with only one bathroom. This wasn't the life she wanted. So even if he dealt with the threat to her safety, what kind of future could they have?

It was the reality that hurt most. For all her naturalness and enthusiasm, Bella had been raised in a kind of luxury he could only imagine. He certainly couldn't see her taking on his load of debt and the

grueling difficulty of his life, and being happy cooking and doing laundry.

Nor could he see himself taking any of her money
to make their life more pleasant. The truth was, he
had nothing but contempt for the kind of man who
would do such a thing.

So where did that leave them?

Bella was right, he thought miserably, curling his
body around her slender form. He should just enjoy
the gift of this brief time they had together, then let
her go without an argument. That was what she
wanted, after all, and it was the manly way to be-
have.

She murmured something and nestled closer to
him. Dan's heart began to pound as he hoped she
was going to wake up and turn to him again. But she
settled back, smiling in her sleep.

Tenderness overwhelmed him again, and tears
stung briefly in his eyes. He brushed at them, then
gathered her close and tried to sleep.

THE NEXT MORNING, a Saturday, Bella made pancakes for the first time. She had a cookbook propped
on the counter, opened to the correct page, and Chris
hovered nearby as an assistant. Josh sat on the floor
in one corner of the kitchen, playing solemnly with
a plastic truck.

Dan appeared in the doorway, already finished
with his morning chores. Bella glanced at him, her
heart melting. She hoped the children couldn't see
any telltale emotions in her face.

''What's all this?'' he asked, smiling at her and
coming over to ruffle Chris's hair.

"We're making pancakes," Chris told him, stirring the batter vigorously.

Dan dropped a light kiss on the nape of Bella's neck, and her whole body turned to jelly. "Okay, I think the griddle's hot enough now," she said huskily to Chris, trying to ignore the man behind her. "Next we're supposed to pour out a spoonful of the batter, like this…"

A couple of minutes later, Ellie came in and stood with the rest of them. Holding her breath, Bella reached out with her spatula, loosened the pancake and flipped it over. The side revealed was smooth and brown and looked delicious.

"Wow," Chris breathed.

When Bella removed the test pancake, she felt a warm surge of accomplishment. Carefully, she poured more pools of batter onto the hot griddle, while Dan went to wash his hands and the girls hurried to set the table and find the butter and syrup.

"Best pancakes I ever tasted," Dan announced a few minutes later, attacking a plateful while Bella finished cooking the rest of the batter. "Aren't they, kids?"

"Yummy!" Josh yelled, banging his spoon happily on the tray of the high chair, his fat face smeared with maple syrup.

"I love them," Chris said solemnly. "Don't you, Ellie?"

"They're real good," Ellie said, causing Bella to exchange a startled glance with Dan over the girl's lowered head.

She carried another platter of golden pancakes to the table and allowed herself to rest her hand on

Dan's shoulder as she set the plate down. But that was a mistake, because the brief touch made her heart pound and her cheeks turn pink.

Nor did it help when he reached around casually, out of sight of the children, and caressed her bottom in the khaki shorts. Immediately her body moistened and ached with hunger.

She moved away, avoiding the laughter in his eyes, and sat down at the head of the table with a couple of pancakes on her own plate.

"Dan," she said, struggling to keep her voice normal, "Chris wants to go with you to feed the ponies after breakfast, and Ellie's going to help me with the dishes. Do you and Chris want to take Josh with you?"

"Sure, he can come along." Dan gave Bella a quizzical glance while Ellie stared up at them in alarm. "Josh loves seeing the ponies, don't you, son?" He smiled at the toddler.

"More," Josh demanded, pointing a sticky hand at the platter of pancakes. "Want more."

The platter emptied in no time, to Bella's satisfaction, and Dan kissed her again in front of all the children before he took Josh and Chris outside, leaving her alone with Ellie.

"Well, here we are," Bella said, feeling a little awkward. She filled the sink with hot water while Ellie moved around, clearing the table and countertops. "Do you want to wash or dry?"

"I'll dry," Ellie said tonelessly. She held up a tin of baking powder. "Where does this go?"

"In that cupboard, second shelf."

Bella set up the drying rack, then began to wash

dishes, starting with glasses and cutlery the way she'd read in the volume on housekeeping that she'd found in one of the cabinets.

"I finished my book last night," Ellie said, rubbing a glass with her towel.

It was the first time the girl had ever volunteered even a scrap of conversation.

"Was it a good book?" Bella asked, washing the forks and putting them in the drying rack.

"Pretty good. There's three of them, you know. I was supposed to get the last one on Monday. But now I won't have time to finish it before…" Ellie stopped and her face reddened with embarrassment.

"Before what?" Bella reached for a plate and immersed it in the soapy water.

"Nothing."

"Ellie…are you thinking about running away?"

Bella saw how the child's hands tensed and clutched the dish towel, how her shoulders went rigid beneath the baggy shirt.

"That's dumb," Ellie said, her voice shaky. "Why would I do something like that?"

"I guess people can have lots of reasons for running away."

"Like what?" Ellie asked.

"Well—" Bella washed a plate carefully "—once I ran away from somebody because I was afraid he might hurt me."

Ellie's jaw dropped and she stared at Bella in amazement. "How did you know?" she whispered, her face pale. "Did somebody tell Daddy?"

"About what, dear?"

"About Cody Pollock and the things he says to me and…" Her voice trailed off.

"I didn't know much about Cody Pollock," Bella said, "except that you had a fight with him the other day. But it's really true that I ran away because a bully was picking on me. And I'm guessing," she added quietly, "that you might be going through the same kind of thing."

Ellie gulped and nodded, looking down to hide her face.

Bella kept methodically washing dishes and stacking them in the drying rack. She didn't want to scare Ellie off by appearing too anxious.

"What does this boy do to you?" she asked. "Does he hurt you?"

Ellie nodded her head jerkily. "Sometimes he punches me or grabs at me when nobody's looking. But mostly he just…says things," she whispered.

"What kind of things?"

Ellie took a deep breath. "He talks about what he'll do to me if he ever catches me alone."

"Like what?"

Ellie's face flamed again. She whispered something, and Bella bent closer. "I'm sorry, dear," she murmured. "I didn't hear what you said."

"Cody says he's going to…to do the same things that Daddy does to you in bed."

Bella's throat constricted with outrage. Impulsively she took the child in her arms and Ellie clung to her, sobbing.

"Ellie," Bella said, patting the girl's back and trying to hide her anger, "have you told your teachers about this?"

The girl shook her head against Bella's chest, gulping. "My teacher can't do anything," she said. "Mr. Kilmer's scared of him, too. Cody's real big and mean, and he has this gang of friends."

"Well, then, how about the principal?" Bella frowned, thinking. "Surely the principal could handle Cody."

"I'd never be able to talk to Ms. Osborne," Ellie said.

"Why not?"

"She's just so…" Ellie paused and turned away, rubbing her forearm across her eyes, then groped in her pocket for a tissue. "I couldn't ever talk to the principal."

"I'll talk to her," Bella said with sudden decision. "On Monday."

"No! Please, I don't want Daddy to know about this!" Ellie said in panic. "If he ever heard about the things Cody says to me, I'd die. Honest, Bella, I'd really die."

Bella was torn. She knew Dan should be told about Cody Pollock's vile threats. But she also remembered, all too well, her own shyness at Ellie's age, and how painfully humiliated she would have been to have her father know about a problem like this.

"Okay," she said at last. "I won't tell your father. I'll just go and talk to the principal myself."

"Promise? Just you?"

"I promise. And I want to know for sure you won't do anything silly, like run away. Will you promise me that?"

"Okay," Ellie replied in an offhand way, but Bella could see the relief in the girl's eyes. "Look,

Bella,'' she said, pointing, "you missed a bit of syrup on this plate.''

"Picky, picky,'' Bella said with a grin.

Ellie smiled back, and all at once the little kitchen seemed flooded with sunshine and contentment.

ON MONDAY MORNING, Bella sat by the passenger window of the truck with Josh strapped into his seat behind her, while Dan drove through the downtown area of Crystal Creek.

The town was drowsy and peaceful in the autumn stillness. Even the streets seemed deserted, though Bella knew the morning coffee crowd was gathered in the Longhorn for their hour of companionship and gossip.

"I need to pick up a load of feed supplement,'' Dan said. "Should I drop you at the school and come back in a half hour or so?''

"I didn't make an appointment, so I have no idea how long this is going to take.'' Bella squinted at the redbrick middle school, just up the block from the courthouse. "Maybe it's better if I meet you down at the Longhorn whenever I'm done. That way you can get Josh a pudding or something if you have to wait.''

"Okay.'' He parked in front of the school and gave her a questioning glance. "You're sure you don't want to tell me what this is all about?''

Bella avoided his eyes. "I promised Ellie I'd look after it on my own. This is sort of…a girl-type problem.''

Dan drummed his fingers on the steering wheel. Bella watched them and felt a deep, involuntary shiver when she remembered the feel of those hands on her body, arousing her to a fever pitch.

The past two nights in that moonlit bed had been even more passionate as they grew accustomed to each other, and skilled at tantalizing and satisfying. But every time they came together, Bella's hunger was both quenched and fueled. She wanted him all the time, more and more. Leaving Dan was going to be the deepest agony Bella had ever known, but she knew it was foolhardy to delay any longer.

She'd already decided to go to San Antonio on Wednesday to retrieve her cash and stock certificates. Immediately afterward, she would buy a plane ticket and leave Texas. And she'd never see Dan or his children again.

Bella had abandoned any thought of staying in Crystal Creek long enough to let Douglas Evans sell her stocks so she could give a substantial amount of cash to Dan. Instead, she planned to send him the money from some distant place without a return address, so he'd be forced to accept her gift.

By now, the danger of lingering at the farm had multiplied. As always, she risked being discovered by Eric, and thus threatening the security of Dan's family. But she also faced another danger, and this one was becoming almost as terrifying.

If she spent many more nights in Dan's arms, she would become too weakened by passion to leave.

"You're sure?" he raised a questioning eyebrow as he glanced at her.

"I'm sure." She leaned over the seat to check on Josh. "I'll see you two men later at the restaurant," she said, stroking the child's plump cheek. "Josh, darling, you be a good boy for Daddy, all right?"

"Good boy," Josh promised, giving her a radiant smile.

Bella climbed from the truck, waved to Dan and started up the walk to the front door of the school. She watched him drive off, then went inside just as the bell rang for recess and children began to pour from the classrooms and head outside to the playground.

In the midst of the shouting, milling throng, Bella stood and looked around wistfully. She had never attended a public school.

Even now she could remember how much she'd wanted to be part of a crowd of children like this— casually dressed boys and girls, talking and laughing together.

But Bella had attended quiet, ivy-covered mausoleums filled with rich girls in uniforms, who'd either been snobbish and unkind or as miserable and lonely as she was.

Suddenly she was conscious of somebody pressing close to her, and looked down to find Ellie gazing at her anxiously.

"Did you talk to her yet?" the girl whispered.

Bella shook her head. "I just got here. Is it all right if I go in now, do you think?"

"I guess so," Ellie said. "Ms. Osborne always works in her office through recess. I'll just sit here and wait for you, okay?"

"Okay." Bella smiled at the girl and touched her shoulder. "Hey, don't look so scared," she murmured. "This isn't going to hurt a bit."

Ellie ducked her head nervously and crossed the foyer to sit cross-legged by the wall, watching as Bella went into the office.

A young woman in a tight sweater told her to take a seat, waving scarlet-tipped fingers at a chair near the front desk. "Ms. Osborne's on the phone," she said. "I'll tell you when she's free."

"Thank you." Bella smiled and lowered herself into the metal chair.

When the secretary opened the door to check on her employer, Bella saw the principal through a screen of potted plants. She froze in panic and utter shock.

A slender blond woman in a gray sweater sat behind the desk. She was still on the phone. Bella sat rigidly in the chair, feeling as if she'd just been kicked in the stomach. The room whirled around her as she struggled to regain control.

The woman was ten years older than when Bella had last seen her and looked different in many ways, but she was still unmistakable.

The respected principal of Crystal Creek middle school was Luciana Delgado, Bella's long-vanished sister.

CHAPTER SIXTEEN

FOR WHAT SEEMED like an eternity, Bella sat staring through the screen of plants at her half sister.

The principal clearly wasn't aware of Bella, and hungrily, Bella studied her sister's face. Lucia was still lovely, though she looked a little thinner.

"Still on the phone," the secretary announced, coming back into the reception area. "But I'm sure she'll just be a few more minutes."

"I..." Bella got to her feet and said awkwardly. "I need to leave. I'm so sorry, but maybe later it'll be..." Words failed her.

"Sure, whatever," the secretary said, looking bored.

Bella struggled out to the foyer, where Ellie sat hugging her knees.

"You're back way too soon," the girl muttered, her face taut with anxiety. "Wasn't Ms. Osborne there?"

Bella reached down to take Ellie's hand and lead her outside. They sat on the grass next to a tree while the other children played around them.

"How long has Ms. Osborne been working here at the school?" Bella asked.

Ellie shrugged. "I don't know," she said. "Ever since I was a little kid. She's always been here."

Lucia.

It was still very hard to believe. What an incredible, unfortunate coincidence that both of them should have been drawn to this town where they'd spent summer holidays in their youth.

"Why didn't you talk to her?" Ellie asked, plucking at a blade of grass.

"Well, I was kind of startled. It turns out your school principal is…" Bella hesitated, swallowing hard. "She's somebody I used to know."

"So you didn't say anything to her about Cody?"

"Actually, I didn't talk to her at all." Bella rubbed her eyes, trying to collect herself. "When I realized who she was, I got up and left before she even saw me."

Ellie's face paled beneath the freckles and a tear slipped down her cheek.

"I knew you wouldn't do anything," she said miserably. "Grown-ups can't help with somebody like Cody. They always promise they will, but there's nothing they can do."

"Oh, honey," Bella said in despair. "Really, I wanted to—"

"And now," Ellie went on with a catch in her voice, "I have to get away before he can do something awful. I have to go to my mother in Nashville, and she doesn't want me, either."

Bella stared at the girl, horrified. "That's where you were planning to go? All the way to Nashville? By yourself?"

Again Ellie shrugged. "There's nowhere else for me to go." Another tear slipped down her cheek.

Bella put an arm around the girl's shoulders. "All

right," she said. "I'll go back and talk to Ms. Osborne."

"Now?" Ellie asked.

Bella took a deep breath, her heart pounding with dread.

"Yes," she said firmly, then got up to brush dried grass from the back of her jeans.

The bell rang for the kids to go back to their classrooms, and before she could change her mind, Bella walked back to the school office. The secretary waved a pencil at the principal's door.

"She's off the phone now. Just go on in."

Bella forced herself to open the door and step in.

"Well, hi there, Luce," she said with a brave attempt at lightness. "Fancy meeting *you*..."

She choked, overwhelmed by a sudden hot flood of tears.

"Isabel?" Luciana stared across the desk, open-mouthed, as Bella lowered herself into one of the visitor's chairs.

Bella groped for a tissue from a box on the desk, wiped her eyes and looked at her sister with a surge of the old wistfulness that had dogged her childhood. She'd always adored Luciana, with her patrician blond good looks and the gentleness she concealed under an exterior of reserve. It had broken Bella's heart when she'd walked out more than a decade ago after a fight with their father, vowing never to set foot in the house again.

"So how...how have you been?" Bella asked, knowing as soon as she spoke how utterly banal the words must sound.

"But...the newspaper said you were dead," Luciana whispered. "Bella, the paper said you drove your car off a cliff and into the river. Ever since, I've been sick with grief."

"Have you?" Bella asked, deeply moved. "I was sure you wouldn't even remember me after all these years, Luce."

"I think about you all the time," her sister said simply. "Leaving you behind in that house was the hardest thing I've ever done."

She came around the desk to embrace Bella. The two of them clung to each other for a long moment.

"It would have killed me to stay, darling," Luciana whispered. "I couldn't stand to have anything more to do with that man."

"With Daddy, you mean?"

"Who else?" Luciana's tone was bitter.

Bella sank into the chair again as Luciana went back around the desk. "I never found out what the fight was about," she said, helping herself to another tissue. "After you left, Daddy refused to allow anybody to talk about you ever again. I don't think he's spoken your name in ten years."

"God, that man's a coldhearted bastard," Luciana muttered, her beautiful face hardening. "I tried many times to get in touch with you, but he'd never allow me to talk to you. At your school they were ordered not to let me near you. I never knew where you went to college. And then, after you got married and left home, I didn't even know where you were or what your name was."

"Luce—"

"Look, I don't want to talk about him, Isabel. If that's why you're here, I can't help you at all."

"I'm not here to talk about Daddy. Nowadays he doesn't know where I am, either."

"Then what are you doing in Crystal Creek?" Lucia asked.

"I'm married to Dan Gibson."

Again Luciana's jaw dropped in astonishment. "You're what?"

Bella mopped her eyes again, struggling to regain a bit of composure. "Don't look so shocked," she said at last. "You must have gotten married yourself at some point in the last ten years, or your name wouldn't be Osborne."

"That marriage didn't last more than a few months," Luciana said. "It was a misguided choice, at best. But at least I got rid of the Delgado name, so it was a worthwhile experience."

Bella smiled, surprised at how comfortable she felt talking with Luciana.

But she sensed that Lucia was already beginning to withdraw again after the initial relief that her sister was still alive.

In the lift of Luciana's chin, the guarded look in those lovely blue eyes, Bella could see her retreating back into the icy reserve that had always been her protection from painful family associations.

"So tell me," her sister said, folding her hands on the desktop, "how did you ever come to be married to Dan Gibson?"

"It's a long story."

Luciana glanced at her watch, then gave Bella a smile. "Well, I have a lunch meeting in a couple of hours, but I'm free until then."

So Bella began to talk, telling her sister all about

her marriage to Eric Matthias, the growing violence before she left him, his threats and obsessive behavior and her father's unwillingness to protect her.

"So Daddy's solution was to save your marriage and send you back to your husband?" Luciana asked in disbelief, interrupting the narrative. "He actually took this man's side against you?"

"You know what Daddy's like. His philosophy has always been to ignore problems at home. If that fails, throw money at them and they're sure to go away."

"That's how he tried to stop your mother's drinking," Luciana recalled bitterly. "Every couple of years, he'd send the poor woman off to Switzerland or Rio to some upscale treatment facility. It simply never occurred to him that what Claire really needed was a little more of his time and attention."

"No," Bella agreed, thinking about her sad mother. "That never once occurred to Daddy, not even when you tried to tell him."

Both sisters were silent for a moment.

"Well," Luciana said, "that's obviously not the whole story. What happened next?"

Bella went on to tell about her growing desperation, her attempts to get away and Eric's unnerving ability to track her down no matter where she went.

"So finally," Bella said, "I decided I was going to have to die."

"Suicide?" Luciana whispered, her eyes widening. "Oh, God, Isabel. Not you, too."

"No, I mean I had to disappear somehow and make it look as if I'd died, so Eric would give up and stop looking for me." As she'd explained it to

Dan that first morning, Bella told her sister how she planned her "death," then stashed money and papers in San Antonio for later use, as well as in the bus depot at Abilene.

"Oh, you poor sweetie." Luciana reached out to take her hand with a return of the impulsive tenderness that Bella remembered, though it would probably have surprised many who knew her now. "How awful it must have been for you. And so lonely."

"It was lonely, all right," Bella said. "And, when I saw them laughing with Eric—" she swallowed painfully "—it was the ultimate betrayal. I just didn't know what else to do."

"Well, of course you didn't," Luciana said.

"Wait, it gets worse," Bella said with a brave attempt at lightness.

She told Luciana the events of that fateful night, how she'd been forced to jump off the cliff behind her car and then, stripped of money and identification, how she'd made her way up the river, battered, hungry and thirsty.

When Bella came to the part about her invasion of Dan Gibson's farm along the river, her sister's face went pale. "You broke into his house?" she breathed. "Like a thief in the night?"

"I was so hungry, Luce! And I was terrified. I thought if I could steal some money, find a few decent clothes, grab something to eat…"

"But instead, Dan Gibson caught you."

"He sure did." Bella smiled privately, remembering. "And then he ran a bath for me, bandaged up the worst of my cuts and let me use his bed. The next day we drove up to Abilene to get my cash and my extra set of ID. But we found that Eric had been there before us and cleaned out the locker.''

Luciana's eyes narrowed. ''So your stalker, this policeman…he knows you're still alive?''

''Oh, yes, I'm sure he does. And my guess is that he's just waiting for me to make a wrong move.''

''So where does this bizarre marriage of yours come into the story?''

Bella thought about the cozy little house, the sweetness of the children and Dan's tender lovemaking.

In many ways, life with Dan Gibson seemed ordinary and comfortable. But Luciana was right—the situation was completely bizarre.

''Dan and I made a deal,'' she said. ''I needed a new legal name I could use to put together a passable ID that wouldn't tip Eric off to what I was doing. That way I could leave the country without him knowing.''

''And marrying Dan Gibson provides you with the name,'' Luciana said, looking bemused. ''But what did you supply as your part of the bargain?''

''I was supposed to give him enough money to buy a new irrigation pump, plus three months of child care and housekeeping while he gets his life in order.''

''Child care and housekeeping? Isabel Delgado?'' Luciana threw back her head and gave a rich peal of laughter.

Bella smiled ruefully. ''I know, our upbringing hardly qualified us to be efficient domestic types, did it? But you know, Luce, it's actually kind of fun.

Cooking and washing and all that. I sort of like it, and I really love Dan's kids.''

Luciana's face softened, and she reached out to take Bella's hand. ''Isabel, you were always such a good person,'' she said, then sat back in the chair, looking businesslike again. ''So you were supposed to keep house and baby-sit for Dan Gibson in exchange for a legal name?''

''Yes, but I can't stay long enough to keep my part of the bargain.''

''Why?''

''Because of Eric and...some other things,'' Bella said, her cheeks warming.

''So what are you going to do?''

''I'm going to give Dan some money. A lot of money, actually.'' Bella lowered her voice and glanced automatically over her shoulder. ''But he doesn't know that. After I'm safely out of the country, I'll send the money without a return address.''

''When are you leaving?'' Luciana asked.

Bella shifted uneasily in the chair. ''As soon as I can, probably before the end of the week. I'm scared Eric's going to find me if I stay much longer, and I don't want that to happen around Dan's kids.''

''How would he ever find you in a backwater like Crystal Creek?''

''Don't forget he's a policeman, Luce. The man has contacts everywhere and all the power of the state behind him. Besides, they got a good look at Dan up in Abilene when he went to ask about the stuff in my locker. This very moment, Eric could be...''

Bella shuddered and fell silent.

Her sister watched her gravely. "You were telling me your plans," she prompted after a moment.

"On Wednesday morning, Dan and I are driving to San Antonio so I can clear out my safe-deposit box. As soon as I have the cash, I'll buy a plane ticket to Canada and fly there the next day."

"Where will you go in Canada?"

Bella shrugged. "I haven't given it much thought. Probably I'll stay in Banff for a while. Remember how beautiful it used to be when we went up there for skiing holidays?"

"And if you're living in Canada with the legal name of Bella Gibson, you think Eric won't be able to find you?"

"I hope not. I don't know what kind of life I'll have," she added, "but at least I'll be safe."

Luciana watched her shrewdly, then looked down at her desk. She picked up a pen and toyed with it. "Well, I'm sure you didn't come here to tell me all this," she said at last. "In fact, I believe you were as shocked as I was to find out Ms. Osborne was your long-lost sister."

Again Bella glanced behind her at the closed door.

"Luce," she said earnestly, leaning across the desk, "we can't let anybody know about this. Not a soul in the world. For all I know, Eric might have tracked you down long ago and be watching you right now to see if I turn up in your life."

Luciana gave her a tired smile. "Honey, I've got problems of my own. And no matter how much I love you, the last thing I can afford to do is get involved with the rest of my family again. You can be sure I'm going to keep your secret."

"And you'll understand if I don't…" Bella paused awkwardly.

"If you need to keep your distance from me, I'll understand better than anybody else in the world," Luciana assured her. "Now, why don't you just tell me your reason for being here?"

Bella hesitated, uncertain how to switch gears and begin dealing with Ellie's problems.

"It must have something to do with Ellie," Luciana prompted.

"How did you know that?"

"Because she's the only one of Dan Gibson's children who's a student in my school," Luciana said dryly, "and I'm assuming you came here to my office today as a parent, not a sister."

"Yes, Ellie's having a problem," Bella said, briefly startled and pleased to be described as a parent. "It involves a boy named Cody Pollock."

"I see. Well, then, tell me the problem." Lucia leaned forward, her blue eyes level and intent.

"Poor Ellie's been going though hell, and she's afraid to tell her father about it."

As Bella described the problem, Luciana listened in silence, her mouth firm with disapproval. When Bella concluded, Luciana sat back in her chair.

"You know, I suspected something like this might be going on," she said. "After the incident in the library when Cody claimed Ellie hit him without provocation, I wondered. It just seemed so unlike her."

"Yes, it is."

"I called the farm over that incident," Luciana said. "Was it you who answered the phone?"

Bella nodded, shivering at the memory. "We actually spoke to each other. You know, I had a feeling that voice on the phone was familiar, but I couldn't think who it was, so I put the whole thing out of my mind."

"Isn't that odd?" Luciana mused. "I didn't recognize your voice at all. But then, in the years since I left home, you've changed from a child to a woman."

"Yes, I guess I have. Tell me, Luce, why did you happen to pick this job and this school?"

"I always wanted to support myself so I'd never need any family money as long as I lived. I got myself the proper training, and when this middle-school principalship at Crystal Creek was advertised eight years ago, it seemed like the perfect job. Remember how much we both loved visiting the McKinney ranch when we were kids?"

"Yes," Bella said with a wistful smile. "I remember. So do you like your job, Luce? Is your life happy?"

Her sister's face looked sad and distant. "My life is pleasant and uneventful," she said. "Nothing much worth talking about. But our concern is with Ellie at the moment, right?" She paused. "So what kind of threats has Cody been making to her?"

"Sexual ones," Bella said bluntly.

Luciana's face hardened. "That won't be tolerated," she said. "I talked with June Pollock recently about Cody's behavior. June's very upset with him, and we've agreed neither of us is willing to put up with any more. This is definitely the last straw."

Luciana tapped her pen on her desk while Bella watched her in silence.

"I need to call Ellie in," the principal said at last. "Before I talk to June, I'll want confirmation that the boy has actually said and done these things. That behavior is grounds for expulsion."

"Ellie will be terrified," Bella said. "She seems so intimidated by you."

"She's a good girl," Luciana said, "and one of the brightest in the school. I hate to think what the poor child's been suffering at the hands of that lout."

She got up from behind the desk and moved to the door, her figure as graceful and elegant as Bella remembered.

"Leslie," the principal said, popping her head into the outer office, "could you have Ellie Gibson sent to the office, please?"

Luciana sat down behind her desk again, and she and Bella talked about inconsequential things while they waited. The years rolled away as Bella entertained her sister with stories of her growing prowess as a homemaker in Dan Gibson's house and her first attempts at cooking.

Luciana laughed at first, then listened in thoughtful silence, tapping the pen on her desk blotter again with a faraway expression.

Finally there was a knock on the door and Ellie came in, looking pale and frightened. She sat in the chair next to Bella, who gripped the girl's hand and gave her a reassuring smile.

Luciana began to question the child gently. She was good at her job, and soon Bella saw Ellie's nervousness fade away as the girl responded. She still, however, seemed to find it hard to meet the gaze of the beautiful woman behind the desk.

When Ellie was finished, Luciana came around the desk and put an arm around her thin shoulders.

"I'm so sorry about all this, Ellie," she said. "If I had known what was going on, I would have put a stop to it a lot sooner. But you can be absolutely sure that Cody Pollock will not bother you again."

Ellie gazed up at the principal. "Really?" she breathed.

"Absolutely. In fact," Luciana said, returning to her desk, "don't tell anybody just yet, but I think Mr. Pollock will probably be on his way back to Lampasas by tomorrow. Now, you may return to your classroom."

Ellie's face blazed with happiness. She paused to give Bella a fierce hug and a shy kiss, then rushed from the room while the two women sat smiling at the door where she'd vanished.

"So," Luciana said at last, "you're leaving on Wednesday?"

"I hope so." Bella got to her feet. "I might not be able to contact you right away, Luce," she said, "but sometime after I'm settled…"

"I'll wait to hear from you," Luciana said quietly. "Will you be in touch with Dan?"

Bella felt pain knotting in the pit of her stomach as she fought back tears.

"No, I can't involve him and the kids in my problems any more than I already have. When I leave, that's going to be the end of our relationship, except for sending him some money."

Luciana looked at her keenly. "And will that be

hard for you, not having any further contact with Dan and his children?''

Bella knew that if she stayed any longer under her sister's keen, sympathetic gaze, she was going to burst into tears again.

''I'll be fine,'' was all she said, moving toward the door. ''Thanks for taking care of Ellie.''

''Isabel, there's more than one way to deal with a bully,'' Luciana said gently. ''Running away isn't always the answer. Sometimes you can get help by asking for it, the way Ellie did.''

''The bully who's been threatening Ellie doesn't have a police badge,'' Bella said. ''I really have no choice, Luce.''

Her sister nodded gravely. Bella crossed the room to give her a hug, then escaped into the school hallway.

She wandered outside, struggling to compose herself before she had to walk down and meet Dan and Josh in the restaurant.

CHAPTER SEVENTEEN

ON WEDNESDAY, Dan awoke in the coolness of early dawn and lay watching the pale light at the windows, listening to the birds.

The house seemed empty and peaceful, as it always did when the kids were away. He'd taken them the night before to stay with Mary and Bubba for a while, because today he and Bella were driving to San Antonio. She would recover her money from the safe-deposit box and purchase a plane ticket.

Tonight he'd drive back home alone, and Bella would be gone forever from his life.

He turned to look at her as she slept. She lay close to him, her face sweet and gentle in repose. Dan smiled, his heart aching, and leaned over to drop a kiss on her hair. People who joked about how women looked in the morning without their makeup had never lived with a woman like Bella.

But his memories of the night before, their final night of lovemaking, belied the gentle sweetness. When Bella was sexually aroused, this woman was a tiger in bed. They'd done things together that he'd never experienced before.

Now, just thinking about it brought him fully erect, aching with renewed lust.

He kissed her again, this time with more purpose. Her eyes fluttered open.

"Mmm," she murmured, then nestled closer to him and licked his neck drowsily.

The feeling of her tongue drove him wild. He rolled over on top of her, knowing how responsive she was when she first awoke. There was no need of foreplay, a good thing, considering his urgency.

He entered her smoothly, gasping at the damp silkiness as she enfolded and gripped him.

"Bella," he whispered against her ear. "Sweetheart, are you awake?"

"No, I'm dreaming." She sighed blissfully, her breath warm against his throat. "Such a lovely dream. Oh," she added with a little moan, "keep doing it just like that. Oh, Dan…"

"This way?" he measured his stroke, knowing the pace she liked.

Her body began to move against his, so well tuned to him that she could have been designed expressly for his pleasure. With one foot she kicked the covers away, leaving both of them free to roll and move in the bed. Then her legs wrapped around his waist, and her heels began to drum softly on his back.

Dan laughed, holding her close while he continued the careful rhythm that was bringing her to a fever of response.

"You're so delicious," he told her. "I could never get enough of you if we had a whole lifetime to make love."

She was silent, and when he drew away to look at her, he could tell she was near climax. Her breasts and cheeks were flushed, and her eyes were closed in rapture.

The sight of her arousal was too much for Dan to bear. He finished in a massive explosion of feeling, then lay on top of her, his body shaken by additional bursts of pleasure.

"I don't know how you do this to me," he told her, drawing her hair back to whisper in her ear. "After you make me come the first time, it just goes on and on. You're like some kind of enchantress."

"Or a witch," she said, and he could hear the bubble of laughter in her voice. "At least I keep you coming back, Dan."

"You could always keep me coming back," he told her. "Just say the word, and I'd cross the earth to have you again, Bella."

She opened her eyes and leaned up on one elbow, her face sad.

"It's Wednesday, isn't it?"

Dan nodded. "Yes. Have you changed your mind?"

"Dan, I can't change my mind. You know how dangerous it is for me to be here."

She turned away to stare at the window while he studied her profile. After a moment he reached out to trail a finger along the dainty line of her nose, then over the fullness of her lower lip and down toward her breasts.

"Bella…"

"What?" she asked, still not looking at him, though he heard the threat of tears in her voice.

"You know that kid the principal sent away yesterday, the bully who was picking on Ellie?"

"What about him?"

"Well," Dan said, touching her mouth again, "I still think there's probably more to the story than you've told me, but I'm satisfied it's okay because Ellie seems so happy now. I just wanted to ask you…" He hesitated again.

She glanced at him expectantly, then turned her head away again.

"You told me," Dan went on at last, "how the principal said there was more than one way to deal with a bully."

"Yes, I did," she said cautiously.

"Well, have you given that any thought? Don't you think we could do something about this guy so you wouldn't need to keep running?"

"What can we do?" she asked bitterly. "Go to the police?"

"I'm not afraid to deal one-on-one with this bastard," Dan said. "You only have to say the word, and I'll be in Austin this afternoon. And I don't believe he'd bother you again."

This time she turned to gaze at him earnestly. "Don't even think about it," she said. "I'm leaving today, Dan. By tonight I'll be far away, and then Eric will never be a part of your life or get anywhere close to your family."

Dan held her chin and forced her to keep looking at him. "Tell me the truth," he said quietly.

"What about?"

"Is this all about Eric, Bella?" he asked. "Or is part of it the money?"

"What money?"

"I think you're reluctant to make any kind of commitment to me because my life's too different from what you've always known.''

She pulled away from him and turned her back, staring out the window. Dan caressed her slim shoulder, forcing himself to say the painful things in his mind.

''I keep thinking, Bella, that maybe deep down you're actually glad of the chance to get away from me. We may be great in bed, but this isn't the life you want to lead, is it?''

She murmured something, and he leaned closer.

''What did you say, Bella? I didn't hear you.''

''I said, you're right,'' she told him over her shoulder. ''I could never live this way. Such a shabby little house, and only one bathroom, and the responsibility of these kids all the time... It just not my style.''

''I thought you liked housekeeping and looking after the kids,'' he said. ''You keep telling me how much fun it is.''

She gazed out the window so he couldn't see her face.

''What's going on, Bella? Were you just pretending?''

She shrugged, still not looking at him. ''It might have been fun for a week or two, but hardly for a lifetime. Come on, Dan. Surely you realize that.''

His throat constricted with pain. ''I thought so.'' Dan tried to keep his voice casual as he climbed out of bed and pulled on his shorts. ''I'll go out and hurry through the chores,'' he told her. ''You make some breakfast and pack your things so we can get on the road.''

''What things?'' she asked, getting up. ''I don't

have anything at all to pack. Which is just as well,''
she added with a sad little smile, "because I don't
have anything to pack stuff in, either.''

He looked away hastily from her naked body,
cursing the aching hunger that never seemed to ease,
no matter how often they made love.

"You'll have to take some clothes," he said, "at
least until you get a chance to buy your own. I'll
give you one of the kid's duffel bags."

"Thank you," she muttered with an odd formality,
bending to pull on her panties and denim shorts. She
still refused to look at him, and Dan knew both of
them were thinking about her chilling admission that
his life was too poor and humble for her.

He lingered in the doorway, watching her dress for
the last time. "I'll be in as soon as I can," he said.

"I'll be ready." She headed for the bathroom.
"Let's get this over with."

BY MIDMORNING, they were at the outskirts of San
Antonio. Bella looked around at the square-fronted
adobe houses, the vine-covered buildings and sleepy,
sun-washed look of the suburbs.

It seemed like years since she'd left this city to
embark on her desperate adventure, and now she was
back for the last time. Who knew when she'd ever
see her hometown again?

Or Dan Gibson and his children, and the little
farmhouse that was the place she would carry in her
heart for the rest of her life.

She shifted on the truck seat, pleating the denim
of her jeans with tense fingers, still thinking about
the early-morning scene in the bedroom, while Dan

drove through more residential areas toward the downtown commercial district.

Dan had been so easily convinced that his life was too modest for her. He must have known very little about her, even though he was a marvelously intuitive lover. Otherwise, how could he possibly believe she would reject him because of his financial situation?

He was passionate, honorable, considerate, tender—everything a man should be. In fact, Dan Gibson was perfect.

And if he'd ever given any indication of loving her, not just sexually but emotionally, as well, Bella would have been lost. But she suspected that in his secret heart he was probably relieved to have her gone from his life, along with all her unsavory baggage. Because if he felt any reluctance about her imminent departure, he was certainly hiding it well.

"Here we are," he said. "I'll find a place to park, then come back and wait for you right there." He indicated a wrought-iron bench outside the bank building, under a row of hanging baskets that trailed flowers and greenery.

"Make sure you get at least an hour of parking," Bella told him, gripping the door handle. "There are a couple of travel agents just down the street, so we can buy a plane ticket as soon as I have my money."

"Fine," he said without emotion, watching as she got out and stood holding the door.

She looked at his face. "Dan…"

"You'd better go, Bella." He shifted the truck into gear. "We're blocking traffic."

She closed the door and watched him drive away,

then pulled her baseball cap low over her eyes and walked into the bank.

The place seemed both familiar and oddly strange. The ceiling soared overhead, at least five stories high in the outer foyer, which was decorated with ceramic murals of Western life and Texas history. Bella crossed to a counter in front of the room where the safe-deposit boxes were kept. "I'd like to access my box," she said to the man standing there.

"Name, please?"

Bella looked around nervously. Nobody was in sight, though she could see a number of cubicles nearby, lined with cork walls that concealed their occupants. None of them seemed to be within earshot. Isabel knew she had no choice. If she wanted to get to that box, she had to identify herself to the attendant.

"Isabel Delgado," she murmured, leaning forward.

The man's eyes flickered a little but he made no comment, simply entered her name on a computer keyboard and indicated the scanner set into a bank of controls near his elbow.

"Could you press the ball of your right index finger on the scanner, please?"

Bella obeyed, then followed the man as he took a set of keys and led her to the door behind his desk. He opened it to admit her, locked it behind them and led Bella to a bank of metal drawers, each bearing a numbered keypad.

"Do you remember your numerical combination, Ms. Delgado?"

"Yes, I do." She entered the numbers of her

mother's birthdate and watched as the drawer clicked softly. The bank attendant pulled it out on smooth rollers, then stepped away to wait at a small desk near the locked door.

Bella removed a metal box from the drawer and carried it to a table in the center of the room. She leafed through the contents, checking them against a master list in a compartment at the front.

Everything was in order, and nothing seemed to have been touched. The largest manila envelope contained almost three hundred thousand dollars in cash, mostly in thousand-dollar bills. After a brief hesitation, Bella took all of the money, as well as a smaller envelope full of cut diamonds.

The stock certificates had a face value of close to two million dollars, and most of them were the shares in their family company that had belonged to her mother. Bella knew her father would happily pay twice the face value to get those stocks in his own name and control a commanding block of his own company.

What a pity she could never let him know where she was, Bella thought grimly. Still, the face value was nothing to be sneezed at. Once she was settled, she'd find somebody to sell the stock for her and send Dan Gibson a cashier's check for one million dollars.

Bella allowed herself a wistful smile, picturing the look on his face when he drove up to get the mail one morning, with Gypsy riding in the box of his truck, and found an envelope containing all that money from an undisclosed source.

Of course Dan would know where the money

came from, but he'd have no way to track her down and return it.

And then all his worries would be over. He could pay off his mortgage, fix up the house, buy new farm equipment and things for the children, even take them on a holiday.

Briefly, Bella wondered if she could put a little note in with the check. Nothing extensive enough to reveal her whereabouts, of course. Just a letter saying, "Darling, I love you, and I always will."

But that was a luxury Bella knew she could never allow herself.

He doesn't love you, she told herself firmly. *It was just a crazy adventure, a week of marvelous sex, but now it's over.*

After some further hesitation, she put all the remaining contents of the box into a second big envelope, even her mother's birth certificate and marriage license. She might need them someday, and who knew when she'd ever be back in Texas?

"Thank you," she said to the attendant, crossing the room with her two envelopes. "I'm ready to leave now, and I won't be needing the box anymore. I've removed all the contents."

"The rental was paid for a full year, so there'll be a refund," he said as he got up to unlock the door.

"I don't want the refund," Bella told him.

"Perhaps if you'd care to leave a forwarding address, we could—"

"No, I'm in a hurry."

Silently he held the door for her, then stood watching as she left. Nobody else seemed to take the slightest notice as a young woman in faded blue jeans, plaid shirt and a baseball cap walked out of the bank carrying more than two million dollars.

BELLA HAD A BRIEF MOMENT of panic as she left the cool interior of the huge building and came out onto the sun-washed street. Dan wasn't on the bench, and there was no sign of his truck.

But he appeared almost at once, ambling toward her from the direction of an umbrella-covered hot-dog stand. He carried a box filled with wrapped hot dogs, fries and soft drinks.

"I thought this would be a quick way to have lunch," he told her. "And I put lots of sauerkraut in yours, just the way you like."

"You're my dream man," she said, keeping her voice deliberately light. "Where shall we eat?"

"There's a little park just around the corner."

Bella smiled sadly. "Yes, I remember that park. My nanny used to take me down there when I got cranky on shopping trips."

She walked beside him, clutching her two envelopes. Dan glanced down at them. "Any problems?"

"None at all. Everything's here. I cleaned out the box."

He looked around nervously. "Is it safe for you to carry it out in the open like this?"

"I don't have much choice at the moment," she said. "But I'll be glad when I'm out of the country and it's all stashed in a bank somewhere."

They sat on the grass in the little park with the envelopes tucked between them, eating their hot dogs and chatting amiably.

As always, Bella was struck by the simple pleasure

of just being with him. Dan had such a quirky out-look on life, a droll humor that made her chuckle, even in the midst of her deepest sadness. And he loved to argue about politics, religion, even the weather.

"Did you know that you argue for the sake of arguing?" she asked. "If I say something, you'll take the opposite view just to get me going."

He gave her a grin, his eyes very green in the sunlight. "That's not the way to get you going, sweetheart."

Her cheeks warmed. "You know what I mean. You'd argue black was white, just to annoy me."

"That's not argument." He lay on his back and extended his legs. "That's debating."

"I see." She fed him the last of her hot dog and he chewed it gravely, his eyes closed, hands behind his head. A withered leaf caught in his hair. Bella leaned over to brush it away, then let her hand rest for a moment on his cheek.

"This is nice," he said, grasping her hand and turning it over to kiss the palm before releasing it. "I should take holidays more often."

Bella looked down at his beloved face. The poor man considered a day in the city a holiday. She thought of the wonderful things they could do with just a small portion of the money in those envelopes. They could pack up the kids and take them to a private island for a month, or go on a luxury family cruise around the world.

"I wish..." she began, then caught herself.

"What?" he opened one eye and squinted at her.

"Nothing."

Bella gathered the residue of their picnic, deposited it in a trash bin and came back to scoop up the two envelopes.

"Come on, Dan," she said, picking up his hand and tugging. "Let's go buy a plane ticket."

There were three travel agencies on the nearby streets, but apparently none of them could find an acceptable seat on any out-of-state flight leaving San Antonio that day.

"Here's one that's going to Oklahoma City," an agent said, frowning at her computer screen. "It leaves the city at four-fifteen. That's less than a couple of hours from now."

Bella shook her head and drew Dan away from the counter. "Oklahoma City's too close," she whispered. "When I get off that flight, I want to be a long way from Texas."

"Here's one! I have a vacancy on an American Airlines flight leaving Austin tomorrow morning at ten-twelve," the agent called. "And it has a Canadian destination, just like you asked for."

"Which Canadian city is it flying to?" Bella asked, moving back to the counter.

"Calgary, Alberta."

"That's perfect. I'll take it."

"But it's first class," the woman said, "and the tickets are—"

"Whatever," Bella told her hastily, rummaging in the envelope bulging with cash. "Please, just get me that ticket."

When they left the agency and started down the street toward the parking lot, she felt no relief, just misery. "By this time tomorrow," she told Dan, "I'll be heading for Canada. I'll be safe."

"Meanwhile we have one more night together," he whispered, putting an arm around her shoulders.

She tensed, clutching the manila envelopes in her arms.

Dan smiled down at her, though his eyes were sad. "Come on, Bella, it's only an hour's drive from the farm to Austin, and the kids are staying with Mary overnight. You might as well spend the night with me and I'll drive you to the airport in the morning."

She hesitated, wondering if it was safe to go back to the farm. What if somebody had seen them here in the city and made note of Dan's license plate? What if—

"Stop worrying," he told her. "You're safe. Nobody's seen us, and tomorrow you'll be gone. Just give me tonight, Bella."

At the note of pleading in his voice, she was undone. "All right," she said. "One more night. Come on, let's go home."

CHAPTER EIGHTEEN

ERIC MATTHIAS GLARED at the file on his desk. He was dealing with a disciplinary matter, involving two cops who'd been accused of unnecessary brutality in their handling of a robbery suspect.

He hated the whole matter, and most of all the fact that the police were increasingly held hostage by the whims of a public who simply didn't understand the dangers and stresses of the job.

The fact was, this punk had robbed a liquor store at gunpoint and suffered his injuries while resisting arrest. In Eric's opinion the punk deserved whatever happened to him. But instead, as acting lieutenant, Eric was forced to review the file and decide on disciplinary action against his own men.

The whole prospect made him tired and irritable, and the beginnings of a headache began to stab at his left temple. When the phone rang, he snatched it up, then winced at a distant crackle of static.

"What?" he said sharply. "This is a bad connection. Who's calling?"

"It's me," a voice said breathlessly, coming in a little more clearly now. "It's Manny Solvito. I got her, Eric."

"You what?"

"I got Isabel. We picked up her trail at the bank, and I'm following them now."

Eric's palms began to sweat, and his heart thudded. All trace of the headache vanished in a flood of excitement. "Where are you?" He lowered his voice and glanced through the window at the squad room.

"I'm on the I-10, heading northwest from San Antonio toward Fredericksburg. She's in a truck just ahead of me with her farmer."

"Have they seen you?"

"No way. Hell, them two lovebirds can't see nothin' but each other."

Pain burned in Eric's belly. "How did you pick her up?"

"She went into the bank to get her stuff from the safe-deposit box, just like we hoped. My girlfriend was quick enough to spot her, even though Isabel's hair is short and she's wearing torn blue jeans and a ratty old baseball cap."

"You're sure it's Isabel?"

"My contact in the bank checked her name on the computer when she was inside with the attendant. Isabel spent about ten minutes in the locked room, then came out carrying two big envelopes. By that time my girl had contacted me, and I was already down in my car across the street from the bank."

"Good man," Eric clutched the phone tensely. "What did she do when she left the bank?"

"The farmer was waiting for her with a box of hot dogs. They went to that little park down the street from the bank and had themselves a picnic."

"A picnic?"

"They lay around on the grass, laughing and holding hands. It was a real sweet sight."

"What does this farmer look like?" Eric asked, his throat tight with jealousy.

"Oh, he's a big, good-looking guy. Sort of a Harrison Ford type. Anybody can tell Isabel's nuts about the guy. She could hardly keep her hands off him."

Eric's heart began to thud so erratically that he wondered if he was on the verge of some kind of attack.

"Eric?" the investigator shouted through rising static. "You still there?"

"I'm here. So what did Isabel do after this picnic?"

"She and the farmer went down the street to visit a couple of travel agencies, then went back to their truck. It looks like they're planning to take off with Isabel's money."

"They're not going anywhere," Eric said grimly. "But if she's already bought a plane ticket, we need to move fast."

"I can't hear you!" Manny shouted. "Look, I didn't have time to go inside the agency and find out what kind of tickets they bought. I'm on my own this afternoon and I didn't want to risk losing them. I had to stay on their tail."

"That's fine," Eric said. "You're doing great, Manny. Just keep them in sight. I'm on my way to catch up with you."

"You'll stay in touch? I need you within cellphone range."

"I'll be in touch. What I plan to do," Eric said, thinking rapidly as he began to pace the floor, "is

take an unmarked car and head for Fredericksburg.
That way I'll be in position to follow them if they
head to Abilene or take the cutoff up to Brownville
or Stephenwood. You have no idea which way they
might be heading?"

"None at all," Manny said. "They're just driving
along, talking and looking at the scenery like a couple of tourists. She's got her hand on his shoulder,
and she keeps touching his hair."

The tenderness and intimacy of this simple gesture
made Eric close his eyes and press a hand to his
forehead. He was chilled and sweating.

"Can you see the tag on that truck?" he asked.
"Pull up close enough to read it for me, then drop
back right away."

Manny did so, and Eric jotted the license-plate
number down.

"Okay, got it," he muttered. "I'm heading out.
Call me back in ten minutes, I should be on the road
by then. And, Manny?"

"Yeah," the investigator said, his voice growing
faint again.

"Don't lose that truck, or you won't ever see another penny from me."

Eric clicked off the phone and knotted his tie. He
withdrew his service revolver from its concealed
shoulder holster and looked at it with a twinge of
anxiety.

The way he felt right now, taking the gun was
probably not a good idea. When he pictured Isabel
with that other man, his anger rose to a level that
frightened him. Besides, he'd already be in enough
trouble if anybody discovered him using an un-

marked car to track his ex-wife. A rational part of his mind told him the whole project was crazy, irrational behavior.

But when he thought of Isabel's face, her sexy body, that elusive spirit of hers that he'd never been able to hold on to...

Isabel had a plane ticket. She was leaving Texas, probably tomorrow. Without further thought, Eric jammed the gun back into its holster, grabbed his car keys and hurried from the office.

"I need to head out of town right away," he told the unit receptionist. "I'm afraid my ex-wife might be in danger. Could you get somebody to run a license-plate check for me, Marian?"

He gave her the number, then worried briefly whether this was going to leave a clear trail back to him if anything went wrong.

But, of course, nothing would go wrong. He just needed to confront her, tell her his side of things and convince her that she really belonged with him. Isabel would leave that farmer behind soon enough if she could only understand how desperately Eric needed his wife and how much he wanted her back.

Soon he was in the car, pulling out of the police parking lot and heading off across the city toward the exit to the highway that ran through Dripping Springs and on to Fredericksburg. He drove through the autumn countryside like a man in a dream, her face and eyes filling his mind.

The police radio and the cell phone sounded at the same time. Eric flipped open the phone and said, "Hold on, Manny," then took down the information from the police computer.

The registered owner of the truck was Daniel Gibson. He had a rural route address, near Crystal Creek up in Claro County.

Eric nodded and flipped open the cell phone. "Manny?" he said. "You still got them?"

"I'm on their tail. Traffic's thinned out a bit up here so I had to drop back a few more lengths."

"You'll be able to see in time if they turn off?"

"Sure I will. Look, this ain't my first tail, Eric," the PI said. "I've done this a time or two before, you know."

"Just don't lose them. I think they're heading toward Crystal Creek, but I need to know exactly where the guy lives."

"I'm on it," Manny said. "If they're on the way to Crystal Creek, they'll be taking the Fredericksburg turnoff."

"I'll be somewhere behind you. Keep them in sight and don't lose them. Call me if anything happens."

Eric folded the cell phone, then turned off the police radio, as well, wanting to be alone with his thoughts for a while.

He'd never known such depths of pain. Emotions surged and boiled within him, completely out of control. Again he pictured Isabel riding with the farmer and resting her hand on the man's shoulder, caressing his hair. Acid rose in his throat, almost choking him.

She must have been sleeping with the guy all this time, maybe even while she was still married to *him*. How else could she have found the guy so soon after her staged disappearance? Because, of course, this farmer had to be the same man who'd turned up in the bus depot in Abilene, asking about the contents of her locker.

Eric pictured the two of them lying in bed, naked and sweaty from lovemaking, talking about him and laughing at how they'd fooled him.

"Oh, God, Isabel." He groaned aloud, opening the car window to let the wind rush though his hair and cool his hot face. "How can you do this to me?"

Manny reported at intervals while the two people in the farm truck drove though Fredericksburg, apparently unaware of the vehicle following just a few car lengths behind, then headed north toward Crystal Creek.

Eric took the cutoff at Johnson City to save time and headed into Claro County, his heart pounding as he realized how quickly he was closing the gap between the truck and his unmarked police car.

After all this time, the woman was only minutes away from him. He felt a fierce excitement, a thrill that sang in his ears and danced in scarlet waves before his eyes.

Manny kept reporting as he followed the truck through the town of Crystal Creek and back out onto the highway, slowing to a safe distance as his quarry turned and drove onto a crushed stone road leading to a farm, mostly invisible below the curve of the hill and a screen of trees.

"I'm at the entry gate now. It says D. Gibson on the mailbox."

"That's the place," Eric said. "I'm still almost a half hour south of Crystal Creek. Tell me how to get to the farm entrance."

Manny gave instructions and Eric listened carefully, then clicked the phone off for the last time. Twenty-five minutes later, he crested a hill and saw Manny's little car parked at the side of the road. Manny was outside his car, squatted by the front wheel with a tire iron in his hand.

Eric pulled to the shoulder behind him and walked over casually, hands in his pockets, glancing around. If anybody saw them, he was simply a passing motorist who'd paused to give a hand to somebody in trouble.

"Do you think there's any other vehicle exit from the farm?" he asked the PI, standing and watching as Manny pretended to tighten the lugs on his tire.

Manny shook his head. "I walked up that rise while I was waiting, and I could see the buildings. The river runs by to the west, and the place has steep cliffs on the other side. You could maybe get out by going cross-country, but it'd be a rough trip."

"You're sure they haven't seen you?"

"Positive."

A minivan passed, and Manny concentrated on the tire again while Eric knelt, pretending to help.

"They stopped on the way in to pick up their mail," the investigator muttered over his shoulder. "That's not the kind of thing you'd do if you thought somebody was on your tail."

"So if they bought plane tickets, they're obviously not leaving tonight. There wouldn't be time to get to any major airport."

"That's what I figured."

Eric frowned at the fields with their clumps of mesquite and peaceful herds of grazing cattle. "I'm going to hide my car in that approach," he said, jerking a thumb over his shoulder, ''and then head out to find a position overlooking the buildings. You stay here and watch the road. Don't call me unless it's an emergency, because I want to get close to the house and they might hear the phone.''

''What should I do if they try to leave?''

''Stop them,'' Eric said curtly. ''Find a way to detain them here.''

Something in his face obviously alarmed the other man, who licked his lips and glanced around nervously, still kneeling by the front wheel.

''Look, Eric,'' Manny said at last, ''I really don't want to—''

''You've got nothing to worry about,'' Eric told him, taking deep breaths to calm himself. ''Nothing bad is going to happen, Manny. I just need to talk with her, that's all.''

He turned on his heel and walked back to his car, pulling it off the road and into the shelter of a heavy growth of vines and shrubs. Trailing branches enclosed the car and almost prevented him from climbing out.

At last he made his way by foot over the rough terrain, creeping closer until he settled into a rocky outcrop less than fifty feet above the farm buildings.

He had a clear view of the small house below him, outlined vividly by the setting sun. A light blazed suddenly at a rear window, a kitchen he thought, and he could make out the form of Isabel's body, almost see her face.

He caught his breath, staring avidly through a screen of brush. She looked different somehow, though her body was as slim and curved as ever, even in the jeans and cotton shirt. Her hair was cut in a boyish style that gave her a winsome look.

Eric had forgotten how long and graceful her neck was. His hands fisted involuntarily, as he imagined the pleasure of squeezing that fragile throat.

The thought alarmed him, and he shook his head to clear it. Sweat broke out on his forehead, and his heart stopped beating for a moment when a man appeared in the room and headed for the door, pausing to say something to Isabel as he passed.

She laughed and replied, then moved to the stove and began to stir something in a saucepan.

Eric's jaw dropped.

Isabel was cooking?

When they were married, she hadn't even known how to boil water. He'd never met a woman who had so few homemaking skills.

And now she cooked for this farmer?

It was unendurable, the final insult.

His pain mounted as the man came back to drop an arm around her shoulder and kiss that slender neck, then cup one of her breasts and bend to nuzzle it. She leaned against him, still holding her mixing spoon, and lifted her face to his for a long kiss.

Eric groaned. He was shaken by a sudden urge to pull out his revolver and fire through the window at them.

"I shouldn't have brought the gun," he whispered. "I should have left the damn thing behind in the trunk of my car."

The two people in the window stood close together at the stove, wrapped in each other's arms, and seemed to be talking. The whole scene was cozy and domestic, like that of a long-married couple.

His jealousy grew. Cautiously he crept from his hiding place and began to edge down the hillside, then drew back in haste when the man headed for the door.

"Bella, I'm taking the truck and driving up to check on that mare," the farmer called from outside. "I'll be back in fifteen minutes or so."

"Well, don't be gone long, sweetheart," she said. Both her voice and the words were like flicks of a whip on Eric's already raw emotions.

He edged toward the house, moving from one dark pool of shadow to another.

DAN STRODE TO THE TRUCK, near where Gypsy lay on her bed of sacking by the barn, her chin resting listlessly on her front paws. She was taking a long time to recover from surgery, and Dan was afraid she might have picked up some kind of infection. If she didn't look better by tomorrow morning, he'd have to take her to the vet.

Then he remembered, with sickening impact, that he was going to drive Bella to the airport in the morning. By this time tomorrow she would be far away and he'd never see her again.

It was hard to believe life would go on, he thought, watching as Gypsy climbed heavily into the box of the truck to ride with him to the horse pasture.

Veterinary appointments would be kept, and sick animals would recover. There'd be new calves and foals, crops to harvest and beehives to move. The kids would grow and change, and life would go on.

But Dan Gibson's heart would be dead.

The moonlit river had carried this woman to him, and she'd shown him a kind of love and happiness he'd only dreamed of. Touched places in his soul he'd never even known existed.

The prospect of her leaving was unbearable. And how was he going to tell the kids she was gone? They'd all fallen in love with her, even Ellie. They were going to be heartbroken.

When the collie was settled in the box of the truck, he drove slowly around the barn and set off across the rutted trail to the horse pasture, wondering how he was going to get through this last night without breaking down and sobbing in her arms.

IF SHE WAS VERY CAREFUL, Bella could keep the reality of her imminent departure out of her mind by concentrating on small things, like setting the table nicely and preparing the evening meal.

She took a couple of steaks from the meat compartment and went outside to check the barbecue, which Dan had started earlier. The coals seemed hot enough, but still, it would probably be best to wait until he got back to put the steaks on; they both preferred their meat rare.

She heard a noise from the cliffs overhead and looked up sharply. It was a small rockfall, probably caused by cattle up on the ridge.

Twilight had deepened and the rugged cliffs were growing darker, illuminated here and there by rays of dying sunlight. As she watched, the light faded and the hills were plunged into shadow. The breeze freshened and Bella shivered a little, hugging her arms, then hurried back into the house.

She stirred the pasta mix in the saucepan, and began to fry some mushrooms in Dan's cast-iron frying pan, briefly diverted by the way they sizzled and browned. Then she set the table, checked her watch and got out another saucepan to cook some frozen green beans. She had to hurry, because Dan would be back soon.

Just as she formed the thought, she heard him in the porch and her heart leaped with joy as it always did at his approach.

"Hi, darling!" she called. "Wait till you see the mushrooms! They're so—" She turned and froze in horror, the words dying on her lips.

Eric Matthias stood in the entry to the kitchen, staring hungrily at her.

CHAPTER NINETEEN

"HOW NICE TO HEAR," Eric said with an odd, strained smile that Bella found more frightening than a spoken threat. "It's been such a long time since you called me 'darling.'"

She looked wildly around the kitchen, searching for an escape or a weapon, anything to prevent what she feared was about to happen. She grasped the hot cast-iron pan of mushrooms.

Eric glanced at her makeshift weapon, then still wearing that same mirthless smile, moved a few steps closer.

"Are you afraid of me, Isabel?" he asked.

"Yes, I am." She backed against the stove with the pan gripped tightly in her hands. "I've been afraid of you for years."

"Why?" He looked genuinely puzzled. "I love you. All I ever wanted was for us to be together."

"Eric," she said in despair, "you don't love me. You don't even know me. You're obsessed, and that has nothing to do with love. And let me tell you, when somebody's obsessed and stalking you, it's a really terrifying experience."

He watched her, breathing heavily. Bella wondered if he'd even heard the words, let alone understood them.

"And this farmer you're living with," he said at last, his face darkening, "does he love you, Isabel? He understands you and knows how to treat you and all those other things I don't?"

"He has nothing to do with anything," she said. "I'm leaving him. Just let me go away, please, Eric. Don't follow me anymore. Then all of this can finally be over, for both of us."

"You're lying." He watched her closely. "I can tell when you're lying."

Slowly, his eyes still intent on her, he reached under his jacket and withdrew a snub-nosed revolver from its holster.

"Eric, for God's sake!"

His pale eyes were filled with such pain and confusion that she was uncertain what to say to make him put down the gun. When he was in this frame of mind, any careless word might be enough to set him off.

"I can't let you go away with him, Bella," he whispered. "It's not right. You're supposed to be with me. You're my wife. I have to stop him from taking you away, Bella"

Her thoughts raced frantically. If only she could see Dan as he approached and shout some kind of warning.

But as soon as she formed the thought, Bella knew it was hopeless. Dan would never save himself by leaving her alone and in danger.

At least the children weren't here. Thank God for that.

"I swear to you, Eric," she said earnestly, "that I'm not going away with him. I'm going by myself.

I won't be with any man. If you'll let me go into the other room, I can show you my ticket.''

His eyes flickered uncertainly, but he still held the gun.

"I can't trust you anymore, Isabel," he said. "Maybe you'll go away alone, but he'll come to you soon enough, won't he? And then you'll sleep with him, and touch him like you…''

His voice grew thick and he paused, rubbing his mouth with the back of his hand.

"Don't, Eric," she said softly. "Please don't torture yourself like this. Look, our marriage is over, but you're still a nice-looking man with a really good job. Some other woman would be—''

"I don't want any other woman!" he shouted, waving the gun. "I want my wife! And I'll kill the bastard who tries to take her away from me.''

"This man is nothing to you, Eric," she pleaded. "It's me you want. Look, I'll come with you. Maybe we can start over." She tried to hide the fear in her voice. She'd do this for Dan. "If we go right now, Dan will never even know you were here.''

Eric stared at her. His hand had begun to shake badly, which frightened her even more.

"If I take you with me now, you'll run away again, won't you?" he said heavily. "You'll go off and leave me the first time we have a little argument. You'll run back to this farmer.''

"No, Eric, I won't ever come back here.''

"He's always been around," Eric said, ignoring her. "He's the one who ruined our marriage. All that time you kept saying it was because of my temper or your ratty old dog, and instead, it was him. You were sneaking off to sleep with him whenever you had the chance. He stole you from me, and he's going to pay."

"Eric, that's crazy talk, and you know it. I never saw this man before in my life, until I drove my car into the river," she said passionately. "He rescued me and helped me, and I've been hiding here at his farm ever since. That's the truth, Eric, I swear it. All the time you and I were married, I never—"

She froze at the sound of Dan's truck. Then a few moments later, the crunch-crunch of Dan's boot heels on the crushed rock of the driveway.

Eric followed her involuntary glance at the door. He moved back against the wall, aiming the gun with hands that were suddenly steady.

Bella could see that his years of police training had taken over. Instead of a shaken, jealous man, Eric Matthias had become a cold-eyed killer.

Now was the time, Bella thought wildly.

While he was distracted by Dan's arrival, she could lunge at him, try to grab the weapon, maybe even throw the hot pan of mushrooms at his head.

Just as she made her decision, Eric moved toward her with frightening speed, grasped her wrist and pressed his fingers into it so painfully that she bit her lip to keep from crying out.

"One word from you," he whispered, "and I shoot the farmer as soon as he comes in the door. Do you understand, Isabel?"

She nodded, wide-eyed with terror.

She heard Dan open the porch door, then the thud of his boots as he pulled them off and dropped them on the floor. In seconds, his body filled the kitchen doorway. He smiled at her as he removed his cap and hung it on a peg.

"No foal yet," he said, "but it should be here by morning. Did you put the steaks on?"

She shook her head.

"Bella?" he said, moving toward her. "What's wrong?"

And then he saw Eric behind the door, standing with the gun trained on Bella's face.

"One more step, cowboy," Eric said tautly, "and she's a dead woman."

Dan stopped in the middle of the room. Bella could see his face hardening with tension as he assessed the situation.

"Are you all right, Bella?" he asked, never taking his eyes off the man with the gun. "Has he hurt you?"

"I'm fine," she said, her voice husky. "Dan, I'm so sorry. I didn't hear him until—"

"Shut up," Eric snapped. "Spare me your love chat." He stared at Dan. "This woman is my wife. Did you ever stop to think about that while you were playing with her?"

"You're wrong," Dan said quietly. "This woman is *my* wife. If you don't believe me, I can show you our marriage certificate."

Eric's face paled beneath his tan. "That's a goddam lie!" he shouted. "If she got married in Texas I would've seen her name on a computer somewhere."

"It's a sealed license. My cousin's the county clerk, and she pulled some strings for us," Dan told him, his tone almost conversational. "You won't find my wife's name on any computer, because she isn't Isabel Delgado anymore. She's Bella Gibson.''

Eric's eyes flicked in her direction "Is that true, Isabel?'' he asked. ''You're actually married to this man?''

''Since last week.''

He brushed at his forehead impatiently with his free hand, then released the safety on the gun.

''It's your fault,'' he said to Dan, his voice shaking. ''You took her away from me. You ruined everything, you bastard. I should just...''

He lifted the gun, aimed it at Dan's face and steadied it with both hands.

Bella held her breath, fighting back waves of sickness. Dan stood unmoving, his gaze level. ''You won't pull that trigger,'' he told Eric. ''Because if you do, your life is over, too.''

''My life's been over since I met her,'' Eric said in despair. ''She lied and cheated all the time. Nothing matters anymore.''

''Bella never cheated on you,'' Dan said gently. ''She and I only met a little while ago, after her car went in the river. She never had another man while she was your wife.''

''Shut up,'' Eric said, still training the gun on Dan's face. But some of the conviction had gone from his voice, and his hands were shaking again.

Bella glanced from Dan to her ex-husband.

''I think she tried to be a good wife to you,'' Dan went on, ''but you kept pushing her away with your jealousy and threats. You're the one who ruined your marriage, Eric. You did it yourself.''

Eric stared at him, then Bella. ''I'm going to kill

her," he shouted, aiming the gun at Bella. "If you say one more word, I'm going to kill her. She deserves to die."

"She doesn't deserve to die," Dan said. He moved across the room and stood close to Bella, resting a hand on her shoulder while Eric tracked him frantically with the gun.

Bella shivered under Dan's touch and resisted the urge to reach for his hand.

"She doesn't deserve to die," Dan said again, still gripping her shoulder. "This is a wonderful woman. I love her and I always will."

She listened, dazed, as he went on, "She would have been a good wife to you, Eric, if you'd ever given her half a chance. Bella's fair and decent and good, and she really cared about you. All she wanted was to be treated with kindness, but you couldn't do that. You let her down. You were so wrapped up in yourself you didn't know how to love your wife."

"And you do?" Eric said, his voice thick with fury and pain. "You're such a hotshot lover, you know how to make a woman happy?"

"I'm not a hotshot at anything. Hell, my first wife was so unhappy with me," Dan said with a bitter smile, "she went off to live all by herself in Nashville to try and become a country-music star."

Dan moved slowly away from Bella and walked back to lean against the counter while Eric swung the gun in his direction again.

"I'm only a farmer, Eric. I have nothing to offer a woman like Bella, and she knows it. She's leaving me tomorrow," Dan added, staring directly at the other man. "Did she tell you that, Eric?"

"Why would she leave, if you're so much in love with her?"

"Well, partly it's because I have no money and our backgrounds are too different. But I think she's also going away because she's afraid of what you'll do if she stays. And when she's gone, my life won't be worth living anymore," Dan said. "I'll have to keep working because I have three kids to look after, but I'm going to miss her every day until I die. I guess that's what it means to love somebody."

"If she'd loved me like that, I wouldn't be in this mess now," Eric muttered.

But most of the anger had drained from his voice. He sounded almost pleading.

Bella watched the two men, stunned by what was happening. Somehow the power in the room seemed to have shifted. Even though Eric still held the gun, Dan was the one whose presence dominated. His face was taut, his green eyes charged with emotion.

"You'll have to leave now, Eric," he said in the same quiet, firm tone he used with the children when they misbehaved. "I want you to walk away from my farm the same way you came in and never show your face around here again."

"And as soon as I'm out of sight, you'll be on the phone to the police." Eric lowered an arm briefly to rub his chest and shoulder in a distracted fashion, then returned it to the raised gun. "My career's going to be ruined, anyhow. I might as well shoot both of you and myself right now."

"I can guarantee your career will be over if you ever threaten my family," Dan said. "But if you walk away right now, I'm going to forget you were ever here tonight, and so is Bella.''

She listened in disbelief.

"Aren't we, Bella?" Dan asked, giving her a quick warning glance.

She nodded.

"Say it out loud," Dan told her. "Eric can't hear you."

Bella cleared her throat. "Yes," she whispered hoarsely. "If you leave us alone from now on, you won't have anything to worry about."

Eric slumped into a nearby chair, still clutching the gun. "How can I trust either of you?" he muttered. "Nobody ever keeps their word."

"You can trust me," Dan said, "because Bella matters to me a hell of a lot more than you do. I hate making a promise like this, when you should be in jail. But if I get you sent to jail, you'll get out someday and start threatening her all over again. If you walk away from here tonight because I allow you to leave, it's going to be over."

"How?" Eric asked.

"Your life and your career will be in my hands," Dan told him. "I'm the one with the power, not you. And you can trust me not to turn on you, because I'll never stop loving this woman."

Eric watched Dan for a moment, then swung his gaze to Bella, his face working.

"You never loved me, Isabel," he said.

Dan sent her another warning glance. Bella held her tongue, watching as he moved closer to the man in the chair and extended his hand.

"Give me the gun, Eric," he said.

Bella held her breath and waited.

"Come on," Dan said gently. "Give me the gun, and it'll all be finished."

After a long, agonizing hesitation, Eric handed him the weapon, his face cold and stiff.

"I'm going to keep the gun overnight and take it to your office in the morning," Dan said. "You can leave now and go back the way you came."

"You've got to promise me you'll bring back my gun," Eric said in a toneless voice. "If they ever find out…"

"I'll bring it back tomorrow morning before nine o'clock," Dan said. "You have my word."

The two men's eyes met for a long moment. Eric was the first to turn away. He heaved himself to his feet and strode toward the door. Bella got up and watched him go, amazed at how he seemed to have shrunk. For years this man had loomed so large in her life, an object of loathing and fear.

Now he was just an ordinary man in a creased, dusty suit.

CHAPTER TWENTY

BELLA AND DAN moved outside and looked on in silence as Eric staggered down the driveway, heading for the road. His figure grew more and more indistinct in the shadows.

"He's gone," she said. "I can't believe he's really gone."

"He won't bother you again. He's finished, Bella."

"I know," she said slowly. "It's just...so hard to believe. I've been terrified of Eric for so long, I can hardly imagine a world where that threat doesn't exist."

She spread her arms as if to embrace the velvet darkness. "It's such a beautiful night, Dan. Everything's so beautiful."

He moved away to sprawl in one of the patio chairs and sat with his eyes closed, legs extended wearily. Bella sank into the adjoining chair and took his hand, squeezing it warmly, but he didn't respond.

"I know *why* it's finished," she said after a moment. "And so do you."

When he didn't reply she glanced at him cautiously. "It's over because you told Eric you loved me," she said. "He knew it was true. Even if he killed both of us, he could never kill the fact that you love me and I love you.''

Dan made an impatient gesture. ''Don't talk about it, Bella.''

''Why not?''

''Because I still want you to leave tomorrow,'' he said without opening his eyes. ''So what's the sense in talking about love? Let's just eat our supper and go to bed.''

Bella stared at him, bewildered.

''Why on earth would I leave tomorrow? Dan, I don't have to leave at all. Not ever. I can stay here in peace for the rest of my life, because Eric's no threat to us anymore.''

''You can't stay here.'' He got up abruptly and moved away from her, walking into the house.

Bella followed and watched as he pulled open the door of the fridge to take out the steaks. ''Dan, what's going on? Look, I just heard you tell Eric you loved me.''

''But nothing else has changed.'' He turned to her, holding the package of meat, his eyes full of sorrow. ''The threat may be gone from your life, but everything else is just the same, Bella.''

''What do you mean, everything else is the same?''

''I'm still a farmer in a shabby house, and you're a woman with more than two million dollars in a brown paper envelope.''

''But that doesn't matter to me!'' she said, stung. ''It doesn't mean a thing.''

''This morning you told me it did.''

''Oh, Dan.'' She came across the room and took

his arm, clasping it tightly. "Sweetheart, I didn't mean it! I just said it so you'd let me go and not try to deal with Eric on your own."

She broke off, puzzled by his grim expression.

"I'm hungry," he said, moving toward the door, "and you must be tired. Let's cook up those steaks so we can go to bed. It's been a long day, and you have a plane to catch tomorrow."

"I'm not catching any plane," she said.

"Yes, you are."

"But...why would I go all the way to Canada now?" she asked. "I don't have to hide from Eric anymore."

"You can go wherever you like," he said. "I plan to drive you to the airport tomorrow morning, and what you do after that is up to you."

He disappeared into the darkness of the patio, and she heard him moving around at the barbecue.

Stunned and disbelieving, Bella reheated the pasta and vegetables in the microwave and put them on the table.

A few minutes later Dan brought in the steaks. They sat down to eat in silence. She could hear the sound of the river and the soft beat of insect wings against the screens.

When their meal was over, Dan helped her clear the table and rinse the dishes, then left to have a shower while she tidied the rest of the kitchen.

"I'll sleep on the couch," he told her, appearing in the doorway after half an hour with a couple of blankets and a pillow. "You can have the bed."

She went to the doorway and watched as he

flipped off the living-room light and settled on the couch.

At last she wandered into the bathroom for a shower. The hot water pelted her face, mingling with her tears.

Afterward she toweled herself dry, put on one of Dan's clean shirts and stared at herself in the mirror for a long time, then sat on the bed and gazed out the window at the darkness, thinking hard.

Finally she padded down the hallway in her bare feet and perched near him on the edge of the couch.

"Are you asleep?" she asked.

"No."

"Good," she said. "Because I'm going to kiss you, dammit, and I want you to feel it."

She nestled beside him and drew his face to hers, kissing him with passion, and was satisfied to hear him grunt in surprise. He reached out to grasp her wrists.

"What's this about, Bella?" He sat up, still holding her hands.

"It's about you being an idiot," she said.

She wriggled one hand free and pulled his face to hers again, hungrily seeking out his mouth. He resisted for a while, then softened and began to respond.

"Why are you torturing me like this?" he asked hoarsely.

"Because you think it makes a difference that I have money and you've got a mortgage. That's so stupid," she muttered, her lips moving over his face. "I don't know why I even care about you."

"You can't pretend it doesn't matter," he insisted quietly.

"I'm not pretending!" She placed her hands on each side of his face, forcing him to meet her eyes. "Listen to me, Dan Gibson," she commanded.

"I'm listening."

"How would you feel if our situations were reversed?"

"Reversed?" he asked.

"If you had several million dollars and I'd just started a business of my own and was struggling to make a success of it? Would that keep you from having anything to do with me?"

"Of course not," he said. "What do you think I am, Bella?"

"I think you're a complete and total imbecile," she said, kissing him again. "Gorgeous and sexy, but not too bright."

He began to look confused. "I'm not sure what you're getting at."

"Then just be quiet," she told him, "and listen to me."

"I'm listening," he assured her again. For the first time she heard a warm undercurrent of laughter in his voice.

Bella almost lost her concentration then. She got up and began to pace the room while she organized her thoughts. Dan remained on the couch and eyed her warily.

"What we're going to do," she told him, "is make a business deal."

"What kind of deal?"

"How much did you say your land is worth?" Bella asked.

"Probably about two million dollars, if I ever wanted to sell. But I'm not selling my land, and there's a mortgage on—"

"I'm going to buy a half-share in the farm," she interrupted. "For cash."

He got up and turned on a lamp, then came back to sprawl on the sofa and gaze at her. "You're serious," he said.

"Damn right I'm serious. I love you and your kids, and I'm staying right here in this place for the rest of my life."

"But, Bella—"

"Thanks to you, I don't have to worry about hiding from Eric," she said. "So I can go to San Antonio and sell my stock to my father. As soon as I've got the money in hand, I'll pay you for my half of the farm."

"This is crazy. You can't possibly—"

She raised her hand to silence him. "You can pay off your mortgage and buy whatever equipment you need. Once the debts are cleared I expect this place to start making money and give me a tidy return on my investment. I'll also use some of my money for improvements to the house, since I'll have a half-share in that, as well."

"Bella—"

"I was thinking we could build a new wing over there on the northern part of the house. Enough space that the kids would each have a bedroom and you could have an office. And, of course," she said thoughtfully, "another couple of bathrooms. Maybe a sunroom for plants, with some nice wicker furniture…''

"You're crazy." He stared at her. "Completely out of your mind."

She crossed the room and sat in his lap, gripping his hair. "Hey, you want me to hurt you? Because I will, if that's what it takes to make you see reason."

He looked up at her solemnly, but his eyes were dancing. "Bella, I…"

"Oh, darling…"

She melted into his arms and felt his hands begin to explore her body.

"Don't distract me," she said with an attempt at dignity, "while we're still in the middle of our negotiations."

"Is that what we're in the middle of?" His mouth brushed her eyelids and moved over her face.

"I want to hear you agree, Dan. I want you to promise you'll sell me half this farm and let me stay here."

"I probably have no choice," he said. "We're legally married, and you have every right to stay."

"Hey, that's true, isn't it?" she said, pleased. "We're married. So you can't refuse my offer."

"Bella, everything I own is already yours. You don't have to buy it from me."

"In that case, everything I own is also yours. Fair's fair."

"But—"

"Look," she said firmly, "this is going to be a real marriage, Dan. I want a legal half-share in the farm, bought and paid for. Do you hear me?"

"If I'd known you were so pushy," he said, kissing her breasts through the thin cotton of the shirt, "I'd never have married you."

"Too late." She smiled at him and stroked his hair lovingly.

"Oh, Bella."

All the laughter had faded from his voice, and she heard the rough edge of emotion that always took her breath away.

She wrapped her arms around him and kissed him. He stood up, lifting her effortlessly, and carried her down the hall to the bedroom, placed her on the bed and lay beside her, his body taut and urgent.

"Oh, Dan," she said in bliss as he embraced her tightly, "I love you."

"A sunroom?" he whispered.

"And a family room with a fireplace. Maybe a second-floor loft—I haven't decided yet." She smiled dreamily. "And of course we'll want a nice little nursery for the baby."

"The baby?"

"Or babies," she said. "I haven't decided yet how many there'll be."

"Oh, Bella, you're going to be the death of me."

She struggled in his arms and rolled over to lie on his broad chest, gazing into his eyes.

"I'm not a victim anymore, Dan," she told him gravely. "And I'll never be that weak again. From now on, you'll just have to get used to having me around as a partner."

He held her hips in both hands, moving her body against his.

"I think I could get used to this, Bella," he murmured.

"Lie still." She lowered her face to kiss him. "This won't hurt a bit."

He laughed again, then held her close to him as she moved her body with rising purpose.

Soon their quickened breathing and impassioned whispers filled the little room, drowning out the murmur of the river and the rustle of leaves just beyond their window.

Come back to Crystal Creek

Turn the page for a preview of
the next exciting story set in this
small town in the beautiful
Texas hill country.

CONSEQUENCES

by Margot Dalton

Harlequin Superromance #928

On sale July 2000

Lucia Osborne was the principal of the middle school in Crystal Creek, a central Texas community small enough that everybody knew everybody else's business, and gossip whirled around town with the destructive speed of a brush fire. She was divorced, thirty-seven years old, and had not had a man in her life during the seven years she'd lived and worked in Crystal Creek.

So when Lucia needed to buy a pregnancy test kit, she couldn't simply walk down the street and make her purchase at Wall's Drugstore, which had been serving the locals for more than sixty years. Ralph Wall, the pharmacist, was one of the most garrulous men in the county, and also happened to be married to Gloria Wall, chairperson of the school board.

As a result Lucia had to wait an entire agonizing week before she could get away long enough to make the hour-long drive to Austin, buy a testing kit and take it home to the privacy of her little apartment.

Lucia had lived for five years on the third floor apartment of a gracious old house owned by June Pollock. Flowered paper covered the slanted walls, and live oaks and pecans rustled against the dormers. Though it was vastly different from the palatial estate she'd grown up in, Lucia loved her cozy little home.

These high airy rooms were her sanctuary and retreat, a place where she could let down her guard and relax, away from the measuring eyes and sharp tongues of the community.

But on this mellow Sunday afternoon in late October, her silent apartment was more like a prison, and the air seemed heavy with menace.

She stood in the candy-striped bathroom with its antique claw-footed bathtub and pedestal sink, holding the little plastic wand in her hand and studying the instructions.

Two lines in the window indicated a positive test. One line meant you weren't pregnant.

Lucia took a deep breath and looked at the wand. Her eyes blurred for a moment, then focused in horror on the two red lines.

She moaned aloud and leaned her forehead against the cool surface of the mirror. Then, with the careful precision that was an integral part of her nature, she took a second wand from the package and went through the whole test again.

Again the two red lines appeared clearly in the little window.

"Oh, *no,*" she murmured aloud, whimpering when she heard her own voice in the autumn stillness.

After a moment she bundled up all the testing equipment, wrapped it in a plastic sack and stuffed it in the trash can under the sink.

A warm breeze was blowing from the south of the Gulf and across the rolling valleys of Texas hill country. At the bathroom window, a white muslin curtain billowed and drifted on the wind, brushing the leaves of a potted African violet on the windowsill.

Moving automatically, her face pale and tense with dread, Lucia closed the window and touched the soil around the plant. It was dry, and she used a little copper pitcher from a nearby shelf to water the violet, being careful not to drip onto the sensitive furred leaves.

Then she wandered out into her bedroom and lay down on the old brass bedstead, gazing up at the ceiling with haunted eyes. Finally, she rolled herself up in her soft green and white quilt and began to cry soundlessly, so the landlady wouldn't hear her from downstairs and come up to ask what was wrong.

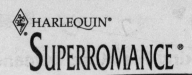

HARLEQUIN®
SUPERROMANCE®

**They look alike. They sound alike.
They act alike—at least some of the time.**

Two Sisters by **Kay David**
(Superromance #888)
A sister looks frantically for her missing twin.
And only a stranger can help her.
Available January 2000

The Wrong Brother by **Bonnie K. Winn**
(Superromance #898)
A man poses as his twin to fool the woman he thinks
is a murderer—a woman who also happens to be
his brother's wife.
Available February 2000

Baby, Baby by **Roz Denny Fox**
(Superromance #902)
Two men fight for the custody of twin babies.
And their guardian must choose who will be their father.
Available March 2000

Available wherever Harlequin books are sold.

HARLEQUIN®
Makes any time special ™

Visit us at www.romance.net

HSRTWINS

HARLEQUIN®
SUPERROMANCE®

*Pregnant and alone—
these stories follow women
from the heartache of
betrayal to finding true love
and starting a family.*

THE FOURTH CHILD by C.J. Carmichael.
When Claire's marriage is in trouble, she tries to
save it—although she's not sure she can forgive her
husband's betrayal.
On sale May 2000.

AND BABY MAKES SIX by Linda Markowiak.
Jenny suddenly finds herself jobless and pregnant by
a man who doesn't want their child.
On sale June 2000.

MOM'S THE WORD by Roz Denny Fox.
After her feckless husband steals her inheritance and
leaves town with another woman, Hayley discovers she's
pregnant.
On sale July 2000.

Available wherever Harlequin books are sold.

HARLEQUIN®
Makes any time special ™

WELCOME TO

Crystal Creek

If this is your first visit to the friendly ranching town in the hill country of Texas, get ready to meet some unforgettable people. If you've been there before, you'll be happy to see some old faces and meet new ones.

Harlequin Superromance® and Margot Dalton— author of seven books in the original Crystal Creek series—are pleased to offer three **brand-new** stories set in Crystal Creek.

IN PLAIN SIGHT by **Margot Dalton**
On sale May 2000

CONSEQUENCES by **Margot Dalton**
On sale July 2000

THE NEWCOMER by **Margot Dalton**
On sale September 2000

HARLEQUIN®
Makes any time special ™